Marion H r exploring
the compl er poetry,
short stories and novels have won prizes, g the bestselling
T rea Badenoch
Fiction Award and the Blackwell Prize. She has an MA in Creative
Writing and has taught creative writing for many years for the
Open University and lectured on Creative Writing MA courses in
Newcastle and Teesside Universities. Marion is married with two
grown-up children and lives in Norton in the Tees Valley.

Praise for Marion Husband:

'Husband's writing is notable for an understated yet intense
sympathy for the movements of the heart. Impressive' *Guardian*

'As with all the best novelists, Husband's talent seems to draw its
energy from the experience of writing from perspectives far
removed from her own as she inhabits other genders, other
sexualities, other eras' Patrick Gale

'Compelling and sensual. Well written' Penny Summer

'The writing is intelligent, and the emotions heartfelt'
Sally Zigmond, author of *Hope Against Hope*

'Winner of the Andrea Badenoch Award, Husband's novels are
compelling page turners with hidden secrets and complex love
lives that vividly convey the aftermath of dreadful conflicts'
Northern Echo

'Marion Husband explores the morality of wartime Britain with
intelligent and compassionate insight' *Mslexia*

'A superbly written book, this is a poignant and very readable novel'
Historical Novels Review

By Marion Husband

The Boy I Love series

The Boy I Love
All the Beauty of the Sun
Paper Moon
Shadows of the Evening

Standalone

Say You Love Me
The Good Father
Now the Day is Over

Shadows
of the
Evening

MARION HUSBAND

ACCENT

First published in 2021 by HEADLINE ACCENT
An imprint of HEADLINE PUBLISHING GROUP

1

Cataloguing in Publication Data is available from the British Library

ISBN 978 1 7861 5783 6

Typeset in 10.5/13pt Bembo Std by Jouve (UK), Milton Keynes

Printed and bound in Great Britain by Clays Ltd, Elcograf S.p.A.

Headline's policy is to use papers that are natural, renewable and recyclable
products and made from wood grown in well-managed forests and other
controlled sources. The logging and manufacturing processes are expected
to conform to the environmental regulations of the country of origin.

HEADLINE PUBLISHING GROUP
An Hachette UK Company
Carmelite House
50 Victoria Embankment
London
EC4Y 0DZ

www.headline.co.uk
www.hachette.co.uk

Shadows
of the
Evening

Prologue

Thorp, November 1962

Adele said, 'She's at peace, now.'

At Margot's graveside, Bea nodded. At least Adele hadn't mentioned heaven, or some *better place*. The vicar in his funeral address had talked of Margot's husband, Havelock, saying that Margot was reunited with him; the man seemed so certain of this that Bea had been appalled. Even if there was a heaven it should be a place where all earthly connections were severed, where no one needed to have anything to do with such men as Havelock Redpath; they would be no more than strangers. And yet, if heaven were such a place she and Margot would only meet again as strangers, too. But this was all nonsense – they would be dead and that would be that: no more Margot just as there was no more Havelock, just as there would be no more of her. Anyway, Havelock had gone to hell; she took a grim comfort in the idea of him burning for ever.

Heaven and hell, then, both or neither; she looked down at Margot's coffin, Bea's own handful of dry earth scattered across the brass nameplate. She had wanted to cover it so she couldn't read the inscription; she could pretend there was someone else beneath the pale oak lid. She could look around and see Margot in her funeral coat, her lovely face shadowed by her funeral hat. Margot would catch her eye and smile, and she would see that the lightest touch of pink lipstick had been applied with her usual uncertainty and that the navy cashmere scarf she had bought her for Christmas complemented her blue eyes, just as Bea had known it would. Margot's small gloved hands would be holding a rose.

'Bea?'

Adele was frowning at her, concerned. Margot's ghost vanished and Bea saw how suddenly old her sister looked, black didn't suit her, didn't suit anyone, what frights they all looked in the November gloom. There was the vicar – she could never remember his name – his face pinched with cold so that he looked pained as a medieval saint, except that his nose was red with broken veins. Margot hadn't much cared for him and so she had stopped going to church so often, making apologies and embarrassed, smiling excuses. Bea glanced towards St Anne's, the pretty little Norman church surrounded by its ancient graves, hardly any space left for Margot, they had squeezed her in beside Havelock and her parents. She should have been buried elsewhere, Bea thought angrily, she should have had some escape from them.

After last night's storm the cemetery's horse-chestnut trees were finally bare, the sodden branches black against the grey-white sky, the smell of leaf mould and turned earth as thick as the mourners' breath on the frosty air. Only the wreaths were colourful, a plump cushion of tight red rosebuds from Mark, a cross of burnt-orange chrysanthemums from Bobby, the cards she had squinted at earlier both written in the same hand, the same sentiment repeated: *To a dear mother, rest in peace.* Couldn't they have written more, these sons? She wondered which one of them had deigned to write such wooden words, only to realise that they had left it to the florist, she could hear Bobby saying *write the usual thing.*

Bitterly, she looked across the grave at Margot's eldest son. At least Bobby Harris appeared suitably unhappy. His disfigured face was grotesque, of course, but from this little distance, without her glasses, he had the air of grieving, even the semblance of the handsome man he once was. An ex-RAF officer, he stood very straight, shoulders back, head a little bowed, his damaged hands clasped together in front of him as though he cared enough to pray. *Rest in peace*, indeed! She glared at him, wanting to make him look up and meet her eye and see how much contempt she had for his piety. He was wearing a poppy in his buttonhole, the modest paper flower a flash of colour against his finely tailored black coat. He was a Harris all right, as vain and aloof as any member of that degenerate family.

Adele repeated, 'Bea? Are you all right?'

'Yes. Don't fuss.'

'I'm not fussing. Do you need a handkerchief?'

'No.'

Adele took a lacy square of Irish linen from her handbag and pressed it into her sister's hand. 'Here. There's no shame in a few tears.' Gently she added, 'Shall we go home?'

'No! We'll see it through.'

'As you wish. Wipe your nose, dear.'

Bea did as she was told and the lace scratched and smelt oddly of her mother – face powder and rose water – although her mother had been dead for years. Not for the first time, Bea thought that Adele was deciding to become their mother, taking up her habits, her mannerisms and ways of talking, even her scents. Things she thought she had forgotten about her mother were returning and this was disconcerting; she was beginning to resent Adele for making her feel like a young girl again, that frightful little beast she once was.

Thrusting Adele's hanky into her coat pocket she said, 'Well, are we going?'

She saw Adele glance at Bobby and Mark who had begun to walk along the gravel path towards the waiting funeral car. They hardly needed a car, Margot's house was only a cock-stride, but she supposed the cars had been paid for; the expense must not be wasted. She watched the two men, noticing how Mark placed his hand lightly on Bobby's back as though to shepherd him; Mark was always a kind boy and more like his mother, he had nothing of his father Havelock in him, just as Bobby had nothing of Margot. Only half-brothers, yet so close, *great friends*, Margot had called them, pleased at their friendship but nervous of it as though she wondered what they might tell each other. Again she had summoned Margot, her timid laugh whenever she talked of her sons. Bea believed Margot was frightened of Bobby; even before he was burnt she hardly knew what to say to him.

3

Adele said, 'Right ho, then.' This was one of their mother's expressions and Bea frowned at her, but Adele was still watching the brothers and the small band of mourners following them; Bea knew her sister would rather go home than face Bobby. 'I never know where to look,' Adele had admitted that morning. 'And I'm sure he's used to the awkwardness of others but it's just that I'm not used to *him*.'

'You just have to look him in the eye,' Bea had told her, and she had been brisk and no-nonsense because that morning Margot's death was still a novelty and not the horror the funeral had made it. She drew breath, holding back the tears because there *was* shame in them, and defeat; she couldn't give in to emotion, where would it end? She squared her shoulders. Stepping out ahead of Adele she said, 'Come now. Let's not dawdle out here in the cold.'

'Thank you for coming,' Bobby said, and he took her hand in his, his deformed fingers briefly light around hers. Boldly, Bea looked at him directly, thinking how he hadn't aged at all, his damaged face frozen on that day in 1944 when his Spitfire had crashed in an explosion of flames. He was still slim as a boy, still the upright officer; and he looked and smelt expensive. She remembered how wealthy his father had made him and felt a touch of something like jealousy. He smiled, and she saw his father, Paul Harris, in him, urbane and charming, the Harris men were nothing if not charming. Bea stepped back from him, she couldn't help thinking of snakes – and turned to Mark.

Mark grinned and embraced her in a light hug. 'Aunt Bea,' he said, and kissed her cheek. 'How are you?'

He was an actor, all front and smiles, handsome as any leading man. Taller and broader than Bobby, he gave the impression of having lived a carefree life, but this was an act: he was Havelock's son and no one escaped that man with their spirit intact. She felt herself soften towards this brave light-heartedness; she realised suddenly that this was what made him such a star in that silly television show Adele loved so much. She found herself looking him up and down and he laughed, saying, 'Do I pass muster?'

'Your mother would be proud of you.'

He sobered. 'Yes, well, I hope so.' He glanced past her as though someone more interesting had just walked in, only to immediately turn to her again as if conscious of his rudeness. 'You were such a good friend to her.'

Bobby said, 'Mark, why don't you fetch Miss Davis a drink?'

Mark nodded. 'At once.'

Watching him edge through Margot's crowded living room, Bea said, 'Well, I should circulate.'

'No, please, Mark won't know where to deliver your drink if you go now.' Bobby smiled, adding, 'It's only sweet or dry sherry. Knowing Mark he'll bring a glass of each for you to choose from.'

'He's a decent boy.'

Bobby looked towards Mark, who had become caught up in a group of Redpath cousins. Turning back to her he said, 'How are you?'

'Fine. How are you?' She sounded cross; she often sounded cross, *blunt*, Adele would say, and she cleared her throat as though this might make her next words softer. But she couldn't think of any next words; she had nothing to say to this man who had just lost his mother and seemed more pained by this than she had ever expected. She shifted uncomfortably, conscious of her own bulkiness. Adele had insisted that she wear a dress – *you can't wear trousers to a funeral, honestly, Bea!* With the dress she'd had to wear stockings and women's shoes, although she had refused point blank to put on a corset. Perhaps she should have worn a corset, it would have been a kind of armour, protecting her from Bobby Harris's piercing gaze.

He said, 'Thank you for everything you did for my mother.'

She wanted him to call Margot Mum and she said too sharply, 'I only did what anyone would.'

'She depended on you.'

He made this sound as though Margot was at fault, a clinging, useless woman. She wanted to get away from him, to find Mark and snatch both glasses of sherry from his hands, downing them one after the other. And then she would leave. She would mourn Margot in private, without this creature eyeing her as though he knew all

5

there was to know. But Bobby all at once touched her arm, saying, 'Miss Davis, I would so much like to talk to you in private – not now, tomorrow, perhaps? I'm going back to London with Mark the day after tomorrow . . .' In a rush he continued, 'That biography that's just been published about my father – that *trash*. I know you knew its author, Charles Dearlove. I need to talk to you about it, about him.'

She was astonished. 'This is your mother's funeral.'

'Yes –'

'And you want to talk about him – your father – today, when you should be thinking about her?'

'Not today, no, of course –'

'But you mention him – them, it –' She was so angry she could hardly speak coherently. She could feel her face flush as though she really had gulped down two sherries, the urge to prod him in the chest almost overwhelming. 'You should be quiet about that father of yours. He wasn't fit to clean your mother's shoes. How dare you speak to me about him today? This is Margot's day – your father ruined her life, I won't have him ruin her funeral too.'

'Aunt Bea?'

Mark appeared beside her, his face soft with concern. She stared at him: the resemblance was uncanny – Margot's ghost was there between them, as painfully ready to placate her as she had always been in life. The room had become still and quiet, everyone intent on her. She was caught out in her ugly dress and pinching shoes, the absurd outfit making her a silly, red-faced, hysterical woman. She should have stood firm and worn her good trousers and jacket but she had been persuaded to wear this dress for Margot's sake, for Margot, who wouldn't have minded what she wore, for Margot, who was dead. She would never see Margot again.

She blinked, unsure for a moment where her anger had come from or where her grief was going – what was she to do with it? She was too old to feel like this, she should have grieved before now – how had she got through life without ever having felt pain like this? She must be some kind of monster to have got off so scot-free. Her mouth was open and she closed it, swallowing hard. As firmly as she could she said, 'I must go.'

In her bedroom she tore off her dress, her stockings, and disgusting, flesh-coloured suspender belt. Her slacks were folded over the bedroom chair and she snatched them up and put them on. There was no mirror in her room, she had never had a mirror; she wouldn't look at her wide hips, those pendulous breasts that were so impossible to flatten no matter how she bandaged them. She pulled on a jumper and found a handkerchief in her trouser pocket. All these tears streaming soundlessly down her face – she couldn't even cry out loud, no practice; she couldn't start blubbing and howling now; she was much too old for such nonsense. Wiping her nose she thrust the hanky back inside her pocket and squared her shoulders. Margot had been ill and in pain and now she was at peace. At peace. She nodded to herself, sensibly. She had always been sensible: Margot had always relied on her sensibleness. Margot had always relied on her.

Bea sat down on her bed, just on its edge; she would just have a moment before she went downstairs and out into the garden; there was work to be done in the garden, always something to do. She closed her hands around the edge of the mattress, steadying herself. Adele had made her bed, all neat, all plumped and straightened. She hadn't put on her shoes, not yet, no harm done if she lay down, just for a minute. She moved sideways up the bed, slowly, slowly, until her head was sinking down into the pillow; she closed her eyes, pressing her fist to her mouth as she cried.

Chapter One

Thorp, April 1964

From the sitting-room window Adele watched the removal men through the gap in the fence. Earlier her brand-new neighbour had brought out a tray of tea and placed it on the bird table and the men had gathered around at once, jostling and joking; four men, strapping and sweaty. One had a tattoo. Adele had peered more closely at this one; he was the boss, she thought; perhaps he had once been a sailor to have a tattoo like that. His arms were very muscular; he had a crooked, gap-toothed smile which he turned on the woman who had brought out the tea and she had smiled back in that way that some women have, accepting such a smile as her due, used to men noticing her and smiling, eyes roving. The woman – her new neighbour – had been brisk. 'Tea, boys,' she had said, and the mugs had clinked together as she'd placed the tray down and a little of the tea had slopped so that the mugs dripped as the men drank, as they watched the woman walk back into her new house, hips swaying: sashaying, she supposed.

Behind her, Bea said, 'Adele, what on earth are you doing?'

'She's moving in.'

'Yes.' Bea stepped closer so that they were side by side at the window. 'I can see that. And I heard the commotion.'

'They're a happy band of men.'

Bea snorted. 'They'll see you spying on them. They'll think you're odd.'

'So?' Adele watched as, tea break over, two of the men manoeuvred a table from the van with grunts of effort and barked directions.

Turning to her sister she said, 'Earlier they brought out a painting. The blanket covering it fell off. A Francis Law.'

'A reproduction.'

Adele turned back to the window. 'Perhaps not if she was Mark's wife. Mark and Law were related, after all. She's an actress. Not as famous as Mark was, of course.'

'Have we seen her on the goggle-box?'

'No. No, I don't think so.'

'Well, we'll introduce ourselves in good time. Won't let on we know too much.'

This was the line that Bea liked to take: innocent ignorance. When eventually they introduced themselves to their new neighbour, Bea would take the lead in presenting a united front of not knowing. They knew nothing but would not feign surprise at anything they were told; they must always be inscrutable, never vulgar enough to ask questions. If information was offered, all well and good, although Bea's interest was a queer thing and rather furtive, Adele thought, like a well-trained dog catching the scent of a roasting chicken.

The two sisters stood side by side in silence, watching as the table disappeared into the house, followed by two dining chairs elaborately carved in an ugly, near-black wood. The men came out again, back into the van; rugs were retrieved, rolled and slung over shoulders to make inverted Vs. A brass bedstead, a mirror, an armchair with greasy, worn-away arms; there was a hat-stand, naked as a winter oak, and a bookshelf. Tea chests followed, mostly carried by the youngest man, no more than a boy, who was teased and chided by the others. Weaving her way through all this was the woman, who pointed into the van and then into the house; who said 'Careful!' and 'For goodness' sake!' and 'That's for the room at the front.' Adele noticed how her hair had fallen from its grips and that she was becoming almost as sweaty as the men. Frazzled, she supposed. She wondered if she had drunk tea inside the house, away from the men and their eyes, or had only got on, unpacking and arranging.

Adele knew her neighbour's house well; during her childhood it had stood empty for years, her own giant play house, there to accommodate any kind of game or make-believe. When Havelock Redpath bought it in 1922 she had been quite put out: wasn't it *her* house? Even if she was too old for games, she had still liked to walk through its empty rooms, imagining what might be made of them because one day Eric would buy it for her and they would live there like proper grown-ups, all their happy childhood memories kept safe. But eventually Havelock brought his own bride, Margot, to decorate its rooms, and Margot's taste was not hers and she had always felt as though Margot didn't understand the house and that she played too much to its darkness. Poor Margot, who couldn't be told this – she had enough to contend with. But oh, that wallpaper, brown and purple like stains, or that other room – a rush of red and black: she couldn't comment on it, couldn't lie so said nothing; only décor, after all.

Now she watched as someone else's furniture was carried through the wide front door, imagining where that table, that mirror, might be placed. She knew the bedrooms and the attics, the pantry and the outhouse and the garden, that place in the summerhouse where the sun slanted through the dusty windows, where she and Eric had hidden from Bea and Charles. Where Eric had kissed her, there, in that shaft of sunlight, amongst all the forgotten hoes and spades and the smell of earth. Years ago now; that kiss was as ancient as could be and it was foolish to think of it after so many years.

Bea drew breath, powering herself up for action. 'Well,' she said, 'no good standing here. We should have some lunch. Eggs, I think. There are far too many eggs.'

The implied fault was hers; they were her chickens, after all, productive little busybodies, clucking and scratching away with such silly lack of foresight. 'Perhaps we could give some to next door,' Adele said, 'when she's settled in. Or I could bake an egg custard.'

Bea's nose wrinkled and her mouth pursed – her thoughtful look, used when she was considering her options. Gazing out of the window at the woman, who was now climbing inside the van, she said, 'I'm not sure she looks the egg-custard type.'

11

'No. I'm sure you're right.'

Bea turned to her. 'Thirty, thirty-five, would you say?'

Adele watched the woman jump from the van, untidy in slacks and an untucked white shirt, her hair still everywhere; there was a bright, determined hardness about her eyes, her mouth was set in a thin line, as though the men had lost or broken something and now there would be hell to pay. 'Around thirty,' Adele agreed. 'Isn't she pretty? Her name is Cathy.'

Bea nodded as though she knew this. Then, all at once brisk, she turned from the window. 'I think we've wasted enough time. Let's leave *Cathy* to it, shall we?'

Cathy stood in her new kitchen and accepted the tray of dirty mugs from the boy. He said, 'I'll wash up for you, if you like.'

He looked so eager and he was blushing, so that Doug the foreman laughed and ruffled the boy's hair so roughly he staggered. Such strength, these men had, even the boy, she needn't have worried so much, nothing had been a problem for them, not even the piano. The piano stood just where she had told them to place it in the front room – she would call that room her study once the removal men were gone – the piano stool full of Mark's sheet music set just so, as though Mark was about to sit down and play.

Doug said, 'Thanks for the tea.'

He had pocketed the money she had given him, along with his tip; she had tipped each man in turn, as Mark would have, thanking them each individually. Mark would have been the one to deal with all this *manly* stuff, the men would have taken him seriously and not smirked as he handed out the money. As she showed them to the door, thanking them again, she supposed they had been more or less respectful, not asking questions about why she, as a single woman, was moving into this great big brute of a house. They had been surprisingly quiet and serious, on the whole, as though the effort of moving her furniture was a grave business and not to be taken lightly. Doug had recognised the Law painting, of course, being a local man. Wonderful, he had called it. Very poignant. She didn't say, 'Oh, do you really think so?' as she usually did when others praised the picture, didn't raise her eyebrows in ironic surprise at such an unsurprising comment. She had been respectful, as he had been, and said nothing at all.

No doubt Doug had believed the painting was a fake – a copy. She had been too nonchalant around it, too careless, she realised now with a little jolt of panic. If Doug had believed it was an original Francis Law then surely he'd believe she would have had them treat it more carefully, she would have warned them and not just flung an old blanket over it. She would have transported it herself in her car, or had some specialist arrange its safe arrival. If Doug had known its worth he wouldn't have left it in the kitchen, propped up against a tea chest full of pans.

The removal men left. Relieved to have the house to herself, she went to the picture and lifted it onto the table, laying it flat. An oil on canvas, it took up half of the Formica table, and was a portrait of a boy of around twenty, lying on his back in a meadow. He wore an army uniform, minus the tunic, his khaki shirt undone at the neck, its sleeves rolled up past his elbows, his braces hanging at his sides. He wore puttees and boots and his cap lay on the grass within reach of his hand. The grass was quite long in places, and full of cowslips and what looked like buttercups and daisies but only the cowslips recognisable and not simply blurs of white, gold, and silver. A sandy-haired boy, his eyes closed against the sun, or perhaps he was sleeping, but not dead, as some boys were in Francis Law's paintings; and he was handsome in that fey way of Law's models. No one knew who the boy was. Mark had believed Law had invented him. The painting was titled *Yesterday*, and she had always thought that this title was horribly manipulative, crassly sentimental. It was worth more than her new house, this pretty picture, and Mark had wanted her to keep it and never give it up.

Mark; she put her hand to her chest because sometimes the thought of him left her gasping for breath; no, not the thought of *him* – the thought that he was dead and that she would never see him again. She closed her hand into a tight fist, pushing it against her heart so that she wouldn't panic or give in to her memories and imagining: his car, skidding across that icy road, how he would have tried to take control but there was no help for it – there was nothing he could do – this was fate. Fate; she took a deep breath; what was there to do other than accept fate, the will of God; there had to be some comfort in this – there was comfort in Christ, the vicar had said at his funeral. The vicar was a good man; if only she had his faith. If only. She mustn't go down the if-only path.

Cathy sat down on the armchair the men had left beside the kitchen range. She lit a cigarette and exhaled smoke impatiently; after all, she had things to do and shouldn't be sitting down, no matter what. There was her bed to be made, at least. Last time she had moved Mark had told her to make her bed first thing. 'Otherwise, come midnight, you'll fall upstairs exhausted and be utterly dismayed by your bare mattress.' The day before she had moved into that London flat he had reached out and touched her cheek. 'Sure you don't want me to help?'

'I've hardly enough to fill my car – I don't need any help.'

'All right, gypsy. I'll bring an aspidistra when you're settled in. No one moves house again once they've an aspidistra.'

He had wanted her to stay put in that little flat above the hairdresser's, *Gina's*, where the smell of peroxide flashed through the floorboards, where the nights were quiet because all the women had gone and only the plastic pink domes of the hairdryers could be seen through the plate glass window, other-worldly amongst the clutter of magazines and hairbrushes, the trolleys spilling over with colour-graded rollers. A short walk from the tube station, Mark could be at her door only minutes after leaving the theatre; the applause would be ringing in his ears still, a part of him still more or less bearing the impression of whatever character he had just played. If he spoke more quickly or more slowly, if he held his cigarette in a way that was quite new to her; if he couldn't sit still, or sat too comfortably, then such un-Mark-ness helped her understand just how high as a kite he was. And she would draw him down with food and wine, with listening and not too many questions asked until he returned to her, not fully – he was Mark again only after he had slept – but at least as the public man she had first met, who was an actor and all front and charm.

These memories were all right; she didn't have to pummel her fist at her breastbone, the panic wouldn't come because the memories were comforting – and there were many of them, happy and glorious, she managed to smile to herself; she was lucky to have met him, to have known him; he was still in her heart, and would be there for the rest of her life, and this was a blessing. She was blessed to have loved him and to have his love in return.

She finished her cigarette and looked around for something that would do as an ashtray; nothing sprang immediately to view and so she stood up and stubbed it out in the sink, turning on the tap to swill the ash away. As it had when she'd filled the kettle earlier, the tap gurgled and shook alarmingly and the water came out brown; she noticed how stained the pot sink was, with a chip the size and shape of a coffee bean. For all its grandeur, the house was shabby and long neglected. There would be mice, she thought, and all kinds of problems that would need men. She turned off the tap, turned it on again, and, as she hoped, the water was a little less tea-coloured, the tap less shudderingly reluctant. There may be less need for men – she certainly hoped so. Already the whole business was beginning to bore her: the house would be a terrible chore. Yet, here she was, against her better judgement; at least she had kept her London flat. She could go back; no one would blame her.

Remembering Mark's advice about beds, she went upstairs, along the landing that dog-legged to another, shorter flight of stairs, and went on further still to the quiet, sunny room at the back of the house that she had decided would be her bedroom. There was a fireplace – rather grand blue-grey marble – a polished wood floor, and two tall sash windows looking out over the garden. She wouldn't think about the garden, but turned her attention to the cardboard boxes and suitcases dumped in the alcoves where they were a dull foil against the heavily patterned wallpaper, a William Morris, she thought, pink and mostly brown and ugly as the brink-of-rotten fruit it seemed to portray. Margot, her mother-in-law, had had some kind of taste – bad or mad, Cathy couldn't decide. Other rooms in this house had walls depicting lambs and shepherdesses; Chinamen, pagodas, and bridges. One room, the nursery, still had its frieze of grinning Humpty Dumpties dangling spindly legs from the red-brick wall. Below the red bricks, nursery-rhyme characters gambolled up and down their hills, a confusion of busyness for a child to lose himself in; she thought of Mark, who had always needed calm to bring him down from the dizzy heights, and knew she wouldn't go into the nursery today, and probably not for a while.

Now, though, her bed needed to be made and she opened the box labelled in her own hand. At once the room began to smell more like hers, her perfume on her sheets. There were her pillows, blankets, and eiderdown, the sheets folded on top ready to cover the mattress the men had placed on the fancy, wrought-iron bedstead she had asked them to reassemble. The bed had seemed enormous in her flat; here, centred on the wall opposite the windows, it looked just right, looked in fact as if it had always been there, a longed-for retreat for all who had lived and died here. Such a lot of sex and death in this room, she had no doubt about that. But she didn't believe in ghosts; the dead were dead and gone.

The sun laid its rectangular patches on the floor and the room became warmer as she worked. Once the bed was made she didn't stop, but emptied the suitcases of her clothes and toiletries, lining up perfume bottles on the mantelpiece to make a pretty display. Next to these, obscuring the wallpaper that little bit more, she placed her jewellery box: midnight blue padded satin, its lid embroidered with a silver chrysanthemum, a lovely box for the rubbish it contained. She had never been a diamonds and pearls girl, although others presumed she was, even Mark, at first.

Mark, at first, had said, 'Would you consider having supper with me?'

They had been introduced a few minutes earlier by David Black, whose arm was still around her waist. She remembered how David had squeezed her to him so that she was squashed against the great, fat bulk of him; she had hooked her own arm around his waist and was happy to lean against him because her heels were too high and the soles of her feet burned. When Mark asked her to supper, David had roared his great, famous laugh and had prodded Mark in the chest, spilling a little from the glass of champagne he has holding; there was a brief frothing of bubbles on Mark's lapel.

'She's my girl, darling boy. Isn't that so, my dear one?'

'Not really so.' She had smiled at Mark, liking him as she liked all handsome men. Of course, David had rather dwarfed him, but David dwarfed everyone, and Mark was actually tall and quite solid-looking, less fey than he appeared on screen. He had been playing opposite David in a television series about an RAF squadron during the war; David as the grand and terrifying Squadron Leader, Mark in the role of the bravest and most glamorous of the Spitfire pilots: the character the camera crew gave the longest odds against being killed off.

David had released her, stepping away so that she wobbled on her heels. 'Now, the idea makes me quite heart-broken,' David said. 'But truly, I do think you two lovelies would make a perfectly gorgeous couple. Now, both of you – stand back to back.'

Mark had looked puzzled; she had found this puzzled look endearing.

'Just do it,' David said. 'It's terribly important. And Cathy – you must take off your charmingly ridiculous shoes.'

She did so, laughing, relieved to have an excuse, and she and Mark had stood back to back. She had felt the press of his buttocks against hers, because what David had suspected was right, without her heels she and Mark were almost the same height, Mark only a little taller. For a long moment they had stood so closely like that whilst David held his hand flat over their heads, his palm gently brushing against her hair. 'Perfect. Perfect partners,' he'd said.

Mark had twisted around to look at her, half his backside still just against hers. He smiled slowly, as though he'd just been given the answer to a question that had vexed him all his life.

In her new bedroom, Cathy sat down on her bed. Last night, her last in the flat she and Mark had shared, she had cried for a long time so that her pillow had become wet with snot and tears – she hadn't cried so messily for months. At 4 a.m., as London's grey dawn fingered its way through the gap in her curtains, she lay on her back and told herself that she could cry if she wanted to, that sometimes crying might even help, and that the brave front she'd been trying on was all well and good, but really . . . But really the pep talk she gave herself had petered out. She had her grief and she could talk around it and through it, strike up a conversation as though it was a fellow guest at one of David's parties, but it was immune to reason, was silent, a black hole; she could pour her whole self into it and be drowned. She could obliterate herself like this, but she wouldn't because Mark would be so appalled. He would say, 'Cathy, live your life,' she could hear him saying it, although he had never said such a thing – he'd no need to, she had been living her life with him.

She stood up, drew breath. There were things to do. First and foremost she should hang the picture of the sleeping boy. He should have pride of place over the sitting-room fireplace. Mark would be pleased to see her doing such a thing.

Chapter Two

Adele had made fairy cakes and was in the process of icing them, a tube of Smarties ready at her elbow to add the final, colourful touch. The house was full of the sweet, eggy scent of just-baked cakes: as soon as Tom and Luc arrived they would know she had baked. She liked to treat Luc, there was no harm in spoiling her grandchild occasionally, although Bea said often that Tom was too soft with the boy and that it would be all too easy to spoil a motherless child. Adele would remind Bea that Luc wasn't motherless – that she shouldn't talk as if Christina were dead. Bea usually retorted that she might as well be dead, and the bitterness in her sister's voice only made her tut because she was tired of Bea's anger and wouldn't rise to it.

Bea came in from the garden, having taken off her wellington boots outside the back door. Her big toe poked through a hole in her sock – men's socks, a pair Adele was sure had once belonged to their father. She was wearing a tartan flannel shirt tucked into tan corduroy trousers, saggy and muddied at the knees, a wide leather belt dissecting her middle. Bea had lost weight, lately, although still that enormous bosom of hers strained against her shirt buttons. Without that bosom she would be mistaken for a man, as she sometimes was anyway, from behind. Soon she would be pestering to have her hair cut again, and Adele would be worn down into getting out the scissors, having failed to persuade her to keep it that little bit longer, that the incipient curls softened her face, even if they were salt and pepper now.

Slumping into one of the easy chairs beside the Aga, Bea said, 'I saw our new neighbour. She was standing on the terrace looking scared to death of venturing any further.'

'Did you say hello?'

'Too far away – I was at the bottom of the garden. I only saw her because I was up the ladder, pruning the apple tree. I waved. She waved back, like this.' Bea waved feebly, making a poor-little-me face. Resuming her normal expression, she said, 'What time are we expecting our boys?'

'About four o'clock.'

'Can I have a cake now – before you cover them all in that rubbish?'

'Help yourself.'

Bea did as she was told. Instead of returning to her chair, she went to the window and gazed out over the garden, eating the cake absently, the crumbs falling onto the shelf of her breast. At last she said, 'I think the apple tree should be cut down. It's old. And the roses. They should be dug up, they're old, too.'

Adele frowned. 'But you love those roses. And the apple tree –'

'Dangerous.' Bea turned to her. 'There's too much work in the garden.'

'You like work.'

Turning back to the window, Bea snorted. 'Yes, I like work.'

'Perhaps we could get someone in to help.'

The cake was finished and she looked down at the smattering of crumbs before licking her forefinger to pick them off one by one. At last she said, 'Perhaps we do need help.'

Adele frowned, the tube of Smarties in her hand forgotten; Bea hardly ever agreed with her, and only when she was most wearily unhappy. Trying to keep her voice light to disguise her concern, she said, 'Tom might know of someone – Tom may even help, if you asked.'

'I wouldn't dream of asking Tom! And you mustn't either – he has enough to do.' Bea glared at her. 'Don't say anything to Tom. I won't have him worried.'

'A little worry won't harm him – is there something to worry about?'

'No. Nothing. Be quiet.'

'Be quiet yourself.' Adele laughed, angry at the childish bossiness that Bea had never seemed able to grow out of. 'Go and have a bath before Tom comes.'

'I've left the ladder against the tree.'

'Leave it for now.'

'No.' She put on her boots again. 'A job's not finished until it's cleared away.'

'Bea –'

Bea turned to her, halfway out the door. 'I'm fine.'

'I never said you weren't.'

'Finish the cakes. Let's be shipshape before the boys arrive.'

Bea sat on the stone bench a few feet from Binky's grave. There was the ladder still against the tree but she couldn't be bothered with it for now. Too much effort to get up and shoulder it to the shed; it could stay there, she imagined the tree growing a callous, incorporating the ladder into itself; the ivy would wind its way around and the robin that followed her around the garden would nest on its highest rung. Perhaps when Luc was a grown man he would find it and wonder why it had been left, because wasn't Great-Aunt Beatrice so tidy, so strict and stern, never one to allow nature to get the better of her?

Bea looked towards the low mound that was Binky's grave. He had been dead for over a year now and still she found herself looking around for him. The Jack Russell had been Adele's idea, bought from the window of Brown's Pet Shop as a puppy. Adele had told how he had climbed over his siblings as if he wanted to be chosen by her, the bravest and brightest little dog; how he would keep the rats away from the chickens and be a good companion and no trouble, none at all. Adele had always wanted a dog. And how much was that doggy in the window? Bea had asked. Hardly anything, Adele had answered, easily affordable: he would eat scraps – dogs didn't need very much. Bea wondered now why she had thought of the expense of such a small, eager creature; except she had always worried about money. Silly, really – there were no pockets in a shroud. She would give a great deal of money to have Binky under her feet again.

Dr Walker had asked after the dog and when she told him he was dead the man had looked quite stricken so that she'd had to reassure him: Binky had lived a good, long life and had died quite peacefully; she had even laughed that no doubt he was up in doggy heaven, good old boy that he was. She hadn't sounded like herself, the words too forced and jolly, almost unhinged it seemed to her now; but there had been an air of unreality during that consultation, she might have been outside herself, observing from behind the tinsel Christmas tree. That day, Walker's surgery was as warm and cheerful as such places could be, with a gas fire burning brightly and the Christmas paper chains fluttering in the up-draught. Christmas cards had been strung on a string across the chimney breast, obscuring the poster informing of free orange juice for the under-fives. And Walker had asked about Binky, and she had made a silly joke, although she missed him terribly and had wanted to cry for him, not for herself. She was outside herself, listening in, and it seemed as if Dr Walker guessed this because he said that she should come back, when she'd had time for the news to settle, that perhaps she might want to bring her sister along with her, to help with any questions she might have.

Gently, Walker had said, 'Miss Davis? Is there anything you want to ask now?'

She had told him, no, that he had been quite clear, and all was quite understood.

Quite understood. Wasn't she an old lady? She'd had her life, a long, interesting, fulfilled life; except now, in the garden where she had worked so hard, her life didn't seem long at all; surely it was only a few months since Tom's birth because she could remember his babyhood so clearly; and then his schooldays, over in a blur of inconsequential busyness. Then there was the war, but those years had been so terrifying that she had put them to one side, her memory

22

would skate over them so that all at once Tom was a married man, showing off that wife of his, his baby.

She could remember further back, to 1906, when she was almost twelve, and Charles and Eric climbing the garden wall, Charles shouting, '*I say – there's a girl in the old man's garden.*'

'I'm not a girl.'

'You jolly well look like a girl.'

Another boy appeared and now there were two of them swinging their legs from the wall, their heels kicking at the bricks. Two boys, brothers, anyone could tell, smiling and quizzical, intrigued by the girl in the garden of the old man's house. Except it was her house now; inside, her mother and father were directing the removal men and she had escaped into the garden because she could sense the row brewing: best to be out of it; keeping out of her parents' rows was her strategy. Keeping close, in an always doomed effort to inhibit their anger, was Adele's.

The first boy – Charles – wasn't Charles always first? – had said, 'You *are* a girl. What's your name, girl?'

Eric said, 'Ignore him. He's the rudest person you'll ever meet in your life. Hello, anyway. I'm Eric. The rude boy is Charles, my cousin. He lives with us, worse luck.'

Worse luck. Better luck if Eric hadn't lived next door; better still if Eric had never been born. How far back in time could she go? Where would the worst luck end and the good begin? There was the wall the boys had climbed. Not fit to be climbed now; fit to topple, hardly a wall any more but a crumbling support for ivy. Perhaps she should talk to Tom, take him through the house and around the garden, pointing out everything that needed to be fixed, shored up or nailed down. 'Tom,' she would say, 'look after your mother when I'm dead.'

She hadn't been back to see Dr Walker. Often she imagined that he had been mistaken; doctors often were. Often she had tidied up after a doctor's mistake. She could tell doctors a thing or two. She stood up. She would put away the ladder because Luc might run out here, climb up, fall down, although this was not very likely – Luc was much too sensible; however, climbing and falling was the kind of thing his father used to do so better safe than sorry. Glancing towards the house, she saw that Adele had turned on the kitchen lights; she should stir herself, get moving before the light became too poor. She took a step, hitching up her trousers: her belt needed another notch – she would wear braces if Adele hadn't drawn the line. 'Why not wear culottes,' Adele had said, her voice bright with desperate persuasion. 'And a blouse – it doesn't have to be very pretty . . .'

Bea smiled to herself. After supper she would take a sharpened screwdriver and punch yet another hole in the belt. For the first time in her life she would have a waist. She thought of Dr Walker and the any number of mistakes he might have made as she lifted the ladder from the tree and carried it back to the shed.

Chapter Three

Tom said, 'Luc, you're only to speak English at Granny's, do you understand?'

'*Oui, Papa.*'

Driving along Oxhill Avenue, Tom took his eyes from the road for a moment to look at his son. In the passenger seat, Luc looked straight ahead, his butter-wouldn't-melt expression all at once infuriating so that Tom's voice was too sharp as he said, 'No French, do you hear me?'

'Aunt Bea understands me.'

'But Granny doesn't. And it's rude to speak a language that someone else in the room doesn't understand.'

'She should learn. It's easy. I could teach her.'

Tom tried to imagine such a lesson: Luc supremely confident, his mother softly indulgent, pretending to be charmed by her grandson's precocity whilst obviously terrified of such a sly child. He wanted to ask, 'Why can't you be nice?' Instead, slowing down for a traffic light he said, 'How was school today?'

'All right.'

Again, Tom glanced at him. 'Really all right?'

Luc was inscrutable. 'Really.'

'If those boys were rotten to you again –'

Luc laughed like a thirty-year-old, turning to look out of the window. He was thirteen. His hands were folded in his lap; he was not a child to fidget or chatter but was always neat in his school uniform – the dark maroon blazer and grey trousers, the white shirt

25

and grey and maroon tie fastened just so according to school rules. His clothes were never stained, his shoes were never scuffed; his short dark hair was always combed into its parting. He was olive-skinned, slight; the other boys at school called him *Frog*; *Frog* was the very least of it. Tom felt himself gripping the steering wheel too tightly as he remembered the blood stains on Luc's shirt earlier that week. Some little bastard was bullying his son; whoever it was, he would like to get his hands on him.

He pulled up outside his mother's house; they had supper here every Friday; this was the start of their weekend – they had battled through another week and their reward was cottage pie, blancmange for pudding. Blancmange: a French word – *white food*. Except it was never white, but pink, so not authentic, then; not any kind of food Christina would recognise. He sighed, not wanting to think of his ex-wife, and Luc turned to him.

'We should stay at home next Friday,' Luc said.

'You like coming here. Don't you?'

'You don't.'

'That's not true.'

Luc picked up his satchel from between his feet. 'So come on, then. Let's go in.'

'Luc . . .'

His son looked at him, eyebrows raised so that he looked like his mother.

Tom shook his head. At a loss to know what else to say he blurted, 'Listen. I could speak to your headmaster –'

'No.'

'No.' Tom exhaled, he could hardly believe he had said such a ridiculous thing; he had only managed to alarm Luc, who had paled, as though he believed they were about to drive back to his school right away. 'No,' Tom repeated. 'Of course not. I'm sorry.'

'Everything's all right, Dad.'

'Yes. Yes of course.' He smiled and had an urge to ruffle his hair, an urge that had to be suppressed: Luc didn't much like to be touched. Brightly he said, 'So, ready for that blancmange?'

Opening the car door, Luc glanced at him. 'No French words, Dad, remember?'

'Our new neighbour has arrived,' his mother said. 'She's very pretty. Did you ever meet her, Tom?'

Tom finished the last of the blancmange. He had eaten too much; he always ate too much at his mother's house. Now he could fall asleep in an armchair, full and befuddled. He had hardly registered what his mother had said and he looked at her blankly. 'Sorry, Mum?'

'Our new neighbour. Poor Mark's wife. She moved in today. I was just wondering if you'd ever met her.'

Tom pushed his empty bowl away. 'Yes, I've met her. Once, when I was in London last year, and again at Mark's funeral, of course.'

Luc said, 'May I leave the table, Grandmamma?'

'Yes, of course, darling.'

'Why don't you go and watch the telly,' Bea said.

'I have homework.' Luc lifted up his satchel, its straps straining across the top of a large book. 'I should make a start.'

'You don't need to do it now, Luc,' Tom said.

'Yes, Papa, I do.'

Heartily Bea said, 'Turning into a swot, are you?'

Luc ignored her, already at the kitchen door, the satchel under his arm. Turning to Tom he said, 'I'll be in the sitting room.'

As the door closed behind him Bea laughed shortly. 'Quite the Little Lord Fauntleroy.'

'Oh, Bea.' Adele began to clear the table. Glancing at Tom she said, 'He's a good boy.'

Bea snorted. 'How's he doing at school?'

'Fine.' He stood up. 'Let me help, Mum.'

'Your mother can manage,' Bea was sharp. 'Come upstairs with me. There's something I want to show you.'

Tom said, 'What are we looking at?'

Bea thought how like his father Eric he looked: slim, handsome, frowning as though he would rather be anywhere else in the world than in this room. Not that he was in the room: he was leaning against the bedroom door frame as though it was far too much effort to stand up straight. He was weary, she supposed. Teaching Modern Languages to a lot of bored seventeen-year-olds would make anyone weary. She imagined teaching to be a particularly draining kind of weariness, sapping one's will to live. All the same, he should buck up; he hardly knew he was born – she had always thought so; Adele had spoiled him, a sneaky kind of spoiling, done behind her back, when she was out at work; she had the idea that they conspired to keep things from her. *Things* – Tom's laziness and lack of ambition; Adele's unwillingness to discipline the boy; Bea grunted, remembering.

Tom repeated, 'What am I looking at?'

'The damp above the window.'

'The guttering, I should imagine.'

He didn't move, only frowned more intently at the water stain. He looked at her at last, his expression softening because they were good friends, really, and knew each other better than anyone. 'What's up, Buzz?'

'The house is falling down.'

He laughed. 'No, it isn't.'

'It's getting too much for us.'

'Is it?' He looked concerned at last. He had always loved this house; but no one should love a house – such a love was too greedy, too complacent; and what were houses, anyway: a burden, an expense, a worry.

Tom went to the window and looked more carefully at the damp that had yellowed the plaster and caused a corner of the ornate coving to crumble. Bea knew that it was most likely caused by loose guttering, or a broken roof slate, perhaps. There was a man she could call who would fix it, most likely at not that much expense. But Tom needed to see that there were things to be done; things that only she worried about, those things that Adele wouldn't notice. And no one ever opened the door on this room, one of the handful of unused bedrooms. The room was chilly; there was a musty smell she was ashamed of. The bed displayed its stained, bare mattress in a way that all at once seemed indecent to her. She wanted him out now, downstairs, drinking tea in the kitchen in a comfy chair. But he was frowning and frowning at the stain, as though it really could cause the house to fall down. She wished she hadn't worried him and wondered now why she had thought to, why she couldn't have been straight with him, come right out and tell him the truth of it all: *You will have to look after your mother.*

Bea sat down on the bed heavily, a pain in her chest as she tried to catch her breath.

'Buzz?' He stood over her, frowning like his father, but not like him, not a great useless lump like him.

She shook her head, as if this might ward off his concern.

Tom sat down next to her and together they stared at the busy wallpaper – wisteria and trellis, repeat, repeat. After a little while he said, 'This wallpaper's really quite something.'

'It's certainly *something*,' Bea said. 'My mother chose it, bless her heart. She hardly ever set foot in here once it was done.'

'The guest room.'

'Not that we ever had any guests. The Old B scared them all away.'

'The rotter.'

'Yes.' She laughed. 'Rotten rotter.'

He looked at her. 'Was he so bad?'

Was he? Her father was just a bad-tempered man, neither kind nor cruel. She gave Tom's knee a quick hard squeeze. 'Your mother's made cakes. We'll have one with a cup of tea.'

As she stood up Tom said, 'Do you want me to sort out a man or something?'

She looked at him blankly, forgetting for a moment the damp which was only an excuse anyway. Remembering, she said, 'No, no need.'

He smiled, obviously relieved. But there was still a question in his eyes, a concern he wouldn't voice if she kept up her talk about tea and cakes; he wouldn't push her. But she had worried him, she knew, and this worrying had been her intention, after all; it was a kind of

29

forewarning, she supposed. Briskly she said, 'Tea and cake, then. That little chap of yours won't turn his nose up at cake, will he?'

Adele watched as Luc ate a cake; she could never quite believe how neat he was, how self-contained and well-mannered, never quite himself and always on guard in the presence of others. Years ago she had seen a film of the Prince of Wales visiting coal miners and she imagined that this was how the prince had behaved in those humble little cottages, and that the miners and their wives and children would feel as if their visitor was encased in an invisible glass dome, absolutely separate, absolutely untouchable, and yet absolutely present; they wouldn't be able to take their eyes off him, just as she sometimes couldn't take her eyes off Luc. Luc with a c instead of a k, she thought as she often did, that missing k making him that bit more foreign. If he missed his foreign mother he never showed any sign of it – he was too proud – proud as a prince visiting his peasants, even as a baby Luc had seemed to look at her as if she would never quite come up to his standards.

She said, 'All your homework done?'

He glanced at her. 'No. I need help.'

She raised her eyebrows in surprise. 'Oh?'

'We have to draw a family tree. I'll have to do Dad's side. Mama would take too long to get back to me. So you need to tell me the names and dates of my great-grandparents, and my grandfather. And then I have to write something about one of them – the most interesting one.' He looked at her frankly. 'It would help if anyone of you did anything special.'

'Special in what way?'

'Interesting – exciting, even. A good story.'

Adele took his slightly crumbed plate away from him. 'I don't think there are any good stories. We're not an interesting or exciting family. But I can tell you the names and the dates – births and deaths? I can tell you all that. As for the rest of it, perhaps you could make something up? Who would know one way or the other? You could make one of us as exciting and interesting as you like.'

'I don't want to cheat.'

'Oh, why not?' She sounded too light-hearted, flippant, she supposed, and he wanted her to be serious, he had even coloured a little at the idea of being encouraged to cheat.

She sighed. 'If you have a piece of paper . . .'

He took a jotter and a pencil from his bag and held them out to her. As she began with her father's name Luc said, 'Was my grandfather in the war in France?'

She didn't look up but went on writing. 'Yes.'

'Was he killed?'

'No.'

'Because I thought I could write about him. Fighting in the war. It's a history project and our teacher loves the war.'

'Does he now? Not a thing to love, in all honesty.'

'Was he an officer?'

'Yes.' She looked up. 'There. Names and dates. Something to build on.'

Taking the jotter from her he said, 'You haven't told me very much.'

'As I say, we are – were – all very dull. Much better if you make something up. Write that your great-grandfather – my father – subdued a cannibal uprising in Bongo-Bongo land, something like that.'

'But he didn't, did he?'

She thought of her father, who certainly wouldn't have taken any nonsense from any grass-skirted blacks, and shook her head. 'No, he didn't. But you need to use your imagination, that's my point.'

He looked at the list of names, then at her. 'Eric. I'll write about him.'

'If you wish.'

'And you're right. No one will know if it's true or not.' He exhaled, obviously pleased that they had reached a satisfactory conclusion, and all at once he looked like Eric – she had never seen the resemblance before, but there it was in that expression of relief – Eric was always pleased when such conversations could be tidied away.

Bea and Tom came down and there was the putting on of coats and all the goodbyes, the walking them out onto the drive where Tom had parked his car, the waving as they drove away. As the car turned the corner out of sight Bea turned to her. 'What's the matter?'

'Nothing. There's nothing wrong.'

'You look put out, that's all.'

Adele turned to go into the house. There was the washing-up to do, things to put away. She was aware of Bea watching her shrewdly, but there was nothing to be done about that. Her sister could think what she liked, as long as she didn't say anything. Briskly she said, 'Come on, let's get in out of the cold.'

In bed, Adele thought about the people whose names she had written in Luc's jotter, her father Bernard, her mother Edna – these two names unfamiliar, and growing more so as the years passed, because in her life their names had hardly been used – they were Mother and Father, and even these titles weren't voiced often. He was the Old B, their mother not enough of a presence even to be given a nickname. Both of them long dead, her mother first, much to everyone's surprise – the quiet ease of her life should have meant something; but perhaps her father's angry cantankerousness had kept him raging against the dying of the light as everyone was meant to, according to poets. Anyway, they were dead and she had never missed them very much, never entertained those sentimental thoughts that she sometimes suspected Bea harboured. Wasn't Bea quite the soft thing at heart, although she hid her softness, suppressed any womanly emotion, of course. Adele thought of how she had ruffled Luc's hair as he was leaving, roughly, as a grandfather might, but there was an expression on her face that belied this ostentation, no masculine gruffness, just an animating love. Her love was so natural yet everything else about her life was as unnatural as she could make it.

'She's just a tomboy,' Eric had said often enough, laughing because Bea's boyishness was never to be taken seriously by a real boy. And Charles would refuse to comment, not being that much of a real boy himself. And what was left for her to say – not much, least said soonest mended, which was her mother's perpetual advice, and on reflection shouldn't be denigrated just because it came from her.

Eric. There he was, grinning into her memory, dangling from the thick branch of the oak tree at the bottom of their garden, jumping down to land at her feet. 'You know I love you, don't you, Del?' He called her Del, no one else ever did, and he told her he loved her so often, from when they were both about fifteen. Did she ever say the words back to him? Oh, she must have. On their wedding day, surely. She *had* loved him – she hadn't merely settled for the boy next door out of laziness, out of a certain lack of interest.

Adele rolled onto her side, curling herself up into the snugness of her bed, taking herself away from her memories to thank God for her safety, her warmth and comfort. Out in the world others were suffering, this was true and always would be true, no matter what. She shouldn't think of Eric – such thoughts only added to the world's suffering. Eric, who was long dead and gone, and only thought of now because she had rushed off his name in Luc's jotter: *Eric Dearlove*, in brackets *Lieutenant in the Durham Light Infantry*. The war should have been the death of him, as it had been the death of so many young lieutenants. Yet he had survived and that was the great pity.

She exhaled; some thoughts mustn't be thought; some memories – most – had to be kept locked down tight and no peeping beneath the lid just because of some such ideas about love or redemption or forgiveness. She imagined her mother's lips on her cheek, although she had never kissed her goodnight, never tucked her in or told her to sleep tight – this imaginary maternal care was a comfort, nevertheless; closing her eyes she attempted to will herself to sleep.

Bea woke as she always did at 3 a.m. She thought that perhaps she should turn on her lamp and read; Adele had borrowed a book from the library for her, a Father Brown mystery. Bea was almost sure she had read it before; she should pencil her initials in the back of library books, that's what Adele did. She would never do this now, Bea was certain. Why change the habits of a lifetime, the *non*-habits, the forgetting of small things such as defacing library books and rinsing out her teacup when she had finished with it – if she had remembered to bring it in from the garden. She knew she exasperated her sister, much as Adele exasperated her. Chalk and cheese, her father had called them – but who was the chalk and who the cheese? Bea smiled grimly to herself. Never mind that. Their differences came down to this: the pretty one and the plain one; the silly girl and the clever girl; the matron and the spinster. Yet here they were, washed up on the same shore, their lives contained within the same walls, the same history, the same future, when all was said and done.

Thinking of the future made her reach out and turn on the lamp, its frilly pink shade casting a dim, rose-coloured light. The shade was Adele's purchase, Adele's beribboned taste; it matched the eiderdown, which matched the curtains. Bea had long ceased trying to keep the tide of pink at bay; her stand against frills had been half-hearted anyway: what did she care? Baby pink or boy blue, some battles weren't worth fighting. Besides the lamp were her reading glasses, a pen, and a notebook; she reached for them, sitting up, and opened the book on a turned-down page.

Last night, at this same small hour, she had made a heading, underlining it boldly: My Funeral. Beneath this was another, less bold heading: Hymns. Last night she hadn't been able to think of any hymns except 'The Lord's My Shepherd'. She put on her glasses and put a question mark beside the hymn's title. *Adele,* she thought of writing, *was this sung at Father's funeral? Perhaps it's sung at every funeral . . . Anyway, can't remember.* Adele would remember; her sister was the keeper of memories.

All she could remember of that day was the new dress she had worn; black wool; no, not so much the dress, but the corset she'd had to wear beneath it. With the too-warm dress clinging to this undergarment she had looked upholstered. Someone might have mistaken her for a chair. And then there were the shoes, of course: shiny black, patent leather court shoes that had belonged to her mother, and yet her mother had been dead for years. Adele must have squirreled these shoes away, knowing they would come in useful. '*I don't think she ever wore them,*' Adele had frowned as she took the shoes from their box, a square of tissue paper wrapping fluttering down to Bea's bare feet. '*Here,*' her sister held them out to her. '*Try them on. Even if they pinch a little . . .*'

Oh, they'd pinched. And her feet had swollen so she could hardly take them off, and sweat patches bloomed beneath her armpits, that corset so tight, leaving red weals. But even so she had felt jubilant that day. And if someone had mistaken her for a chair and sat on her she would have laughed and been quite jolly, which wasn't proper funeral etiquette at all; not proper not to care that her father was dead. Not proper to tell Reverend Thomas that actually she hadn't much liked the Old B. Thomas had made one of his understanding faces, not shocked because he was a priest and besides, no one had much liked her father. All the same, it *was* his funeral and really the dead were owed a respectful word on the day of their internment, perhaps. Anyway, no one made the mistake of sitting on her, just as no one mistook her happiness for a brave, if slightly maniacal, front. The Old B was dead, and wasn't everyone relieved?

So, she did remember a little of her father's funeral: Reverend Thomas's faux understanding; the dress; those shoes; the pork pie she didn't dare eat with her body all squashed as it was. Not much of the church service, certainly not the hymns. She thought back to other funerals; her mother's had been a sadder affair and she seemed to have blocked it from her memory. Then there was Eric's funeral, of course, but that was such a very long time ago, she had been immortal then. And then there was Margot's funeral, which she thought of sometimes; she had made a fool of herself in front of Margot's sons; and now one of those sons was dead, his widow moved into Margot's house. At least Margot had been spared such grief – how could one lose a son and survive? She thought of Margot sitting up in bed with the new-born Mark in her arms – how beautiful she had looked, and pleased to see her, which was always surprising, Margot's pleasure in her company. Bea closed her eyes, seeing her face again, her pleasure again, hearing the smile in her voice: 'Bea, of course you're not disturbing us.'

Bea shook her head; she mustn't wander off down memory lane but focus on the job in hand. She tapped her pen against her teeth; perhaps she should leave the hymn choices to Adele, she would be the one who had to sit through them, after all. About to cross out the question mark, she left it in place; it would remind Adele that she didn't know about hymns, didn't much care. Below this heading she wrote *I leave the details to you. Don't go to much expense.* As an afterthought she added, *Flowers from the garden, whatever is blooming.* She thought about this; it seemed a shame to cut flowers only to throw them on her grave, but why shouldn't she have flowers? If she lived until the summer she would want the roses. Perhaps she should make this her goal: to live to see the roses, to show Adele which ones she should cut for her wreath.

She heard Adele's bedroom door open, the click of the light switch. Bea thought of turning off her lamp, not wanting her sister to tap on her door, asking if she would like a cup of cocoa. But then she heard the bathroom door close, so perhaps Adele was not so wakeful, this was just a sleepy stumble to the lavatory. She waited, keeping quite still until she heard Adele return to her room, the light that had leaked beneath her door all at once extinguished. Satisfied that she wouldn't be disturbed, Bea looked down at her notebook: only a few scrawled lines, hardly anything at all; she had never been one to make notes. But then it came to her, that thing that she must insist on, that Adele already knew but must be reminded of. She wrote *I want to be cremated.* She wanted to add *Don't bury me with the parents.* This last was unnecessary of course; Adele wouldn't do such a thing. Their dislike of their mother and father united them.

Eric had said, 'He seems decent enough to me.'

Bea remembered laughing, full of scorn and outrage. '*Decent!*'

In the garden, years after he had first climbed the wall, Eric had blushed. Even though he was in his uniform, so smart and shoulders-back tall, he had turned quite red; she had refused to feel sorry for him, didn't say anything to soften her show of contempt as Adele might have. She had only watched him as he glanced away towards the house, as though he wanted to go back inside and find her father, to study him, perhaps from some hidden corner as one might study a dangerous animal, and satisfy himself that Bernard was a decent chap really, despite all the rot his daughters spouted. A man would understand the Old B. He swallowed hard, his Adam's apple bobbing above his too-tight-looking collar. He turned to her and she saw that his high colour had drained away; he looked pale and so anxious she was afraid he might cry. She wouldn't be able to cope with crying so she said heartily, 'Do buck up,' and this was such a change of tone that he laughed.

Eric said, 'When I said decent I meant that he might not be so bad.'

'No, he might not.' She agreed, a concession; she didn't want him to appear so scared. The Old B couldn't stand any show of weakness. To steady him further she said, 'Just be straight with him.'

'Yes.' He took a deep breath. 'Yes, of course, you're right.' In a rush he said, 'I just wish we could simply elope. No fuss. All done and dusted, a done deal, as it were.'

Yes, she thought; that would be better. That's what she would do, if she were him. She said, 'You do look marvellous, Eric.'

'Do I?' He seemed genuinely unsure and looked down at himself. 'It's rather like a slightly more complicated school uniform.'

'No! Much smarter.' Had she sounded envious? She had certainly felt jealous. In her more elaborate fantasies she thought of disguising herself as a man and joining the queue outside the town hall, now a temporary recruiting station. She would be a soldier; all she had to do was fool whoever it was that needed to be fooled. She could pass for a boy – *had* passed for a boy, and in a uniform . . .

Eric said firmly, 'I should go in. Be straight with him as you say.' He put on a slightly deeper voice. 'Mr Davis, I would like your permission to marry Adele.'

In bed, Bea closed the notebook on her pen, took off her glasses and placed them all down on her night stand. She turned off the lamp because she should try to sleep – sleep was meant to be healing, after all. For some time she stared into the darkness, thinking of Eric and how he was when he came home from the war. Scared of his own shadow, the Old B had said, adding *bloody fool* for extra relish, like salt on an open wound. Thinking of Eric she couldn't help remembering Charles and how the war hadn't changed him at all, except to make him more of what he already was. It was as if the war had been waged just for Charles's ratification.

Charles was coming to see her. Yesterday he had telephoned, the poor line distorting his voice so that she could only make out every other word. All she knew was that he was coming and that he wouldn't be stopped no matter what she said to discourage him. He needed to be told that his biography of Paul-Harris-who-became-Francis-Law hadn't caused damage, not so much anyway, and that she and Adele didn't mind about the way he'd dragged out Margot's past like a stinking corpse to be prodded and pulled apart. He needed her reassurance, and that was why he was travelling all the way back to Thorp. Charles – still the naughty boy looking to excuse himself and be soothed by the adults; she could almost smile at his desperation to be forgiven, to be liked again. Poor little orphan Charles; she could feel her heart softening for him, her resolve to be angry with the foolish man slipping away. Charles Dearlove had been her friend once, still was, she supposed. And Margot wouldn't have cared so much about his book; why should a dying woman care about the dramas of her youth?

She wouldn't think of Margot, nor Charles, not even Eric. She would go to sleep and maybe her body would do some healing of itself and then she wouldn't have to give Tom tours of the house and all its worrisome dilapidations. She saw Tom smile, heard the lightness in his voice when he called her Buzz; she would think of this and try to sleep.

Chapter Four

Charles, winter 1923

Margot said today, 'You were in the war,' and I said, yes, I was, I distinctly remember, and I smiled at her, hoping to make her smile. We were sitting on a bench in the park and she didn't smile, only went on staring out over the duck pond, her hands in her lap, her fingers plucking at a stray thread hanging from one of her coat buttons. I noticed she still wore her wedding ring, a cheap, thin band loose against her knuckle, and the pity of it gave me the idea of placing my hand over hers; but I knew this would cause her to pull away, perhaps even to stand up and say that we must be getting along. She can be all at once brisk in this way, the kind of puzzled briskness that puts me in mind of a man about to snap, the kind of man I take care to avoid. But there I was, on the bench, so close to Margot I could consider covering her hands with mine. I saw her mouth open and close, as if she thought better of what she was about to say. She bit her lip and her fingertip became white as she wound the thread around and around. At last she said, 'The war made Paul mad.'

'Yes,' I said, 'I think so.'

She looked at me. 'You do?' She seemed relieved that someone – even I – should agree with her, and also surprised. 'You really think so?'

I wanted to say that the war made us all mad, not just him. But that would make Paul less of a uniquely special case and she wouldn't be able to give him such a noble excuse. I think she knows that the war can't be blamed and that what Paul did to her was all down to Paul and him alone. Paul Harris would have buggered that man in the park's lavatory, war or no war, because he's as selfish as can be. I

39

couldn't say any of this of course. But I did concur that the war had made him mad because it had, only not in the way that could excuse his sin against her.

Bobby was in his pram, stoically watching the ducks. He is a placid child and no trouble; his mother has withdrawn so completely from the world that he expects little from her as far as I can tell. I picked up his teddy bear from his lap and waved it half-heartedly at him, putting on a gruff, teddy-bear-type voice to say some nonsense. The toy is an odd thing, knitted in blue and yellow wool, very homemade and humble, the stuffing coming out where the child has chewed its foot. As I made the bear dance about, its limbs waggling horribly, Bobby only stared at me and made me feel self-conscious; I don't think I have ever met such a serious child, although I haven't met many, in all honesty. Handsome little fellow, though – very much like his father, Paul.

Paul *is* very good-looking. His brother Robbie was good-looking, too. Handsome men are so rare that one is always surprised by them, especially in Thorp. I tend to believe that anyone in the least exceptional leaves Thorp at their very earliest opportunity and that Paul's parents could only have met in London – even Paris, because he has a dark foreignness about him, just as poor Robbie had. I decided that none of this would have happened if they'd been plain men.

I pondered this: it might not be so true; perhaps even an ugly man in a uniform might have garnered the kind of soft-hearted pity that Margot had so disastrously dispensed. Thinking of Paul and Robbie Harris my usual sadness came over me and the bear became still in my hand; I found myself staring at it, and it seemed to me to represent all the pain in the world, if that doesn't sound too over-blown.

Margot said, 'We should go home.' She made no move. I saw that her coat button had broken from its single thread and she had placed it on the bench between us. I picked it up because all at once I had a terror of losing it which made me worry again about my own state of mind. Holding the button as though I was about to hand it to her, I glanced at Margot. She was looking straight ahead, her lips pressed together. In a rush she said, 'Daddy says I must divorce him.' She looked at me; there were tears in her eyes that she swiped away. 'I must, mustn't I?'

'Yes.'

'I couldn't have him back.'

'No.'

'He wrote to me.'

I imagined Paul in his prison cell, writing to this woman he'd betrayed. I imagined standing at his shoulder, trying to read the words but I couldn't for the life of me decipher them. What could he write? I could hardly believe he had written to her – what nerve the man had. Then Margot rummaged in her handbag and took out an envelope, raggedly torn open, and handed it to me. 'Read it, I don't mind.'

'No, Margot.'

She laughed harshly. 'He writes he's sorry and he loves me and he's truly, truly sorry and ashamed –' She stood up suddenly, stumbled towards the laurel bushes behind the bench and vomited. I made to go to her but she blindly thrust out her hand to stop me. Bobby began to cry. I sat half on, half off the bench and I must have looked the biggest ditherer. I'm sure she didn't want me to see her vomit splashed on the shiny evergreens or notice the savagery in how she wiped her mouth with the back of her hand. Her eyes blazed with anger and disgust and made her powerfully forbidding. So of course I dithered – she'd become a strange beast and I am a coward. I slipped her coat button into my pocket, and although Bobby was crying I'd forgotten him. Remembering him I stood up, charged with purposefulness, and pushed his chair back and forth. 'There, there,' I said, 'everything's going to be all right,' and I couldn't help thinking of Aunt May, who had said this even on the day she died.

I walked Margot home when she'd collected herself. I saw her to the vicarage door and then walked home through the cemetery. All the way I thought that I should have read Paul's letter and that it might have given me some valuable insight; but I have become scrupulous and this is for the best, I think.

41

I have been friends with Margot Harris since 1918, when, home on leave, I'd visited the cemetery surrounding her father's church to visit Aunt May's and Uncle Arthur's grave. They had died within a few months of each other and neither Eric nor I had attended their funerals – Eric was in the asylum by then and I was apparently too indispensable to be allowed home from the stinking trench I'd made my home. I remember that she had approached me shyly and told me she was sorry for my loss. I could only nod because in those days the smallest display of sympathy could undo me. Margot had stepped closer; she had touched my arm so lightly and briefly I might have imagined it; she seemed to understand my predicament because she waited until I could pull myself together enough to make some light-hearted small talk, and we found ourselves strolling around the graves as though we had known each other all our lives. Eventually, hesi-tantly, she asked if I knew Robbie Harris and I said yes, a little, since we were children, and this answer pleased her because she was so obviously in love with him. I asked if she'd met his brother, Paul, and she had shook her head. It seemed we both wanted to talk about the Harris brothers and only decorum prevented us. I wrote to Mar-got from the front, and she wrote back, little, stilted notes – she was never one for words. The men believed these notes came from my sweetheart; I didn't enlighten them.

When I arrived back from walking Margot home Eric was just where I left him, in his father's chair by the fire he'd allowed almost to go out. He hadn't lit the lamp and all I could see through the gloom were the whites of his eyes, which spooked me somewhat. He's so gaunt now, his cheeks so sunken that I can't help being reminded of a corpse. One particular corpse, but I was stern with myself, *you'll not think about that poor old body, Charles, simply don't think about it.* This sternness works sometimes; other times it's all wallow-ing and misery and a charging inability to think of anything but.

I switched on the ceiling light and Eric squinted but hardly moved at all. As I knelt in front of the fire to poke it back to life he said, 'There was someone knocking on the door for such a long time. I kept very quiet, kept my head down. They went away.'

'It would have only been Adele.'

'I don't want to see her.'

The fire revived and I put on more coal. Sitting back on my heels I looked up at him. 'How about some supper?'

'How can you eat?'

'How can you not?'

He snorted. 'Where did you go?'

'For a walk.'

'With that girl.'

'Margot.'

'Another fat girl.'

'She's not fat. Not any more.'

'Good. I can't bear fat women.' Panicked he said, 'That Bea can't make me go next door. She can't. I won't go.'

'You don't have to go. I'll go, say you're busy, they'll quite understand.'

'You'll have to be convincing, she's very cunning.'

I laughed, thinking of Bea, the least cunning woman in the world. But nothing is very funny when you're in a starkly lit, near-freezing room with a lunatic. Still kneeling at the hearth, I looked up at Eric and had the urge to tell him that I was weary of his game, because often I felt that it *was* a game, he was only pretending to be mad, just as he might pretend to be an Indian Brave when we were children.

When we were children – I often think of this. Our shared childhood binds me to him in a way I wouldn't have thought possible when we were both eighteen and ready to flee Thorp. When I was eighteen I was preparing to leave Eric behind without the thought of leaving him crossing my mind. I was just going to Durham University to read English Literature, and he was going somewhere else, I forget where; perhaps he was staying. Our childhood had ended and we had grown apart quite successfully. I liked him well enough. We are cousins but I think it would have been all the same if we had been brothers. We would have met up at Christmas and Easter and he would have become someone only seen when the world was that

43

little bit out of kilter, the hum-drum suspended for whatever imita-tion of celebration Aunt May and Uncle Arthur had put on. Our childhood would have been remembered differently, or at least not so easily; we would have left it more securely behind us. I wouldn't be thinking of Indian Braves, at least.

Adele had left a pie on an enamel plate outside on the kitchen windowsill, covered with a striped teacloth. Beneath it was a note: *mince and potato. Bring back the plate and tea towel when you can.* Her notes are always instructive and to the point and this lack of fuss always surprises me because she is so mild and timid and smiles apologetically when she's crying. But this was only a note about a pie; there should be no *Dear Charles and Eric*, no signing off with love. I've no idea why I want so much more from her, except to reassure myself that she hasn't given up on us.

I brought the pie inside and shared it between two plates; there was a tin of peas in the cupboard and I heated them in a pan, gazing down at them idly as the green water bubbled and a scum like pond algae began to form. Sundays before the war Aunt May would roast a joint – beef, a leg of lamb, a chicken occasionally. Uncle Arthur would carve, making a pantomime of it, smacking his lips and wav-ing the long carving knife about like Sweeney Todd. The first time I saw him do this I was alarmed: five years old and scared of stran-gers, of strangeness. Arthur looked like my father, but kinder, a sweeter man, and beneath that initial, short-lived fear I remember feeling fascinated by him, I'd had no experience of kind men. I would watch Uncle Arthur carefully, waiting for him to be harsh, but of course the harshness never came. I began to think he wasn't manly. Not that I minded; I've never much rated manliness even as a child and I enjoyed the kindliness and the jokes and silliness. All the same I knew there was something lacking in him, something *essential*.

The peas almost bubbled over and I turned off the gas and strained away the water in the sink. Heating and draining tinned vegetables, frying or boiling eggs, and not burning toast is the limit of my culinary skill. Adele makes her pies, her soups and stews, and I wash

44

the pots and take them back to her, her tea towels folded, damp and neat. She never asks if we enjoyed the stew, or the pie or the cake she baked, doesn't seem to care, but I make a point of saying it was delicious. So delicious I ate nearly all of it myself, although I don't tell her this, or that Eric vomited up what little he did eat. Adele has become very thin; I would like to tell her to save more of the food for herself because Eric and I don't need so much. But she has an idea that we are men and men have huge appetites, like that father of hers. Her father is without doubt a man full of manliness and we are as scared of him as he wants us to be.

I called Eric in, I refuse to minister to him hand and foot – he would sit in that chair day and night if I wasn't here to chivvy him. I ate and he didn't very much, as is the way of things; I made tea and smoked a cigarette and suggested that perhaps he could wash the pots, but he only looked at me blankly as though I'd asked him to fly. He told me again that he would like to die. I only nodded and began on the dishes.

In the past when he has talked about dying – and he talks about it often – I would tell him that he has a wife and son to live for. He would only become indignant and deny that he had ever laid a hand on Adele, let alone married her. And then he would add, 'As for that boy, I don't know who the little bastard belongs to – he could be yours for all I know – he has the look of you.' He looks like Eric; like Eric before the war.

The dishes washed, I took the pie plate back to Adele, tap-tapping on the back door in my usual way so that she will know it's me because sometimes I think she still expects to see Eric standing there, miraculously back to his before-the-war self. But it was Bea who came, stepping aside without a word to allow me in.

Their kitchen is a mirror image of ours, only warmer and cleaner, this evening full of the smell of the linen airing in front of the range, the bright flannel stripes of Tom's pyjamas standing out amongst the white sheets and pillowcases. Bea took the plate from me. She said, 'I suppose you were out this afternoon?'

'Yes. Am I allowed to go out, Bea?'

'You do what you want.'

She sounded like her father. They call him the Old B, but this was the young *Bea* angry as I have ever seen her. She repeated, 'Just do what you want – as long as you lock the door behind you.'

I sat down at their kitchen table. 'Am I his gaoler now?' I looked up at her, and all at once thought of Uncle Arthur, who was the only one who didn't comment on her strangeness, who would make a joke to bring her round. For the life of me I couldn't think of any jokes.

She sat down opposite me, scowling so that she looked even more like a man. She was wearing a shirt and a cravat of all things, perhaps she was experimenting with a new look, as women do – she is a woman, after all, for all she pretends not to be. I wanted to tell her that a man wouldn't wear such a thing as a cravat in such a way unless he was a certain type of queer, and Bea wants to be a heterosexual man, I'm sure. Her hair is terribly short, I wonder how she gets away with it at the hospital. But she is matron; matrons can do as they like and perhaps beneath that ridiculous head gear she has to wear as matron no one can tell its length.

She stopped scowling – Bea's anger blows over quickly, as though she can't be bothered with anything that might be called 'show' – and she looked merely exhausted. She said, 'I should run away to the circus.'

'We'll run away together.'

She smiled grimly. 'We could get married – make a really good side-show. Remember how you asked me, all those years ago?'

Not so many years ago – Bea has a knack of making me feel as old as the hills – but I played along. 'We *were* very young.' I smiled. 'Even so, the offer still stands.'

'But you want to marry Margot Harris.' She got up and busied herself folding the sheets. 'How is she?'

'The same.'

'Poor thing.' She glanced at me. 'I saw Dr Harris today at the hospital. He'd come to see a patient. I wanted to say how sorry I was but it didn't seem appropriate. Unprofessional. His son broke the law, after all.'

Bea often dismays me like this. For a few seconds I can believe she understands – shouldn't she understand, after all? – but then she becomes that man she's so hell bent on impersonating, that ordinary, bigoted man the world is so thick with. If we were married she could be the man and I would hide behind her, completely unseen, completely without responsibility. The idea was compelling, like a scream.

Emphatically she said, 'Paul Harris did break the law.'

'Yes. Quite the master criminal.'

'Of course you would side with him.'

'Actually not.' I thought of Margot vomiting into a bush, her baby howling, and my own impotency in the face of it all. I said, 'I would side with him if he hadn't married Margot.'

'Of course for *you* to marry Margot you would have to wait for her divorce.' She looked at me slyly, 'Although there's talk that their marriage will be annulled.'

I pretended to be scornful. '*Annulled*. They have a child –'

She snorted.

I stood up. 'Thank Adele for the pie.'

Bea got up too. As though she couldn't get the words out quick enough she said, 'Any change in him?'

I shook my head, unable to think of a thing to say about Eric, but she was waiting for me to say something because I knew it had taken all her nerve to ask. I thought of lying, of saying that yes, there was some change, that Eric would be fine, he would become responsible for his wife and child – she had my word; all we had to do was wait for that muddled brain of his to unmuddle. I imagined bashing his head with a hammer as though he was an infuriatingly faulty machine.

At last I said, 'No. No change.'

She nodded. I knew that she didn't want any change, that he should only be a prisoner in our house with no chance of parole.

I don't want to write about Eric. I think he will die soon – he wants to die and I'm tired of giving him reasons to live. Probably I'm just tired of Eric and if that's unkind and selfish, well there you are. I've done my best. Ha! That's a nice excuse – excuse me, your honour, but I did my best wheedling and cajoling, reasoning and ranting. There isn't a court in the land that would find me guilty. Here I stand, hand on heart: I did my best. I despair of myself. Tomorrow I'll go and see Dr Harris again. Together the good doctor and I might try once more to persuade Eric to live.

Dr Harris has been shunned by most of our neighbours because of what his son Paul did. For my part I have an almighty crush on the good doctor and have done since I was eleven and he treated me for chicken pox. Dr Harris became something of an *ideal* man to me, kind and steady; I couldn't believe that he'd be given to silliness like Uncle Arthur, or nastiness like my father. And of course, sitting at my bedside with his cool fingers on my pulse, all I could think was how lovely his face was – and so intent on me and whatever he was measuring. I must have stared at him because he caught my eye and smiled as if he knew and understood all about me and didn't mind one bit. He said, 'You're in very good company with this rotten rash, both my little boys are covered in spots, too.' He was married with children: he must have interpreted my look of bitter disappointment as some development of the disease because he frowned and put his hand to my forehead. 'You'll be all right,' he said. He leaned a little closer. Confidingly he added, 'A few days off school, eh? Reading your books tucked up in bed, what could be better?'

He glanced at the pile of novels by my bed – *War of the Worlds* open and face down on top, and because I sensed he was about to leave I blurted, 'What are your little boys called?'

He snapped his bag closed and looked up at me. It seemed to me that he had never been asked this question before, as though no one knew him well enough to care. I was afraid I'd made him sad but he said quite happily, 'Robbie and Paul.'

Desperate to sound grown up, I asked what I imagined a grown-up might, 'And how is Mrs Harris?'

He laughed; I had an idea he might ruffle my hair – I had charmed him and this was appalling to me. Worse, he said lightly, 'My wife died a few years ago. Any more questions before I go?'

I shook my head, dumbstruck with love.

I made up stories about Dr Harris from that day on; all of them included me in a heroic role. But this is the true, un-heroic story.

There was once a fine, handsome doctor with two fine, handsome sons who were quite the talk of the whole town because they were so handsome, so charming and well-mannered that the girls would swoon whenever they walked by, swooning even more because the brothers were motherless, but never mind that. Their father, who was kind and good, had brought up his sons to be kind and good, too: handsome, kind, and good; not very bright, but there you are – you can't have everything.

But ah – even this dimness had its rewards because if a war seems all at once a good idea, better not to be too thoughtful, just salute and look snappy, which is what the brothers did. Robbie and Paul Harris snapped off to fight the war without hardly being asked. As I say, not very bright, but in their uniforms they looked like heroes, and one day one of these heroes smiled at me in a London café.

He said, 'Charles?' He stood up; in his haste to make himself known to me he almost toppled his chair. He laughed self-consciously. 'It *is* Charles Dearlove, isn't it? Paul Harris – Rob's brother.'

This was 1917 and the café had become one of those self-service places, all the waitresses having gone off to make bombs. Still there was some pre-war grandeur I liked, crystal chandeliers mainly that tinkled light on the dusty potted palms and the small, crowded-together tables with their starched white linen and frail golden chairs. A string quartet played Vivaldi just about audibly above the chatter and clink, putting me in mind of the musicians on the *Titanic* – I'm sure those men were similarly ignored.

I had been peering around short-sightedly for a table, a cup of tea in one hand and a sticky bun on a plate in the other. The bun was very white, white-iced and filled with white cream and I was very much looking forward to it, hoping that I wouldn't have to share a table so that my lust for the bun wouldn't be closely witnessed. I was in uniform, too, believe it or not – I couldn't quite believe it myself; and if I looked the very model of a fancy-dress fool, then Paul Harris was much too kind to laugh or fake astonishment. He only smiled at me, as genuinely pleased to see me as I think no one else has ever been. He said, 'Such a small world.' Indicating the other chair at his table he said, 'Will you join me?'

I could hardly say no. I could hardly say anything in fact because I was juggling the tea and the bun and my coat over my arm almost trailed to the floor, and other customers were bumping past me, and past Paul, turning their heads to look at him because he was obviously one of the fighting boys, unlike me. Paul smiled back at them and I thought how smiley he was – happy like he'd been sprung from a box. I had the urge to press down on his head, make him sit and be still. I thought of cutting the bun into small pieces and feeding it to him slowly, a way of calming him, but I only sat down heavily on the dainty chair, edging the cup and plate onto the too-small table before diving after my coat that had crumpled to the floor. When I resurfaced, he had sat down and was handing me a napkin; I noticed the puddle of tea in the saucer. 'That cup'll drip,' he said, and smiled. 'The buns are quite good but the cream is ersatz. Disappointing. Still,' he lowered his voice and leaned towards me confidentially, just as his father Dr Harris had all those years ago, 'there *is* a war on.'

I looked up from pouring the slops back into my cup; his face was close to mine, his eyes bright and searching; his cheek began to twitch and he put his fingers to it with a fleeting, puzzled look. All at once he was searching his pockets for cigarettes and matches. He held the open case out to me, raising his eyebrows when I didn't take one. 'No? I can't stop smoking lately. Filthy habit.' Inhaling deeply he glanced around the busy café, then back to me. For a moment I felt he had forgotten who I was and then as if to remind himself he exclaimed, 'Charles Dearlove! I went to the very best Christmas party ever at your house. Your father dressed up as Father Christmas. I remember being terrified of him because he pulled this alarming face as though he would eat me alive –'

'My uncle.'

He frowned at me.

'Not my father – my uncle Arthur. He could be frighteningly jolly –'

Paul shook his head as though mentioning his terror had been a grave faux pas. 'I think it was the false beard that scared me, really.' He smiled, but less manically, and it seemed that talking of the past had brought him back to earth. With moving sincerity he said, 'It's marvellous to see someone from home. I can't quite believe it. I've been wandering around London all day . . .' He looked down at his cigarette. Rolling it to a point around the ashtray, he said, 'Short leave. No time to get to Thorp. Back to France tomorrow. Back tomorrow,' he repeated, and looked up. 'How about you?'

I cleared my throat, self-conscious in my pristine uniform, a ridiculous fraud. 'I'm at the War Office.'

Paul only nodded. He drew on his cigarette again then clamped it between his lips as he patted down his pockets with both hands. At last he brought out a photograph and handed it across the table to me. 'Here. Rob. He's just been made captain – showing off by sending me this photo of him and his girl – Margot. I think she's much too pretty for him, too pretty and plump – Rob's much too stern for a soft little girl like that.'

I looked at the picture of Robbie Harris and Margot. I recognised her as the daughter of the new vicar of St Anne's, where Aunt May worshipped every Sunday. An avid gossip, May had told me all about the little family almost as soon as they had moved into the vicarage: vicar – who was too godly, May thought; vicar's wife, who seemed friendly enough if a little stand-offish; and Margot – only child. She made the most of Margot, as though I might go to the vicarage and begin courting her at once. May would be disappointed to know Rob Harris had snapped her up – she would know I didn't stand a chance against him.

I handed the photograph back to Paul and he studied it briefly, frowning, before shoving it back in his tunic pocket. 'Anyway,' he said, 'anyway . . .'

I thought I should rescue him with small talk but I found I hardly knew what to say to him. He was very pale, dark rings under his

51

eyes standing out like bruises, and that twitch had begun in his cheek again so that he dragged at his face as if to smooth it out. His cigarette had burnt almost to his fingers and he surprised me by lighting another from its stub – the first time I had seen anyone do such a thing. His hands shook a little and I noticed how bitten his nails were. I noticed too the faint whiff coming off him – like damp, dirty blankets left to scorch in front of a fire. I'd heard about the lice in France and I sat back from him and was ashamed at once. Shame or no, I wanted to scratch and I curled my fingers into my palms to stop myself.

'So,' I said, 'on leave in London, eh? Out on the town.'

I sounded terribly hearty. He was only two years younger than I but I might just have well been his father for all my bright pomposity; thankfully he seemed not to have heard me, his eyes on the café's door as two military policemen came in and scanned the place as though they'd like to arrest every man there. Paul turned to me and laughed shortly. 'They'll be hunting down some poor bugger.'

I shifted, thinking they should arrest me for being such an impostor; he must have mistaken my expression for something else because he laughed. 'They're not looking for me, Charles, don't worry. I'm too much of a coward to be tied to a post and shot.' He looked at me more carefully. 'You've grown a moustache.'

I touched my top lip defensively.

'It's all right,' Paul said. 'You suit it. I just prefer to shave.' He went on studying me and I willed myself to look back at him, feeling daring because meeting another man's gaze is something I rigorously avoid. Despite my daring I began to blush.

He didn't seem to notice my blushing and said, 'I have a room in a hotel close by. Anonymous kind of a place – not grand at all.' He flicked ash casually. 'People come and go all night long.'

As dryly as I could I said, 'It must be difficult to sleep.'

He laughed again as though I was a great wit. He said lightly, 'You should eat that bun. If you don't want it, I'll have it, I'm not proud.'

For all my self-consciousness I couldn't help but look at him. He looked like his father, so of course all the old longing came back and if I could have only sat and gazed at him for a while that would have been enough for me. But he was so matter of fact and no time to waste and I think he was puzzled by my mooning, perhaps even charmed, but still he didn't know quite what to make of me because he glanced away, drawing on his cigarette as if to steady himself. Glancing back at me he said, 'I'm sorry, I didn't mean to offend you.'

'You haven't.'

'That's good. I did rather spring on you – as if we were the most long-lost of friends. And you're Rob's friend, really – don't know me from Adam . . . Anyway . . .' He stood up. 'I'd best be off. Leave you in peace.'

'Stay,' I said. I wanted to say again that he hadn't offended me, that I only needed more time, more *hints*, I supposed, because I'd realised that just looking wasn't enough any more and all at once it seemed fate had led me to this café, to this table, to this frankly smiling boy; he had to sit down and go on talking, there should be a slower conversation that wouldn't make me feel as though the whole world had speeded up. I repeated, 'Stay,' and I smiled to try to make less of my request. 'Unless you have somewhere to go?'

'Only back to my hotel.' Another hint and he smiled back at me wryly, obviously relieved. Sitting down he said, 'But it's a dive, really. Terrible smell of damp. Where are you staying?'

I thought of my landlady, a kindly, respectable widow. She had told me that I could have guests and the front parlour was mine on request. I hadn't asked how much notice she would require for the use of this room, I hadn't expected to entertain. I tried to see myself sneaking Paul past her and imagined him giggling on the stairs. I would have to hush him and be the serious grown-up; the idea was too nerve-wracking to contemplate.

I cut the bun in half and the cream that wasn't cream oozed onto the plate; impossible to eat it in front of him so I pushed it away a little and sipped my tea. I said, 'I live in digs, comfortable enough.' I wondered what else to say; sweat trickled down my back and that itching began again because I could still smell him, knee to knee as we were at the little table. I had asked him to stay and now I should be entertaining him with anecdotes; or making eyes at him, perhaps – I had no idea how to do this. He thought he had offended me and I had to think of some way to prove that he hadn't. Lamely I said, 'Quite a coincidence bumping into you.'

'Don't you think the war leads to coincidences? Everyone is everywhere – bound to see someone you know bumbling about.' He flicked ash with expert nonchalance. 'I went to see a show earlier today and the whole audience was just a sludgy mass of khaki. Every one of them looked like someone I knew – not that I *did* know any-one, thank God, but the possibility seemed likely.'

He seemed to lose his train of thought and frowned. Drawing on his cigarette, his eyes lighted on a girl at the next table then on to the civilian man she was with. The man shifted under his gaze and Paul snorted, only to turn his attention to the girl again who studi-ously avoided his eye; at once I pictured the whole place in uproar, tables overturned and noses bloodied, women screeching as I left him to his brawl. He made me uncomfortable with those looks of his – he might decide to include me in his contempt. I surprised myself by saying, 'You look like you're spoiling for a fight.'

He turned to me. 'Actually I feel as if I'm soaring about the place, you know? Someone should shoot me down.'

'Which show did you see?'

'*Peter Pan*. A story about not growing up. Ha bloody ha, eh?'

'Quite.'

'Quite?' He laughed. 'Listen, *may* I eat that bun? I'm starving and it seems to be calling out to me.'

I pushed the plate towards him. 'Be my guest.'

He ate greedily and licked his fingers when he'd finished. Wiping his mouth with a napkin he said, 'Thank you.'

'My pleasure.'

In a suggestive, nancy-boy voice he said, 'I'm only wondering how I might repay you.' He frowned as though he was going over his words again in his head. Closing his eyes he said quietly, 'Christ, I can't stop.' He looked at me in dismay. 'I'm sorry.'

'It's all right.'

'No, it's not. I have to go.' He stood up. 'Please don't tell anyone at home.'

I stood up too. I touched his arm. 'I'll walk with you, back to your hotel.'

'Would you?' He sounded like a child.

'Yes, of course. Now,' I smiled at him, 'lead on, Macduff.'

I often think of that walk to his hotel. We walked in silence, quickly, as if to get it over and done with without any companionable, meandering diversion, although Paul stopped once to light a cigarette. I stood a step away from him, noticing that in his greatcoat he looked less frail and that his lieutenant's cap made him appear to be someone to be reckoned with, like one of those military policemen. The London traffic streamed past us, no more than a backdrop but all speed and busyness, all as it should be and would be when this act in my life was over. I was about to do something irrevocable – didn't this have to happen one day? Only it was happening this day, with this man, and this was unexpected and not something I could have imagined because my imagination is a florid thing and the unlikely reality would never have occurred to me.

We reached his hotel and it was just as he said – a dive, the staircase painted a shade of yellow that made me ache for whoever it was that had thought this colour of stains might be cheerful. That ache – I was all pathos and sentimentality. The baby screaming from behind a closed door was a poor orphan; that soldier passing us clumsily in his haste a hero. And the man who had painted the staircase – well, he had been a philanthropic optimist – I could almost hear him whistling; I was everywhere: comforting the baby, storming the wire, smiling at the yellow paint. I was holding the banister lightly, letting its stickiness pass swiftly against my palm, and my tread was light as though I wasn't worried at all, and all I could see was his back, his worn-in boots, his puttees, the way his unbuckled, deeply vented trench coat hung too large from his narrow shoulders, how its belt sagged and the pockets at his hips gaped as though his hands were always fists inside them, how his cap cut into his shorn head above the coat's upturned collar. How strange he was from behind, an animated uniform, wisps of cigarette smoke added by the puppeteer to make his creation seem more alive. At the top of the stairs he turned as if to check I was still there and his cap shaded him very efficiently because he was still a uniform without even a mask for a face.

He fumbled with his key; he opened the door; he saw that the room was too bright with daylight and closed the curtains, both hands tugging at them, experienced in their snagging ways. Still there was a gap and he tugged again until there was only a narrow shaft of light and the room became a sickroom where there was only a bed you should climb into quickly, shuddering at the insistent day. I thought he would begin to undress. I thought he would ask me what I was waiting for. In the time he had taken to draw the curtains he had become real and I stood in the doorway, unable to move a step in or out. I wanted this to be over as much as I wanted it to have happened, just another of those paralysing conundrums I have faced all my life.

He didn't undress; he didn't even take off his coat, only his cap, which he held in both hands as he sat down on the bed and stared at the oblong of light on the floor. Where had his cigarette gone, the one he had smoked on the stairs? There was only the smell of it exhaled on his breath; he must have crushed it between his fingers and tossed it down without me noticing. I had been looking away, off down the hotel corridor, wanting to escape. Now he wanted to escape because he said, 'I'm very tired.'

'Then I'll go.'

'You came all this way.'

'It doesn't matter.'

He bowed his head; after a moment he placed his cap gently on the bed beside him. He said, 'I have to go back tomorrow.'

'Yes.'

'I've wasted my leave.'

'How?'

He shrugged. 'I promised myself I'd sleep. Only get up to bathe or to eat. Sleeping, food, well, it all went by-the-by, even though I'd looked forward to it. Wasn't enough time. I didn't want to waste time.'

I stepped inside the room, making a floorboard creak so that he turned towards me warily. I stopped and held up my hands in a way that would show I wasn't about to step any closer. The width of the bed was between us and the poor light helped: he wouldn't see me so clearly and be reminded of how unsullied I was – all a picture of rude health – he shouldn't be comforted by such a man. I said, 'Sleep now, all warm and safe. Bacon and egg in the morning, fried bread, sausages, sweet tea, and then you won't feel as though your leave was wasted.'

'I don't want to go back.'

I felt as if he had reached a hand inside my guts.

He said, 'Isn't it funny? It's like the Sunday evening before you go back to school, but how can it be compared to school? As if I have only so much fear inside me.' He picked up his cap again as if he was about to put it on and go at once – better to be on his way than hang about worrying. But he only looked at it and kept looking at it as he said, 'I'm sorry.'

'No need to be.'

'Do you get back to Thorp much?'

'Not much.'

'If you do, if you see my father . . .' Quickly he went on, 'Sometimes I think he knows about me, other times I think not. Thinking he knows is horrible, humiliating.' He glanced at me as if he might be able to tell whether I understood or not. I did, in a way – I'd had similar feelings, but suspected, fatherless as I was, that I'd felt them less intensely.

But it seemed at that moment that I felt everything less intensely than this boy. If I'd so much as touched his shoulder at that moment I knew he would have reacted violently one way or the other. But I could no more touch him than if he had been an actor on a stage and I was his audience way back in the stalls. I watched him, waiting; it was a good show and interesting to me and so I tried to look sympathetic. I was sympathetic, of course – he was beautiful: I absolutely believed in him and he'd given voice to his fear of going back to the front, which made him even more believable because it had been so shocking and unexpected. I wondered what he would do or say next.

He said, 'You've come all this way.'

I thought of the long journey back to my room in the widow's house, several changes on the tube with all that walking through the underground's seared, exhausted air, and said, 'Don't worry about me.'

He stood up and took off his coat, folding it onto the floor. He placed his cap on top of it then lay down on the bed and pressed the heels of his hands hard into his eyes. He said, 'Do you remember that Christmas party when we were children?'

'Yes.' I sat down on the end of the bed, my feet firmly on the floor, my body angled towards him. I forced a little laugh and said, 'I so wanted there *not* to be a party . . . But in the end, well, I enjoyed the cakes and the presents.' I remembered him, such a vivid memory that I might have invented it that moment, a small, shy child of six or seven, never leaving his brother's side. And his brother Rob was embarrassed by him, and brusque, telling him not to be a baby when he shied from Uncle Arthur's looming face. I'd wanted to go to him and say something kind and reassuring, but Eric was there, and Rob, and boys don't do such things, so I watched him and thought how nice it would be to be alone with him. I had the thought that I might sit him on my knee. This memory was true, I was sure of it. I said, 'I remember you, Rob's little brother.'

'That's who I am. Robbie's brother.'

'You're Paul.'

He laughed shortly. 'No one calls me that. I'm Harris. Or *sir*. Sir. I should call you sir, shouldn't I? Don't you outrank me?'

'I'm just Charles.'

'*Just*, eh? Captain Dearlove, am I really not to worry about you?'

'No, you mustn't worry.'

'I probably won't ever see you again.'

'You will, I think, in Thorp, after the war.'

He frowned at me as though he'd come to his senses. 'Would you go back to Thorp?'

'Yes, to visit.'

He nodded. Staring up at the ceiling he said, 'I've had a rum kind of day. I wanted to go to the National Gallery, I really did. Thought I'd look at the paintings, you know – a real, serious look and it would be a serious, proper thing to do. Except I couldn't bring myself to go there. Just because I draw a little bit, and I can draw a man so you would say, *yes, that's so-and-so, the very spit of him* . . . But that's not enough, I know, and the idea of the art gallery made everything seem even more pointless than it is already, so . . . *pointless.*' He glanced at me. 'So I went to that show instead. And all the time I was thinking of that view of the Thames by Turner and how I should have gone to look at it. Just stood and looked at it and tried to work it out . . . I wish I had gone.'

'You'll get there, one day soon.'

He gazed at me. For some time he didn't speak, there was just a questioning look in his eyes that made me want to blurt something out; but I made myself stay quiet and at last he said, 'Do you want to stay?'

'Do you want me to?'

'I don't know, to be honest. I feel like a fire that's burnt out.'

'You should go to sleep.'

'I *should.*' He smiled as though he was trying to become again that manic boy he'd been in the café, but the effort seemed beyond him and he rubbed his hand over his face, his eyes bleak with exhaustion. At last he said, 'I'm sorry I've wasted your time.'

I stood up, relieved that I hadn't taken off my coat and I could leave quickly without any fuss. At the bedroom door I glanced back at him; already he was asleep.

Chapter Five

Cathy woke in her new bedroom wondering where on earth she was, sitting up and clutching at the bedcovers in fright, like the grandmother confronted by the wolf. When she remembered she groaned unwittingly and this seemed to her to reveal a truth she had kept from herself: she didn't want to be here; she wished she was in London, in her own flat, in the room she had shared with Mark. This room smelt of damp; the busy, hideous wallpaper sucked up all the light and all sound, too, it seemed; this silent house, on a so-quiet street, in a quiet town. Why was she here? She didn't have to mark territory like a cat. She should have sold the place unseen because Mark wasn't here, there was nothing of him here, no haunting spirit, no essence, nothing at all of her true love. He was dead. Stop all the clocks.

She fell back on the pillows. She could always go home; there would be the expense of moving her stuff back, but still. Besides, money didn't matter now she was an heiress. She snorted, thinking more clearly; how could she go home? Home with her tail between her legs, defeated, and there, then what? Audition for more parts she wouldn't get? She couldn't play the ingénue any more – too old; and her *look* wasn't in – if it ever truly had been. So what would she do in London? But then, what would she do here?

No one knew her here and that was a balm: she didn't have to *be* anyone; she could hide away, do nothing. She was quite good at doing nothing – *resting* – and then, when doing nothing became a drag she would think of doing something. She didn't have to think of that something yet; it was too soon, after all. This was her time to mourn: hadn't she decided to give herself this time? He deserved her time, her remembering and prayers. She thought of the prayers she might offer to hasten him through purgatory, if she believed in such a place. Closing her eyes she asked God to bless him before tossing the bedcovers aside and getting up.

Someone had left a bottle of milk on the kitchen windowsill, a used envelope folded beneath it on which that someone had scrawled *welcome from number 96 (next door)*. Stepping outside, Cathy glanced towards her neighbours' house but there was no sign of life, no one watching from a bedroom window to see if she had found this small offering. She wondered which of the old ladies had made the trek along their own drive, to her gate, down her drive and around the back, whether she had cupped her hands around her eyes to peer into the grimy window before setting the milk down, ready to smile and call out a brazen hello if she should be seen. Perhaps she had knocked on the door, perhaps hoping to be invited in.

Cathy took a step back, the better to see more of number 96 and catch a glimpse of the neighbours she had all at once decided were busybodies, a bottle of milk a small price to pay for a poke around. She read the note again, turned it over and saw that the envelope had been addressed to Miss B Davis in a child's painstaking hand. She remembered what Mark had told her about his mother's neighbours, how they had always been kind, and felt ashamed of herself for thinking of them with such suspicion. She looked across at their house again, smiling a little in case they were watching.

In the kitchen she made coffee and toast and sat down at the red Formica-topped table that looked too small in this room that was sized for a cook and a scullery maid, perhaps even a parlour maid or two. There was a row of bells on the wall, each named: dining room, drawing room; study, master bedroom. None of the bells could be made to ring any more; each was tarnished and dusty. She wondered why they had been left there: not for their quaint curiosity value, she was sure, because Mark's mother, Margot, was of a generation that would have only seen them as redundant, perhaps even a reminder of a failure to afford servants. Most likely the effort to remove them had been too daunting, attached as they were to a great slab of wood – the wall would need re-plastering, redecorating, a whole series of disrupting jobs coming one after the other. A choice had to be made: to live with the silent bells or face the consequences. The house was full of such choices. Cathy found herself sympathising with the mother-in-law she had never met, Margot, a widow, like her, alone in this house that needed optimism and vigour when all she had was sadness and lethargy.

'Margot – my mother – is a child, really,' Mark had once said. 'I suppose I've always thought that for as long as I can remember. A rather sensible, downtrodden child, but a child, all the same.' He laughed shortly. 'She always seems surprised to find herself with children – wasn't she too young for the little what-d'yer-call-'ems?'

How had they come to talk of mothers? That play he was in, of course, just after they met, a farce – something about babies being swapped at birth, the consequences of this swapping less hilarious than the playwright had supposed. Two mothers, one dotty, the other stern, and she had asked him about his own mother, which of the two was she most like? So he had told her that Margot, his mother, was really rather an unknown when it came down to it, but that he supposed she had loved him in that distracted way. Mark had looked at her then; until that moment he had been gazing at the ceiling, squint-eyed against his cigarette smoke. He had smiled, such a soft, puzzled, in-love expression on his face, as though he couldn't quite believe his luck that she was there next to him, in bed, as the gentle twilight of a wintry Sunday afternoon settled around them.

He'd turned back to the ceiling; perhaps she was too much of a distraction: he couldn't look at her and speak of his mother. He'd said, 'And of course, she had once, for a short time anyway, been married to the very great artist Francis Law, although she never spoke of her first marriage, never ever not never because my father forbade any talk of the *degenerate*.' He looked at her again more briefly, perhaps assessing her reaction, before stubbing out his cigarette in the ashtray beside the bed. Lightly he went on, 'I tell everyone that Law is related to me, of course.'

She'd laughed. '*Of course.*'

'Of course – a famous name can always open a door or two – use whatever advantage you have, that's what I say. Wasn't it one of the very first things I told you?' He put on the Hooray Henry voice he used in the farce, '*Did I mention my half-brother's father is the war artist Francis Law?*'

In fact David Black had told her just before he had introduced her to Mark at that party. She wondered now if David had wanted to make Mark seem as interesting as possible, because David had always told her that actors were the most boring of men. 'Truly, my dear, they are deadly – yes – even I – but Mark has intriguing depths.' David had looked across the room to where Mark was helping himself to a glass of champagne and laughed shortly and it seemed to her that he was remembering some small humiliation. 'And, what's more, he lets one down very, very gently. I think he's quite a prize and you deserve him, my duck. So, allow me to introduce you.'

There was a knock on the back door, an insistent knock as though she hadn't heard a first, more polite rat-a-tat-tat. The knocking brought her back; she had been out of herself, far away from the pain of the present – the past like a warm bed she so often escaped to. She stood up too quickly, automatically twisting back her hair and securing it with a clasp from her skirt pocket.

Adele said, 'I'm terribly sorry – I do hope I'm not disturbing you.' She thought, *I am disturbing you, you look so cross.* Dismayed, she looked down at the box of eggs in her hands. 'It was just we had so many eggs this morning . . .' She managed to look at the girl and thought how foolish she must appear to her, like a flustered hen. Bea had told her not to fuss. But there were so many eggs, and she had already left the milk and that note: the Rubicon had been crossed. Holding out the eggs she said with idiot brightness, 'Anyway, here they are. Eggs. From our own hens.'

The girl held the door open. 'Come in.'

'Really, I don't want to intrude.'

'You're not intruding. Come in.'

Adele glanced over her shoulder, half-expecting to see Bea glowering over the wall at her. But Bea was still in bed, complaining of a cold, which wasn't like her. She remembered her worry but decided not to think of it now; the girl was smiling at her, suddenly welcoming and no longer cross-looking. Adele remembered that she was an actress and was used to composing different faces on command. All the same, her curiosity got the better of her and she smiled back, stepping through the door into the kitchen she knew almost as well as her own.

But the room was altered; somehow this girl had made it lighter and more spacious. Margot's clutter had gone, of course, the two, tired armchairs that had faced each other across the Aga; that huge dresser crowded with the detritus of her life – scraps of torn paper Adele remembered mostly, scribbled notes – aides to Margot's failing memory. And of course, Francis Law's *Machine Gunner* had been taken down – she noticed a corner of the poster still sellotaped to the wall. 'He gives me strength,' Margot had said once of the *gunner*. 'Look at all that power he has. That anger.' She had laughed. 'And why shouldn't I have one of his pictures? There's no one to throw a fit over it now, after all.'

The girl – Cathy – said, 'Sit down. Would you like a cup of coffee?'

Adele sat at the table. Her eyes still on the poster's torn corner, she said, 'Coffee would be lovely, thank you,' and thought of Margot, her neighbour for so many years, her friend. 'You are my only friend,' Margot had told her, 'Havelock tolerates my being friends with you.' Adele had wanted to ask why she should be tolerable to him – that bully Margot was married to – but guessed that it came down to her terrible meekness and was ashamed. She must have looked ashamed because Margot had reached out and touched her hand briefly – Margot was not given to touching others – and smiled, ashamed too. 'Adele,' she said softly, 'lovely Adele.'

Cathy was saying, 'Do you take milk and sugar?'

Adele cleared her throat; her memories had brought her to the brink of tears, and said, 'Just milk, thank you.'

64

Holding up the milk bottle, Cathy smiled. 'Thank *you* – it was so thoughtful.' Her tone was too bright, an actress playing a part and badly at that, false and rather flashy. She seemed to realise this because her smiled slipped a little and she turned away, placing the milk bottle down gently. More evenly she said, 'Coffee, then, milk, no sugar.'

To lighten the atmosphere, Adele said, 'I think you may have met my son, Tom Dearlove. Tom was a friend of poor dear Mark.' At once she realised that this remark had only made the atmosphere more charged; invoking Mark's name had made the girl stop quite still, her hand grasping the electric kettle as though she had forgotten what to do with it. Adele found herself wanting to say how sorry she was, but made herself hold her tongue and watch and wait: she was interested in this woman and wouldn't allow her own bluster to obscure her.

At last Cathy placed the kettle down and plugged it in. She said, 'Tom. Yes, we met.' She glanced over her shoulder at Adele. 'He came to a party we had. Bobby Harris introduced us. He came to Mark's funeral, too.' Turning away again to spoon Nescafe into two mugs, she said, 'Do you know Bobby Harris?' Again she glanced at her. 'Of course, you must, he was Mark's brother.'

Half-brother, Adele wanted to correct her; he didn't belong to Mark's family, a little outsider. She remembered Bobby Harris as a very beautiful child, a shy will-o'-the-wisp playing alone in the garden, and how she would call out to him *Hello, little man,* standing on the garden bench so that she might see him over the wall. She had wanted to lure him into her house with sweets, to sit him on her knee and cuddle him close. She wanted Bobby to be hers and imagined going to Margot – although she had hardly known her then – and saying, *I'll take him, if you don't want him.* She had been certain that Margot and Havelock hadn't wanted him.

Cathy was looking at her and Adele guessed she had said something she hadn't heard, too caught up in her memories. 'I'm sorry – miles away.'

'I was just saying that Mark was pleased Tom came to that party. They had lost touch, I think.'

'Yes, I should think so.'

A cup of coffee was placed in front of her and Cathy sat down at the table, saying, 'You didn't tell me your name – I mean, I know you're Mrs Dearlove – I presume you are, anyway.'

'Yes. Adele. My name's Adele. I'm so sorry – I do that – forget the formalities, Bea's always telling me off about it.'

'Bea?'

'My sister. We live together . . .' She sipped her coffee, feeling a little ashamed that she had, as ever, made Bea out to be a Tartar. And to say that they lived together made them seem like a couple of old spinsters. Adele set down her cup. 'I'm a widow.'

'I'm sorry.'

Adele laughed, lightly dismissive; she even fluttered her hand to swat away her commiseration, although she had wanted the mention of her widowhood to lend her dignity. But she couldn't be dignified, not even for a moment. She was a silly old woman who laughed even at the fact that her husband was dead. 'He's been dead a long time,' she heard herself saying, and laughed again as she said, 'Tom doesn't remember him.' And why was she laughing about this? This Cathy didn't know how very little Tom's lack of a father mattered; she would only think that she was quite mad. No, not mad: giddy, the giddy goose. She took another longer sip of her coffee; it was too strong, almost black, but all the same she wanted to drink it quickly so she could escape the mortifying turn this conversation had taken.

But it seemed that Cathy was settling in for a chat, because she lit a cigarette and sat back in her chair, her long legs stretched out in front of her. She was as slim as a girl, confident as a man: a modern young thing, Eric would have called her, admiring such women as he did.

Blowing smoke down her nose, Cathy said carelessly, 'I suppose you were Mark's mother's friend?'

Adele managed to look at her properly for the first time, eye to eye, wanting to be confident herself for Margot's sake. Firmly she said, 'Yes. Margot and I were friends. Great friends.'

Cathy narrowed her eyes against the smoke, perhaps even against the starkness of her next question. 'What was she like?'

'Margot?' Adele had to stop herself from laughing again – always her response when she was embarrassed, or cornered. She certainly felt cornered, as though there would be no escape from her quizzical gaze until the question was answered to her satisfaction. She glanced away, towards the torn piece of *Machine Gunner* stuck to the wall. Seeing *Machine Gunner* on Margot's wall had made her feel that she didn't know her very well at all, that she certainly couldn't describe her to this woman who seemed to want so much to be critical. She wondered what Mark had told her about his mother; that she was cold, perhaps, uncaring; preoccupied. But this was her friend, a woman she knew to be none of those things.

'Margot was very kind.'

Cathy nodded, allowing a silence that she couldn't help but wade into.

'She had a difficult life –'

'Of course – the great Francis Law scandal.' She frowned and flicked ash from her cigarette. 'All the publicity around that biography would have been hard for her.'

Adele felt herself stiffening. Primly she said, 'No, I don't think so.'

'Really?'

'Really. All a very long time ago.'

Cathy nodded again, but this time as though she had simply lost interest. Why fish for information she surely must know already about Margot's first husband's promiscuous homosexuality? All that filth had been turned over and picked through so thoroughly, how he had left her each night alone with a new baby so that he might *go* with men, how he had been arrested and imprisoned; how prison had broken him, but still his wife wouldn't allow him anywhere near the baby, although he pleaded and begged to see little Bobby again. And everyone loved Law, of course, the great hero, the feted artist who had left the world with such a legacy, with *Machine Gunner* – that icon of war. No one these days seemed to mind that he'd done those unspeakable things; certainly no one cared that he had done them to Margot, ruining her life.

Cathy met her gaze. Gently she said, 'I'm sorry.'

'What for?'

'I've upset you, prying like that. She was your friend.'

'And your mother-in-law. I understand why you're curious about her. It's a shame the two of you never met.'

She looked uncomfortable. 'We left it too late.'

'Yes. Well. I'm not criticising you.' Although she was, she supposed. She remembered Margot's hurt at not being invited to Mark's wedding. Later, Margot had shown her a photograph of Mark and this woman, Cathy, standing on the steps of a registry office – Chelsea registry office, Margot had told her. They had looked at the photograph in silence, not commenting on the details as they would have for any other wedding photo. She had been too afraid of saying something facile – *what a handsome couple* – although they were; or *I'm sure they'll be very happy together*. Margot's hurt was too deep for such triteness. At last Margot had said, 'I suppose we make our beds, don't we?' She'd picked up the picture from the table between them. 'Should I put it in a frame, do you think?'

Adele pushed her half-finished cup of coffee away. She stood up. 'Well, I should leave you to it. I'm sure you have lots to do . . . Unpacking . . .' She glanced around the room, unable to help her curiosity – it seemed no sadness could overcome it. Her grief for Margot was still a queer fish; she couldn't quite believe she was dead but felt she was only avoiding her, sulking over some slight. Not that Margot had ever sulked; she had only been kind to her, and warm, in her shy way. Adele drew breath. She smiled at the girl. 'Thank you for the coffee.'

'I hope we'll be friends.'

Adele nodded, feeling that she was too old to make friends, that she couldn't be bothered. But she had left the milk on the windowsill, brought the eggs, and accepted the offer of coffee. If there was only nosiness behind these gestures then really she was a bad person, one of the busybodies Bea so abhorred. So she smiled, polite as ever, and said, 'Yes, I hope so too.'

Chapter Six

Bea had decided that it was no good lying in bed, better to be up, dressed – she wasn't dead yet. But, she conceded, there would be no going out into the garden today, her body recoiled from the thought of the cold, of the weeds and the dank piles of leaves – the colossal effort of it all. So she dressed in her second-best corduroy trousers, a plaid shirt, and a grey cardigan she liked for its wooden buttons. Actually, she could fill the cardigan's pockets with stones and walk into the River Tees, a sturdy Virginia Woolf. She smiled to herself because of course her sturdiness got in the way of such doings.

Not that she was so sturdy today. There was a kind of wobbliness that might be something or nothing, and a pain in her hips that might only be old age. In the mirror set on the inside of her wardrobe door, she saw only herself, a little thinner; she peered more closely, wondering if Adele had noticed that her face was becoming gaunt. Adele noticed most things about appearances. '*Oh, your hair,*' she would exclaim, '*you would have such lovely curls if only you would grow it a little longer!*' And, '*Oh, your face! Why not a touch of cold cream? A little protection for your poor skin, at least!*'

Downstairs, Bea looked around for Adele, surprised when she couldn't find her and when she didn't answer her call from the back door: she wouldn't go out into the garden to look for her – after the effort of going downstairs the thought of going outside was even more appalling. She made tea, and it came to her that Adele had gone next door – last night she had been hinting at such a visit. 'A neighbourly welcome,' Adele had called it. She had only grunted; at least Adele didn't suggest that she should accompany her on the mission.

She sat down with a cup of tea, pleased that she was alone and didn't have to lie about feeling better – her 'cold' nothing more than a sniffle, really. She found herself straining to hear voices from next door, but there was only the usual quiet – voices would have to be raised to shouting pitch before anything could be heard through these walls. She tried to imagine Adele shouting – having a bust-up with the girl – she understood Adele's anger at the woman who had snubbed Margot so badly; but Adele would never shout; her sister had gone next door only to satisfy her curiosity, not to seek revenge for her dead friend. Adele could never understand how shallow her curiosity made her seem to others.

She had told Eric, 'She's a ninny, you know.'

He had only laughed. 'Oh, Bea – you mean she's a *girl*.'

They had been watching Adele dance with Charles and it seemed to her that Adele couldn't stop smiling or prattling, not that much interested in the dance steps but only in her partner, Charles, in his brand new uniform, so smart, as men seemed to be in 1915. If Eric had been jealous he didn't show it, only smiled and smiled, unable to take his eyes off Adele – his fiancée of no more than a couple of months. Hadn't he been dancing with her almost all night? How could he begrudge his cousin a dance with the prettiest girl in the whole place? Eric had surprised her by taking her hand and squeezing it. 'Bea. You'll look out for her when I'm away, won't you?'

'No.' She had tugged her hand away from his, outraged. 'I'm not staying! If you think I'm going to sit at home playing nursemaid –'

Charles had appeared before her then, Adele in tow – she noticed how he held her sister's hand as though she was his girl. 'Bea,' Charles had said, 'what are you so cross about now?'

Eric grinned. 'She doesn't want to sit it out at home while we have all the fun.'

Charles had raised Adele's hand to his lips and kissed it, all the time keeping his eyes on Bea. 'Adele, why don't you dance with Eric? I need to have a serious word with your sister.'

And Charles had kept his gaze fixed on hers as Adele protested that no one was to be serious tonight, as Eric laughed and led her away. Bea remembered how her face had burned under the intensity of his gaze and that she had looked away, so angry she had wanted to punch him in the face.

Imagine if she had punched him and knocked him out cold; how surprised he would have been when he came round. Perhaps he would have been changed – some sense knocked into him, some seriousness. But she had only stretched out her fingers at her sides, deliberately not making fists, and looked past him, unable to face that sneering expression of his. She heard him strike a match and smelt his cigarette smoke. He said, 'Girls like Adele will need girls like you, here, at home.'

She managed to look at him. 'I'm going to France.'

'Why do you want to be a nurse? Somehow I can't see you mopping the fevered brow.'

'Why not?'

He frowned at her, seeming to reconsider. 'All right. Perhaps I'm wrong. Perhaps you won't scare the whole Expeditionary Force to death.' Then, 'Why don't you marry me – it will be the perfect cover for us both – a gentleman's agreement, as it were.'

Remembering, Bea sipped her tea and thought that she could almost smile at this now. At the time, aged twenty – and twenty was so very young in those days – she had been so outraged that tears had come to her eyes and she did, at last, curl her fingers into fists, imagining again that knock-out blow. But Charles had only laughed and said, 'Oh, it would be sensible, you know, supportive – two crooked trees leaning into one another.' She had stepped back from him; this was a joke too far, and Charles's expression changed, no longer confiding, just his plain, ordinary self. Rather stiffly he said, 'Sorry. Don't look so shocked.'

Adele and Eric had come back then, saving her. She had said stoutly, 'Would you excuse me?' and had walked away, out of the church hall with its five-piece band on the little stage, into the cold of that October evening. No one had followed her. Her face had cooled as the band played a waltz, the last, slow dance of the evening, the tune muffled by the hall's heavy wooden doors.

She had gone to the dance on her own stern order – she would dance; she would talk to men as Adele did – or rather not talk to them, only listen and smile – and she would be normal in her pretty, cornflower-blue dress that Adele had been so pleased with. The waltz played on and she had wanted to tear the dress in two, right down its front like the skin of a butchered animal. If only she had worn her black skirt and grey blouse – he wouldn't have dared talk to her like that. He wouldn't have thought her soft and vulnerable – even if those were the attributes she had been trying on for size.

She would never wear a pretty dress again. She had chosen that night, just as Charles said she should, to only be herself.

Charles. His visit should prove interesting now her imminent death gave her a licence to say what she pleased. At least she supposed it gave her a licence, if only she could pluck up the courage. With enough pluck she would have travelled to London and hammered on his door weeks ago, when that book of his had been published (she pictured a fancy apartment in Mayfair) and, when he appeared, she would have said . . . *Boo!* She smiled to herself, imagining his face. But his face was all she could imagine – pinched, as though there was a bad smell he couldn't quite place, bloodless, reptilian. She couldn't imagine what she might say to him or how far the licence would take her, from childish glee at his discomfort all the way to bitter incriminations.

There was such a lot to incriminate him and he would admit to some of it, she was sure. A few weeks ago she had watched a programme on television, *Arts' Review*, and there was Charles, smoking and smoking as the interviewer – that hapless girl who was too ready to flatter – tried to coax him into talking about the scandal his biography of Francis Law – Paul Harris, as they had known him – had caused. But Charles had been unfazed as he flicked his cigarette ash, as he smiled superciliously and asked, '*Scandal? My dear girl, in this day and age it's impossible to scandalise.*'

The girl had smiled and nodded as if to put the lie to her next question. 'But hasn't Law's son, Bob Harris, refuted many of your claims about his father's early life?'

It had seemed to Bea that Charles was sweating only because the television lights were too hot. No doubt he was wearing makeup that ran into his eyes and stung, because he took out a handkerchief and delicately mopped his brow, taking his time, no one would hurry him. Pocketing the hanky again, drawing deeply on his cigarette, exhaling, at last he said, 'I have great admiration for Mr Harris.'

So, the interview went nowhere, as she had guessed it would, and, as the programme ended with its irritating music suddenly blaring out, she had laughed harshly, gratified to have her expectations met. But Adele had been angry, turning on her.

'How can you laugh? Poor Margot's name is being dragged through the mud because of that man and his wretched book.'

'Poppycock! Everyone knows she behaved exactly as she should have in keeping that bugger Harris – Law – whatever he liked to call himself – away from her son.'

'Such language, Bea!'

'Then what would you call Paul Harris? A sodomite? What do people call such men nowadays? Poofs? Like that nancy on *Round the Horne*, that what's-his-name –'

'Paul wasn't like him. Margot wouldn't have married a man like that!'

She had laughed. '*No one* would have married a man like that, not even Margot.'

Adele chose to ignore this implied insult against her friend. Primly she said, 'Paul Harris was just a boy who had lost his way, that's all.'

Bea had frowned at her. 'Why are you defending him?'

'He was Bobby's father. Bobby – remember? That lovely little boy who used to come and play with Tom, who was always so polite?'

So polite, Bea thought now as she finished her tea. And so scared to death of that creature Margot had married after her divorce from

73

Harris. Harris was Francis Law by then and might just as well have been a different person altogether. Law certainly never visited his son, not that anyone would have allowed such a visit, she was sure.

She thought of Bobby Harris, how he would knock on the front door, '*Is Tom coming out to play?*' She used to feel sorry for him; she used to hold the door wide open saying, '*Come in, come in – let's see if we can find him,*' and she would feel self-conscious in her heartiness because the Harris child was not only polite – in fact not that dull at all – but watchful and keenly intelligent, the kind of intelligence she would have wished for Tom, despite its power to unnerve her.

And lately she had seen Bobby Harris on the telly, too, another show, late at night after Adele had gone to bed, and he was talking about his father's paintings – not about that biography, it was the paintings that mattered, after all, his father's legacy. But Charles's book had come up, of course; no doubt it was the reason behind his invitation on to the show, although Bobby had refused to be drawn into discussing it. Bea had found herself sitting on the edge of her chair, willing Bobby Harris to stick to his guns and snub Charles and his book because being snubbed would hurt him more than anything.

The back door opened and Adele came in. She seemed disgruntled – their new neighbour had obviously upset her but this was unsurprising, Adele was primed to be upset by this girl who'd had the audacity to marry Margot's son. Bea thought of saying that she shouldn't go round there if she was so ready to be offended, but couldn't be bothered; Adele's motives for visiting their neighbour were too complicated and would lead to too much talking. She really didn't feel like talking.

Adele glanced at her. 'You're up. How are you feeling?'

'That I should go back to bed.'

'You do look peaky.' Frowning in concern she said, 'Should you go and see Dr Walker again?'

'Probably.' She smiled because lately, strangely, she had been feeling more cheerful than usual. 'Don't worry, old thing.'

'Don't call me that. *Old thing!* Like you were a man – like one of those silly boys in 1914. It's so affected.'

'I'll go back to bed, I think.'

'Yes, you do that.'

As Bea reached the door, Adele said hurriedly, 'I'm sorry. Shall I bring you up a cup of tea?'

Bea turned to her; she looked like she had when they were children, all soft and sad and pretty, anxious as they had both been. She had wanted to protect her then; she still did. 'No tea, thank you. Perhaps some soup later.'

Adele nodded, her purposeful self again. 'Yes, I'll make soup.'

Chapter Seven

Bobby Harris said, 'Sir Edmund, thank you so much for agreeing to see me.'

'Not at all, Mr Harris, truly the pleasure is mine.'

So, Edmund thought as he shook Harris's hand, this is Bobby grown up. He had met him once, long ago now, when Harris was a small child clutching his father's hand, and he had looked scared then, as though he would hide behind his father's legs if he had so much as smiled at him. Such a beautiful child, one that no doubt would have garnered many smiles, many admiring clucks if he hadn't been so off-puttingly timid. Edmund remembered how Paul Harris had swung the child into his arms, holding him with a kind of fierce possessiveness; Edmund had been compelled to step back, as if this man he had been fucking only that morning had become a danger: he would kill for this child. Actually, it was very easy to believe that Paul would kill full stop.

But no, he shouldn't think of this man's father, of *fucking* this man's father, because that's what Paul had called it – *fucking*. Really, Paul Harris could be vile. Edmund glanced away from Paul's son because it felt that his own memories of his vileness were plainly exposed on his face. He saw the bottles of gin, whisky, and Dubonnet, the glasses, ice bucket and the thin slices of lemon artfully overlapping on their Spode platter that Roberts had arranged on the sideboard and said, 'Drink? Oh, look, do sit down, let's not stand on ceremony. And please, call me Edmund – none of this *Sir* nonsense. Makes me feel as if my father's just walked in . . . Anyway . . .'

He stepped towards the bottles, indicating them with a sideways sweep of his hand. 'What will you have?'

'I don't drink, I'm afraid.'

'Really? Is that something to be afraid of? Do you mind if I indulge?'

'No, of course not.'

'Do sit down,' Edmund found himself repeating, and was dismayed to hear the edge in his voice. He thought that perhaps he should offer him coffee – or tea now that it was late afternoon. But he was sure Roberts had gone out and he really couldn't face the kitchen, that feeling of being an intruder in Roberts's holy domain. Half hidden behind the bottles was a jug of iced water and, inspired, he said, 'How about a glass of water?'

'Yes, thank you.'

'Slice of lemon?'

There was no answer, and Edmund glanced over his shoulder to see that Bobby Harris was studying one of his paintings, a watercolour he had recently acquired of grazing sheep. His hands were clasped behind his back, shoulders squared: a tolerable impression of a minor royal dutifully taking an interest. But of course there was his face, those hands – no prince could be so disfigured and still do the rounds.

Edmund allowed his gaze to linger on Harris's injuries, wondering about how he might paint him, remembering Paul's portrait of this man. That portrait – *The Artist's Son* – hung in the National Portrait Gallery and was as famous as any work Paul had produced. Hadn't he himself pontificated on it at length on his telly show? He couldn't paint Bobby Harris then, much as he would like to.

He turned back to the tray of drinks and slopped water into a glass, thought again about the slice of lemon and decided against it as being too frivolous. Harris radiated sternness – as Paul had, of course. Oh, he did seem determined to compare father and son, to find them similar, and he should give the son the benefit of the doubt with no preconceptions. He would think of him as the shy child Paul had hoisted into his arms, and smile and be kind, and not

77

morph into the condescending nincompoop he knew he could sometimes be.

He poured himself a gin and tonic and handed Bobby his glass of water. Together they looked at the grazing sheep. 'It's by a little-known Victorian artist called Monty Grey. I say *little-known*, but he was quite the thing in his time. His *View of Loch Ness* hangs in one of the sitting rooms in Balmoral, so perhaps *forgotten* is more the word. Unfashionable, perhaps? Anyway, I was rather drawn to the colours.'

Harris turned to look at him. 'It's pretty.'

'Quite. I only ever buy pretty pictures nowadays.' He smiled at him. 'Your father would have liked the prettiness, I'm sure. Now,' he became brisk in case Harris thought it too soon to mention Paul. 'I want you to sit down, all this standing around is making me feel as though we're at a poorly attended cocktail party.'

Roberts had plumped up the blue cushions on the yellow silk couches that faced each other across the fireplace. Edmund could see that a feather had escaped this plumping and now drifted against the skirting board – a dull, brown and white feather, a chicken's, perhaps. He wanted to pick it up, spoiling as it did the room's otherwise immaculate orderliness, but he refrained from such fussiness – he had an idea it would make him appear deranged. Instead, he sat down, placing his drink on a side table and offering the cigarette box to Harris. He took one, and Edmund was relieved – not such an aesthete, then, nor, as he had begun to fear, a simple out-and-out bore.

Holding his lighter to Harris's cigarette, Edmund caught his eye and found that he couldn't look away, hearing himself say, 'Good Lord, you're very much like him.'

'I was.'

'No, you are. I'm sorry – I'm staring at you now.'

'I'm used to staring.'

Edmund sat back, still staring – he felt as though Harris had given him permission to stare and that he didn't much mind. He even seemed to relax a little under his scrutiny as though his gaping might help the situation.

Edmund said, 'Do people recognise you on the street?'

'Very occasionally.' Bobby flicked cigarette ash into the onyx ashtray Roberts had left polished on the coffee table between them. He laughed, surprising Edmund. 'Sometimes they want to shake my hand.' Holding up his damaged right hand he went on, 'Then they become a little embarrassed, worried they might hurt me, I think. Actually it's all very embarrassing. And lately we're in vogue – there's that series on television, have you seen it? *Blue Sky Boys*? My brother,' he paused, then went on quickly, 'my brother, Mark Redpath, played one of the leading roles.'

He had heard of the brother, who hadn't, after all? The boy hadn't been to his taste, too *boyish* – much too boyish to be dead. Edmund thought of offering his condolences but the moment seemed to have passed because Harris was on his feet again, inspecting one of his father's paintings. Obvious that he had never seen this picture before, he smiled slightly, glancing over his shoulder at him. 'Amir. I met him, the first time I visited Dad in Tangiers.' He turned back to the head and shoulders portrait of the old man, smiling still so that Edmund wondered at the memory the picture invoked. He had met Amir, too; he remembered how the two men had worked together in Paul's garden, Amir so much older but lean and fit as Paul, who was in his prime then and so full of that volatile energy that he seemed never to sleep – or even sit down – so that in comparison everyone except Amir was cumbersome, even Patrick, especially Patrick.

Bobby Harris said, 'Patrick would say that Dad should stick to portraits like this.' He stepped still closer to the picture, peering at it before turning to him. 'Patrick hates the war pictures. When Dad died Pat sold them all – of course, you know that. You know Patrick.'

It seemed this man had no side to him, no guile, because this last statement was merely matter-of-fact, as if he knew nothing of the jealousy between himself and Patrick. 'Listen,' Paul had said, 'Pat knows we've fucked but we all have to behave as though he doesn't know. No – we must take the lie further – behave as if you don't much like me.'

'I don't much like you.'

'There you are – you won't have to put on much of an act.' Paul had grinned at him over his shoulder. Edmund had been following him along a narrow street that led to his house, newly arrived in Tangiers, sweating in the fierce sun, red-faced no doubt, although Paul appeared cool and tanned in pale, loose clothes – extraordinary clothes that transformed him completely from the buttoned-up man he had known in London. He had hardly recognised him: the man who waved at him from the quayside as he walked down the boat's gangplank was too young to be Paul, too bright with smiles and chatter, like one of the boys he had known at school, a younger boy, insisting on carrying his bag. And, as he struggled to keep up with him through Tangiers' confusing, crowded streets, he felt more and more as if he wanted to board the next boat home and that he didn't care for this chameleon. And Paul was wearing sandals; he could see his bare brown feet. He had never ever seen a man in sandals before.

Edmund heard Bobby Harris clear his throat and came back to the present. He said, 'Sorry. I find lately my mind wanders about like an old stray dog.' Going to stand beside Harris he said, 'This portrait of the old man *is* very fine, I think.' He kept his eyes on the picture, unable to look at Paul's son because all he could see was Paul, on his belly in bed, that taut, muscled backside of his. He blinked: there he was in Paul's bedroom in Tangiers and where was Patrick? – out, hardly ever there – and Paul had woken and looked at him, looked and looked, and only looked as though he shouldn't be there, as though he regretted his being there in the room Paul shared with Patrick.

Self-consciously Bobby Harris said, 'Edmund?'

Edmund stepped away from him at once; how like his father he sounded, how unbearably like him. The man should get to the point now and explain why he was here. He would hurry him along. He said, 'So, sit down. I'm sure you're not here to look at my pictures.'

Harris did as he was told, first stubbing out his cigarette. Paul would have lit another from the stub but his son only sipped at his water, his damaged hand seeming to grasp the crystal glass too tightly. He dabbed at his mouth with his handkerchief as though afraid he had dribbled; perhaps he did dribble; his mouth had obviously been worked on – the surgeons had done their best, he supposed. Yet he was still very ugly, although he was getting used to the shock of him and would quite like to sketch him, an excuse to peer more closely.

Harris cleared his throat again. He said, 'I believe you know Charles Dearlove?'

Edmund snorted. So that was it; he had guessed as much. 'Yes, I know him. Everybody does.'

'I wrote to his publisher to request a meeting, but he won't see me. Perhaps he's too ashamed. But I do need to talk to him.'

'Why?'

Harris laughed painfully. 'Why? Because I need to know the truth. If I have been lied to all my life then I want to know. And I don't care about all the other stuff – I know what my father was like . . .' He shook his head as if to clear it. 'If he *was* my father and not my uncle, as Dearlove claims.' He took another sip of water, hastily dabbing at his mouth again. 'Now, Patrick insists that Dad would have told him if I wasn't his, he says I should take Dearlove and his publishers to court. But I just want to see him, face to face, in private. I'll know if he's lying.'

'How will you know? He'll insist that every word he wrote is true. How can he not?' More gently Edmund said, 'Whatever was written in the biography, Paul was your father –'

'You don't know that. He took me on – *became* my father – that's what's important – that's what Patrick says. But I need to know.' Quickly he said, 'If Paul wasn't my father I would be relieved. I would rather be a step away from him.'

Harris glanced away, fumbling in his pockets and bringing out his own cigarettes and lighter. He was ashamed, Edmund thought, as he watched him light a cigarette. Edmund felt that he should say something to alleviate this shame but he thought of Paul and wanted to spring to his defence; and then he would betray himself – another old queen falling over himself to defend the great artist. He sat down on the couch and crossed his legs; he wanted to appear easy, steady, and not cowardly, as he felt now.

Harris said, 'Do you have Dearlove's address?'

'I really don't think you should see him.'

'I need to know who told him – his *sources*, is that the word?'

'I'm afraid I don't have his address.'

Harris drew breath. 'Sir Edmund –'

'*Edmund*, please –'

'I know you and Dearlove were –' he shook his head impatiently; with some distaste he said, 'I know you had a *relationship*. You have his address, I know you do.'

'I don't.' Edmund stood up. He was a tall man, commanding, he often thought that other men forgot how physically intimidating he could be; they were too easily taken in by good manners. Standing over Harris he said, 'Now, I think perhaps you should leave.'

He left, and Edmund stood at his window watching him walk down the street towards the underground. That morning he had wanted Paul's son to stay for lunch and had asked Roberts to leave something suitable in the kitchen: cold meats, salad, that kind of thing. There was a bottle of champagne in the fridge, he had intended to open it, not expecting Paul's son to be anything as dull as teetotal. But what would they have celebrated? Edmund snorted and stepped away from the window. He went to the tray of drinks and poured himself a large scotch. What a prig Bobby Harris was. Paul couldn't be his father – couldn't possibly. Charles was right about that if he was wrong about everything else.

Edmund was rarely angry. He had lived a quiet, interesting, easy life and he thanked God for it; his own, superstitious version of God was thanked almost every night, when he remembered. And this present anger was a petty thing, really, that stemmed from disappointment and irritation; irritation because no one was supposed to know that he had a relationship with Charles Dearlove but everyone did; it had been going on for too long for people not to know, on and off for years; and disappointment because Harris was not the

82

man he had expected. He had expected to fall in love with the expected man; he had wanted to feel that bitter-sweet sentimentality that only falling in love with the wrong person could bring.

He sat down and lit a cigarette, his anger ebbing away. He thought of Charles, of telephoning to warn him that Bobby Harris was seeking him out. The thought made him look at the phone as though it might suddenly ring and it would be Charles's voice on the other end, sardonic and bitter, mercilessly mocking if Edmund should mention Harris. Charles would guess at those expectations he'd had of Bobby; he always could see through him.

Edmund sipped his drink; now that he had thought of Charles he couldn't unthink him – he was here, in this room, circulating amongst his guests. Some were wary of him, others foolishly hailing him, sure they could get the better of a camp old queer. Edmund had winced for these men and all their faults that Charles could so easily target. He would wonder at the masochistic urge that had had him invite Charles in the first place. Charles was best kept secret, kept to his shabby flat in Notting Hill where he would serve pilchards on toast, protesting it was all he could afford. Then he would grin at him, 'Why don't you give me money, Edmund?'

'Because you'd spend it on rent boys.'

'You can't know that.'

He had given him money over the years and he didn't know what Charles spent it on; not boys, he was almost sure. Charles was fastidious. 'I'm not like your beloved Paul,' Charles had told him. 'I don't fuck around. There,' he'd laughed shortly, 'that's a truth I won't bore you with again.'

Edmund drew breath; he glanced at the telephone again. If Charles wasn't going to call him – if he really couldn't read his mind over the small distance between their two flats – then he could always call him. About to pick up the receiver, he sat back in shock as it began to ring.

Chapter Eight

Everyone should leave Thorp, Charles thought, only to remember that he'd believed this as a young man and really he should have grown up in the intervening years. But he had only grown old, and the belief remained – best to leave Thorp; anyone with any gumption did.

He'd just arrived on the 9.50 a.m. train from Kings Cross, his London newspaper already thrust into a bin on Thorp Station. The station seemed smaller than he remembered, shabby with pigeons, he was sure there were never pigeons; he was sure there was a waiting room with a coal fire always burning in an ornate grate and a café with tea urns and Chelsea buns. And in 1918 there was bunting, red, white, and blue, and a uniformed station master to salute him. Now there was only a row of padlocked doors and an exit sign pointing up the cracked concrete steps. The fancy wrought-iron benches he remembered, the hanging baskets filled with begonias, the guards with their whistles and trolleys, had all gone. The platform was deserted, even the pigeons had taken off down the line; no one else had alighted, giving him the sense that he had made a mistake: there was nothing and no one in Thorp.

But there was Bea, of course, and thinking of her he decided to walk to her house. The walk would give him time to re-acclimatise himself; also he hadn't forgotten that it was market day; on market days the Green Dragon pub opened outside its normal hours. Market day and a mass of dirty-white canvas would stretch from one end of the High Street to the other, stormed by all the many housewives and buses: diesel exhaust fumes and the smell of cold apples and cabbage stalks and oranges squashed on the road. A tramp would pick up the less rotten fruit and secrete it in the pockets of his coat; Charles remembered his furtiveness so well that it seemed to him now that he must have seen him often, that he must have stared and stared, as interested as he would be in a cat found stiffly dead on the road. Remembering the down-and-out – the string-for-a-belt, itchy-bristly stink of him, even the bruised apples he imagined fermenting in his pocket – he was eight years old, the stallholders packing up around him as Aunt May – late as ever – was panicked into buying whatever they had left.

And so, walking from the station towards the market, the memories came to him as he had known they would: there was Aunt May lifting her skirts a little as she stepped off the tram, distracted and checking again for her purse in the depths of her handbag. There was Eric, whining, causing his mother to all at once remember him, to whip her handkerchief from her bag, to spit on it and swipe a smudge from his cheek: there was the scent of face powder and Yardley's English Rose all confused with May's licked-glass breath. There was Eric, squirming and squirming, his chin clenched in May's pincer grip, she seemed to lift him from the pavement, his neck impossibly stretched, his feet treading air. Late afternoon and the poles of the dismantled stalls were clattering to the cobbles, a noise like broken dinner gongs reminding May to hurry. Her grip on Eric was released, her handbag snapped closed, her humiliated son forgotten again as she barged through the thinning crowd. He followed in her wake, trying to ignore Eric's whines as imperiously as she did. She had promised cake if they were good and he wanted Eric to be quiet; he remembered seething with this want, his agitation as easy to recollect as the tentative glow from the newly lit gas lamps – that particular yellow – and the smell of the cold fruit and vegetables, that particular green.

Last week, because of his impending visit, Edmund had asked him about Thorp and Charles had trotted out his one true fact as he always did. 'Thorp has the widest High Street in England.'

'Really?' Edmund had raised his eyebrows in that way he had, as though he hadn't properly listened and was anyway regretting his question.

Charles wasn't silenced by this expression: only that morning he had decided he wouldn't be so alive to Edmund's boredom; daringly he would say whatever he wanted to say: it would be a test, and so he said, 'In 1556 two Protestant priests were burnt at the stake in front of Thorp's Shambles.'

'That doesn't tell me much about Thorp.' Edmund closed his eyes and blew an undulating lavender-grey smoke ring at the bedroom ceiling. Charles had watched it, quite mesmerised so that he forgot about Thorp, about everything, there was only the immediate pleasure of watching the expensive smoke disperse. Edmund was a magician, bent on entertaining him, and he felt flattered and grateful, so when Edmund said, 'I do want to know, you know,' he had only stared at him blankly and Edmund had laughed, saying, 'I think Thorp is a mythical place – somewhere you and Paul invented.'

Unable to resist his jealousy he said, 'What did Paul say about it?'

'Oh, you know,' another smoke ring, not quite as perfect as the last, squashed itself against the ceiling. Edmund flicked ash into the ashtray on the bed beside his hip; the sheet was draped artfully just below his nipples – it might have been carved in marble except the body beneath it was too fleshy, too warm and golden. Charles remembered how he had wanted to climb back into bed beside him but knew that it was too late, his side of the bed would be cold, crumpled, and sticky, there would be *that* smell and he would be disgusted and that would be that. Also Edmund had distanced himself with his questions about Thorp, his throwaway remark about Paul. Worse, Charles had tried to be himself, without censor, and this endeavour had backfired because he *was* a bore. No, it was time to dress, to hurry up and go.

But he didn't want to go too quickly. Buttoning his shirt he said, 'Thorp exists. I'll take you there one day. We'll stay at the Grand Hotel.'

'As long as it *is* grand.'

Ridiculously, this remark had panicked him. He was Aunt May, unable to decide for the best now that the best was gone. He fumbled with his buttons; from the corner of his eye he saw Edmund crush out his cigarette and toss the sheet aside. Charles was about to ask him when he might see him again when Edmund said, 'Paul said Thorp was like a model town an unimaginative child had arranged on his bedroom carpet – that long –' here he smiled at him – 'wide High Street with all its shops and pubs and hotels. There's the Empire Theatre at one end and the elegant, eighteenth-century parish church at the other, its war memorial like a boundary marker, as strange and white as an afternoon moon. Next day the child had better ideas and threw down a river and a sugar factory so that there could be boats and bridges and a lovely, candy-floss smell to enjoy. Then there had to be a train station, then the cobbled streets, the scrubbed-step terraces and the cane-swishing schools. And Paul's father's early-Gothic revival mansion was beyond all this, a stroll across the band-stand park, opposite the cemetery with all its Victorian angels and obelisks.' Naked, Edmund took a silk dressing gown from its hook on the door and shrugged it on. Tying its belt he said, 'Does that sound like Thorp?'

It sounded like a distraction, Charles had thought, because Paul wouldn't have wanted to talk about Thorp, just as he himself didn't. But Edmund's worldly-yet-sunny demeanour discouraged indifference: he had to have stories and cleverness. Charles was afraid he wasn't clever enough and that his story of the burning priests was too much out of the gaudy pages of *A Boys' Own History*. To redeem himself he tried to think of something about Thorp that would interest Edmund, but there was nothing. Only Paul made Thorp interesting to Edmund; only Paul made *him* interesting to Edmund – Edmund wouldn't have glanced at him had it not been for his connection to the great man. In Edmund's bedroom as he laced his shoes he said with transparent nonchalance, 'Why not come with me? See Thorp for yourself.' He had almost said, '*see Paul's Thorp for yourself*,' but had decided he wouldn't stoop so low.

But Edmund had had other plans, although he'd been tempted, Charles had thought at the time. A look had passed across his face that Charles interpreted as intrigued consideration. But he often forgot how well-mannered Edmund was and that this look was almost certainly faked to save his feelings. He had probably been thinking about lunch.

So now he was in Thorp, alone; how could he have brought anyone along on this mission, let alone Edmund? He suspected that Edmund had never left London, unless it was to leave England entirely, and his ideas about The North came mainly from Victorian novels. Edmund didn't know that Thorp was an island, cut off by the gentle Cleveland Hills and the River Tees. Durham's coal mines were an hour north by train, York an hour's journey south. Thorp was a place one passed through, then, thinking how pretty the silhouetted hills were, that perhaps one day you would alight at Thorp Station with hiking boots, sandwiches, and a flask. And if in the unlikely event you did break your journey like this you would be disappointed, because the hills were quite far away from Thorp and really at the unimaginative child's bedroom door rather than beside his bed. But perhaps you would be diverted by Thorp's very wide High Street, by the medieval shambles and the neat Georgian cube of its town hall; you would read the plaque commemorating the Protestant Martyrs and not quite believe in the sacrifice – surely the child had only read this in a book – because Thorp seemed too shrewdly mercantile to carry on so. There was that eminently sensible width of its High Street, after all.

Now the market stalls crowded the High Street, narrowed it; Charles found himself elbow to elbow with Thorp's merciless housewives, in the way and out of place. The smell of cold apples was everywhere and the stallholders shouted about cheap cauliflowers, the Fyffes Banana boxes edging from their canvas enclosures and blocking escape routes. He needed to escape, there were too many women, too much shouting and jostling, he was ankle deep in what looked to be the brightly printed squares of tissue paper used to wrap tangerines. *Look*, he would have said to Edmund, *the litter in Thorp is unexpectedly exotic, all flaming flamenco and castanets*. Spying an exit route beside the egg man's stall, he was pleased that Edmund wasn't here to compel him to say such things.

Charles found himself dodging buses to reach safety outside Woolworths, part of its window display devoted to trowels and trugs and ladies' gardening gloves. He paused, thinking of Bea in her garden and wondering if he should buy her a present. He thought not, deflated by the memory of Bea's unrelenting no-nonsense idea of herself. She would think he was *trying to get round her*, to *soften her up*, although she knew that he knew she couldn't be softened: Bea was set hard in her ways, although she could crack under pressure. Charles smiled to himself – what use were these metaphors anyway? Bea was not a lump of badly mixed concrete; no – she was unfortunately much more complicated than that. He walked on.

The peculiar thing about Thorp was that it seemed to have turned its back on the River Tees and was trying its best to ignore it completely now it had enough bridges and the ferryman was no longer needed. He could smell the poor river, though, polluted as it was by Thorp's more industrial-minded neighbours. He didn't suppose Phumphrey's Sugar Factory could turn the waters so scummy, or decorate the muddy banks with such iridescent rainbows. There was Thorp's smell of burnt toffee if the wind was in the right direction, but that was only sugar, benign and rather comforting, especially in winter – Dickens would have smacked his lips around it, made the stink even stickier, an olfactory feast. The idea made Charles weary; even alone he was still trying to entertain Edmund. He should tell him that Thorp was just Thorp, the place where he grew up and escaped when he had grown up enough.

Past Woolworths, past Richard's Shops with its trio of party-dressed mannequins, their net skirts as stiffly gregarious as their unlikely poses, Charles slowed, anxious not to miss the easily-missed entrance to the Green Dragon Yard. The yard's narrow alley opened onto a cobbled square where the pub's painted sign creaked overhead like a prop from a Bela Lugosi film.

The dragon was very green, a shot of red and orange fire blasting from its mouth, and was there, unchanged, as Charles emerged from the alley. He would have a drink, a gin and never mind the look the burly barman might give him. The barman would have to be burly, of course, all Thorp men were, those who hadn't escaped: their bulk stopped them slipping the net. The man would be suspicious and there would be no bright *What can I get you, sir?* as there was in some of the more knowing London pubs, only that surly, tight-lipped tilt of the chin, the question asked with the eyes only. And Charles would read his mind: *A gin, for fuck's sake*, before the man turned to the paltry row of optics, his contempt still visible in the *Guinness is Good for You* mirror.

But nothing is as one expects. The girl behind the bar appeared no more than twenty, and she smiled at him nervously like a child left to mind the fort. The pub was busy, warm and dim with smoke from the coal fire and all the many cigarettes, the tables taken so that he stayed at the bar, conspicuous in his London clothes – his second-best suit and the light mac he had bought in New York. No, he flattered himself – no one took any notice of a portly man in a beige overcoat. Too warm, he took off the coat and folded it over his arm and felt as though he was waiting for a train. He gulped his drink and asked for another. More settled, he remembered that this pub was a favourite amongst the many backstreet pubs in Thorp that Paul frequented.

I would slum it in Thorp's hard-man pubs, Paul had written to him after one of his requests for information on his early married life. *I was scared but brazen, then after a while those pubs lost their aura of danger and became places I went simply to get away from Margot – from everyone I knew. Thorp is not so small that you can't find a hidey-hole and I was hiding in plain sight. Those pubs weren't hunting grounds – of course not – and although Thorp had a pub that queers had – with some spite and aggression – commandeered I rarely went there. I went to the Castle and Anchor or the Green Dragon, the Stag if I was feeling dour. There were spittoons and sawdust – hard to believe, and I seem to remember the Stag was beer only and only the most poor went there. I could be completely alone and ignored – there is nowhere like a pub in Thorp for being ignored. Usually I am noticed, or rather I make myself noticeable; in those pubs I was just another drinker. Better, I didn't have to sit across the kitchen table looking at Margot, being reminded of the absurd mess I had got us both into and having to keep myself from telling her all about Patrick – how she would love him too, because how could anyone not love him?*

You ask about my marriage, my answer is I loved Margot. I'm not true – I love the one I'm with and want to share with that love everything that's in my heart. Margot, meet Patrick – Patrick, meet Margot. How I loved them both. How I longed to be alone in Thorp's pubs. To say I loathed myself is much too crude; my life seemed much too complicated for mere self-loathing.

There; as usual I am staggered by my own vanity. I hope this letter helps but feel it doesn't. Ask anything you like in your next letter. I don't paint now and have all the time in the world to reminisce. Even better, you should visit us again – Patrick sends his best wishes.

A table became free and Charles sat down gratefully because thinking about Paul had made him want to slump into his misery and not bother with any other mood. Thinking about Paul made him want to groan and cover his face with his hands, and when he dropped his hands the world would be looking at him, hands on hips, foot tapping impatiently in Aunt May's cartoon show of anger. *Now say you're sorry*, the world said in Aunt May's voice, *Say that you were only showing off, as usual, and you won't do it again.* No, he wouldn't grovel: dignified silence was all. He wouldn't even explain that what he had written in Paul's biography was only what Paul had wanted him to write. *I think Bobby should know the truth*, Paul had said, *only I can't tell him myself, the lie is too ingrained in me. I can't even tell Pat the truth.* Paul had laughed and started a coughing fit. Recovered he said, '*Don't let Pat go on thinking the worst of me, eh?*'

Paul had coughed up blood. He was dying and they both knew it and never said a word about it. They both ignored the blood because blood made all Charles's cowardliness fizz from his bladder and through his entrails to trickle down his legs. Paul's ignoring came from politeness, Charles thought. Paul wasn't disgusted, Charles was certain, entrails intrigued him – life in all its messy horror was a fascination. For a slight man Paul had a very large cock. Now, Charles, where did that thought come from?

He looked around the pub – it seemed no one had noticed his face-twitching and rapid blinking that had accompanied this recollection. In his defence, Paul's cock had surfaced only because he was in that sickroom in Tangiers, a bright, white cube of a room, plain, like an anteroom to a Spartan's heaven, and there was Sparta's administering angel, Patrick, helping Paul out of his bloodied pyjamas and carrying him to the bath at the foot of the bed. Charles hadn't averted his gaze; he didn't want to seem like a prude in front of these men. It seemed to him now that he'd behaved with a mannered carelessness ruined by his inability to take his eyes off Paul's penis. But even if he had looked away neither Paul nor Patrick would have noticed; they were intent on each other, this wasn't a show for him or some test he might fail; he was there, of course, and they chatted to him as they went about their business; he was free to observe, even if he was too blatantly shocked to take proper advantage of the freedom.

Not observing, he remembered the stink of blood from the soiled linen, the compensation of jasmine winding its way through the open window, the perfumed oil Patrick had poured and stirred with his hand and forearm into the water. The bergamot scent of the oil began to take precedence as Pat's gentle questions and Paul's murmured responses went to nothing and Paul closed his eyes to give himself up to the water. Patrick had looked at him then; Charles would come to imagine that Pat had put his finger to his lips to silence him, but Patrick had only pressed his mouth closed in a grimace of concern. His shirtsleeve was still rolled to his elbow, the dark, thick hair on his arm flattened and made darker still by the water; Patrick was so dark, such a contrast in that white, shadowless room that he couldn't help looking at him quite openly and without excuse – he didn't care what Patrick thought of him any more, he would sacrifice his pride for the pleasure of looking at him. Patrick Morgan was the most beautiful man and everything he did confirmed this.

He finished his gin in one swallow. Time to get a move on – off to see Bea and no more shilly-shallying – *My old man said follow the van . . .* The breezy song came and went, dilly-dallying him through the obstacle course of pub tables and drinkers.

Chapter Nine

Tom watched as Cathy made tea. He thought of saying something that would break the silence that had lengthened between them, impregnable as glass. But what could he say? Not sorry again. *I am sorry for your loss. You have my deepest sympathy.* All true, of course – more than true; he had very much liked Mark and his death was sickening, not least because it left him feeling as though anything might happen. That stepping in front of a hypothetical bus seemed more likely since Mark's accident. Accident. Such an innocuous word – tripping over a rug was an accident. Having to be cut from the car you'd wrapped around a tree, well, there should be a more portentous word to describe such horror. Perhaps there was, although watching Cathy he couldn't think of it, he couldn't think of anything: from the moment he'd met her she left him witless with desire.

He watched her, trying to find some clue about how she was coping with her grief in the way she took cups from the cupboard and took the tea caddy from the shelf. Her grief was a year old now, perhaps she was almost free of it, she might not think of Mark so often. He thought of Mark, but bloodied in his MG's driving seat – it surprised him how easily he could picture this *event* as this lovely woman spooned tea into the pot. Mark and Cathy had made such a glamorous couple, so lively and vivacious, shouldn't he be thinking of some other image – one from their wedding – Mark with a champagne flute in his hand, toasting his bride? Yet Mark was dead now and the image of him in that concertinaed car was so much more vivid.

Cathy said, 'Milk and sugar?'

'Just milk, thank you.'

She turned to smile at him, tucking a strand of her hair behind her ear. Wasn't she glamorous still? Thinner, with dark rings under her eyes, and that strand of hair was lank – unwashed, he thought, not that it mattered. She was wearing slacks, those with stirrups to hook under the feet so that her legs seemed even longer. Her feet were bare and large with long, straight toes. It seemed she was wearing one of Mark's shirts, its tails tied at her navel, its buttons undone and showing off a pale blue T-shirt. Such small breasts she had – he had thought them larger; perhaps they had been when Mark was alive – before she lost so much weight, so much of her spark.

Setting a cup of tea in front of him she said, 'So, you're playing truant?'

'I have a free period on Wednesday afternoons.'

'That sounds like an excuse truants make.' She sat down and took a packet of cigarettes from the shirt pocket. He shook his head when she offered the open packet to him.

'I'm trying to give up.'

She raised an eyebrow – the first actress-like affectation she had shown so far. 'Giving up? Why?'

'Luc has asthma.'

Nodding as though this was a good enough reason she said, 'You're a good father.'

'I try to be.' He thought how pompous he sounded. He was treading too carefully; he should talk about Mark, some memory of him that they both shared – something light-hearted that would begin with *do you remember*. But wouldn't that, for all its forced sentiment, be just as bad as saying nothing? Besides, she was too lovely to be encouraged to remember her dead husband. Lightly he said, 'How are you settling in?'

'Too early to say.'

'But you like the house?'

'Should I?'

'Well, it is quite grand.'

She laughed, flicking cigarette ash into a saucer. 'Grand!'

'Impressive, anyway.' He felt foolish, that his standards were too low and certainly didn't match hers. He glanced around and saw how shabby everything was and realised he was cold. He remembered Bobby saying how much he had hated this house, how he would escape to his grandfather's house along the road as often as he could. Bobby hadn't thought this house *grand* either – it wasn't compared to his grandfather's home, Parkwood.

All at once she was on her feet. 'I'll show you around, if you like.'

He stood up too eagerly – to be on his feet and following her about from room to room seemed the most perfect idea – a game to play while the adults were out. And she would lead the way and he would have the perfect view of her backside as she climbed the stairs.

What had Mark said about Tom Dearlove? Cathy, aware of this man's eyes on her, remembered that he hadn't said much – only that he was Bobby's friend. Tom was older than Mark – Bobby's age – Mark had said he remembered him vaguely from his childhood when Bobby and Tom would exclude him from their games. Bobby Harris had re-introduced Mark to Tom at some first night party. Mark had told her, 'I only remembered that I'd liked him back then – he was never as difficult as Bobby – never as sternly serious.'

So, Tom Dearlove wasn't serious, then. Good, she didn't want a serious man, only one with some wit – some spark, she supposed. He was handsome, in his way: she wouldn't be ashamed to be seen out and about with him. She wondered if she was truly ready to be involved with someone – half an hour ago, seeing him on her doorstep with his disconcerting bunch of burnt-orange chrysanthemums – she had thought yes, she would like to be held tightly again. Held tightly; she glanced at him – did this euphemism mean she wasn't ready to go to bed with him? Go to bed! She almost laughed – the euphemisms only meant that she was ashamed of wanting sex. She stopped herself from twisting her wedding ring round and round her finger, as though she was trying to remove it. He had noticed her doing this, she was sure – all the little signals, all the looking and smiling and awkwardness – she should just say that she was sorry – she really thought he should go and come back next month perhaps. Perhaps another month would be long enough. Yet she said nothing, only stood beside him at the nursery window, with all the Humpty Dumpties grinning down at them, the rag-and-bone man's cart clip-clopping by on the road below.

He turned to her. 'We should stop that man, tell him to come in and take what he wants. He'll give you a goldfish. Fair exchange.'

'I don't think I want to get rid of anything yet. Besides, some of it is my stuff – mine and Mark's.'

'Sorry, that was crass.' He returned to watching the horse and cart. 'I did notice Mark's piano, of course, but also some of his mother's things I remember from when I used to visit, years ago. The Francis Law is yours, though, I think?'

She had hung *Yesterday* in the drawing room, where she thought it looked rather small compared to the grand scale of the marble mantelpiece, the French doors, and high ceiling. Even the ornate plaster coving seemed to dwarf it and she had taken to standing before the painting, frowning, at last realising that it was too modern for the room. She felt the painting had wrong-footed her.

She said, 'Bobby gave it to Mark just after Law died. Mark could have sold it – he was always on his beam-ends – but he wouldn't, of course – he would have thought it a betrayal. So, I can't sell it either. It's both priceless and worthless.'

'Not worthless, surely? It's very beautiful.'

She watched as the rag-and-bone man drew on his horse's reins; the horse dutifully stopped, a slow, blinkered beast with its compensatory nosebag, and the man leapt down, quick as a frog: one of her opposite neighbours had left a broken old pram on the pavement and it went onto the back of the cart with greedy alacrity, its three remaining wheels spinning wildly. There was a playfulness about this frog-man, she half expected him to look up at her, knowing he was spied on, and salute her. She touched the window, wanting him to do just that – she should stop him, invite him in, say yes – take

96

the old rubbish, all the mahogany wardrobes and horsehair sofas. There were beds in the attic that she imagined maids had once slept on, narrow, metal, cold as January. There would be scrap-metal value. She pictured a goldfish swimming round and round its bowl.

'Cathy?' Tom's voice was concerned.

She said, 'I miss him so much.' She looked at him. 'There are times when I want to run around screaming.'

'Then run around and scream – this house is used to containing screams.'

She laughed, astonished. 'You're odd!'

'Yes. Why are you surprised?'

'Because you look like the straight man.'

He snorted. 'My ex-wife used to say I was the most boring man she'd ever met and that somehow I had fooled her at the start. She was blinded by my exotic Englishness – I don't think she'd met any Englishmen before.' He drew breath. 'She's French – actually Parisian.'

'How did you meet?'

'During the war.'

'That was when, not how.'

'How? I can't remember.' He grinned. 'I'm working on forgetting – forgetting's a good thing – underrated in my view.' At once he said, 'Sorry – I didn't mean to imply that you should forget Mark –'

'No, no, I know, of course I know you didn't mean that.' She looked around the room. Jack and Jill climbed their vivid hill towards the Humpty Dumpty wall, a corner of the frieze coming away to reveal another layer of wallpaper, a glimpse of forget-me-not posies. She said, 'You think this was an unhappy house – all that containing of screams?'

'No, not really so unhappy – Mark was always a cheerful little boy, in my memory . . . If there were screams I think they were the grown-up, silent type. I know Mark's father Havelock was difficult . . . At least my mother and aunt disliked him . . . Anyway.' He became brisk. 'All in the past.'

'Your mother came to see me – she brought eggs.'

'Sounds like Mum.'

She went to the door, holding it open and gesturing that he should step out ahead of her. He hesitated, glancing at the peeling paper. 'I'm not very handy – but I can strip wallpaper, if you would like any help,' he looked at her, 'that is, if you're not so horrified by it all to want to shoot off back to London.'

'I'll stay for a while, I think. Thank you for the offer, I might even take you up on it.'

She followed him downstairs – her turn to look, to notice that his dark, neatly cut hair was slightly thinning, that perhaps there was even a touch of grey all of a sudden shown up by the sun streaming through the half-landing window. His clothes seemed chosen for quality rather than style, although there was a stylishness about him and a care for appearances: his conker-brown brogues were polished – there was no scuffing, no stains or fraying of cuffs or collars, as though a woman looked after him – his mother, perhaps; she hoped not. But of course, he had been in the war. As Mark would say, he had been, seen, and done. A spit-and-polish man, like Bobby. Curious she asked, 'Were you in the army or RAF?'

They had reached the hallway, both of them reflected in the hall-stand mirror, domestically framed by her hats and coats and furled umbrellas. 'Army,' he said, 'nothing as glamorous as the RAF.'

She saw him outside. Standing on the doorstep she said, 'Thank you for coming.'

'My pleasure. Thank you for the guided tour – brought back memories.'

'Well, I hope it didn't interfere too much with your efforts to forget.'

He leaned towards her, mock conspiratorial. 'It's just my ex-wife I'm trying to forget.'

Watching him walk down the path she called out, 'Call again some time.'

He held up his hand in a salute-cum-wave as he stooped to unlock a battered-looking Austin Morris. Perhaps she should have left the last word to him – she wondered if she had sounded desperate. She decided no, that all through his visit she had been fairly cool, cool as she used to be, before Mark. Or had she been frosty, said too little, smiled too little? She thought she liked him; he was presentable, kind, not as dull as he might be. So what, she thought, so what, so what, so what. Cool or frosty, nice or nasty, desperate or indifferent, it didn't matter, *he* didn't matter.

Back inside the house she closed the door and the hall became dark and forbidding – this wasn't her house, this was nowhere – worse than nowhere: a place too full of the dead. She closed her eyes, told herself it was only so dark because outside was so bright. She must be sensible – the dead were everywhere, wherever you went, no point running from them. Opening her eyes, the hall was less dim; she would go out into the garden, scout around, claim her territory. 'Sensible,' she said aloud. A good, brave girl.

Chapter Ten

Adele had taken the bus into town, her shopping bag weighty with library books, her raincoat buckled, her navy-blue felt hat pinned resolutely in place. She had looked at herself in the hall mirror and said, 'There – best of a bad job,' as she always did, and Bea had said, 'You'll do,' as she always did. Adele had frowned at her. 'Are you sure you don't want some tonic wine – I'm going to Boots anyway.'

'I'm fine.'

'Well, you don't look fine.' Adele had been exasperated but she seemed to decide to say no more, only looking down at her bag in something like dismay.

'Don't miss the bus,' Bea said, afraid that she would if she dawdled, and then she would come home, full of huffing and puffing grumbles; and then she would see Charles and be outraged, both at his presence and at the fact she had kept his visit from her.

In the kitchen, setting out her mother's best teacups on the tray and wondering how many bourbon biscuits would be enough to serve without seeming mean, Bea calculated the time it would take Adele to get to the library, then to Robinson's to browse the various departments without buying, then to the market to fill her now empty bag with cabbages, onions and carrots. She might even go to Boots the Chemist, although Bea doubted this. All in all, if the buses were on time, she would probably be home by four; she glanced at the kitchen clock: ten to two. Charles had said he would be here at two o'clock. Perhaps Adele would spy him from the bus; perhaps she wouldn't recognise him if she did, and anyway, it wouldn't occur to her that it was Charles Dearlove – more likely to see the king of Siam strolling along Oxhill Avenue.

Charles would be on time, he was always punctual, right and proper. She spilled the bourbons onto a plate and pictured Charles nibbling at one before placing it just so on his saucer. Somehow he would manage not to allow a single crumb to fall; he would sit straight-backed but nevertheless quite at ease. His sparse hair would be Brylcreemed very neatly over the shiny dome of his head. He would smell almost subtly of that cologne that seemed to her absolutely unique to Charles – he would have a little man somewhere in Morocco distilling it, under instruction to keep the concoction secret. The scent of Charles Dearlove was for Bea what madeleines were for Proust.

She gazed down at the biscuits, palms flat on the kitchen counter because she felt faint suddenly and unsure how she would cope with this visit. If Adele were here it would be different – she would be a different person with her sister around. That person would be gruff and no-nonsense to compensate for Adele's flustering and fussing. But even then Charles would see through to the real person – the person she was when she was alone. Odd that she was only truly herself with Charles: no show, no stuff-and-nonsense. He would see that she was ill and wait for her to tell him all about it. She wondered if she would cry as she told him – he was the only person besides Adele who had ever seen her cry. No, there would be no tears. Besides, Charles wouldn't allow her to cry – he would say only that she should buck up.

'Let's face it,' he had once said, 'we could all weep buckets if we were minded to – life is sheer bloody horror after all.' He'd handed her a handkerchief, all pressed and smelling of that cologne of his. 'Be brave, now. Be *Bea*.' He'd ducked his head to look up into her face. 'All right, old girl?'

She'd nodded, wiping her eyes and nose quickly because he was right: bravery was all – what else was there, in the end?

The kettle boiled; she made tea, so certain was she that in a few minutes the doorbell would ring and there would be Charles, as if he had never been away, as if they spoke every week rather than just exchanging Christmas cards. She set the teapot just so on the tray – a nice display of blue and white Spode: Charles appreciated such things. She drew breath, steady now and calm.

Charles was shocked when he saw Bea; he had thought that perhaps she was someone else – a long-lost cousin, despite knowing all there was to know about Bea's tiny, almost extinct family. There could be no cousins, and this diminished woman really was Bea and unmistakably Bea at that when she said, 'Charles. Always on the dot.'

She had opened the front door wide, standing to one side and ushering him in with a gesture of her arm, like Edmund's man-servant doing his impression of Jeeves. Leading him into the house she said, 'I've set out tea in the sitting room – it gets all the sun at this time of the day. Shall I take your coat?'

His mac was over his arm as it had been since entering the Green Dragon – he had forgotten about it but now it seemed like a terrible encumbrance and he handed it to her, almost not caring when she threw it over the newel post, the belt slithering to the floor. She strode on, flinging open the sitting-room door, and there was the tea tray on an occasional table between two chairs. The room was sunny, and he found himself blinking after the gloom of the hallway, feeling as slow and disorientated as an unearthed mole. First the shock of Bea's appearance, now the surprise of her welcome: tea and biscuits, an armchair with a plumped cushion, the sun streaming in as if even it was in on the act. He saw how little the room had changed since the days when he, Eric, Adele, and Bea had run rampage through this house playing hide-and-seek when the Old B was out at work and Bea's mother was having one of those days when she didn't care what they did. There was the chest he'd once folded himself into, a budding Houdini. The others hadn't found him that day – wasn't he much too clever for them?

Bea said, 'Sit down, Charles. How was your journey? Train on time?'

'Yes.' He managed to look at her. 'Fine.'

'Good show. Now do sit – you would like some tea, I expect – travel is such a thirsty business, in my experience.'

He sat; he took the dainty cup and saucer from her, then took a biscuit he couldn't imagine eating, and watched as she settled herself in the opposite chair. He knew he was staring but couldn't stop himself. Bea caught his eye and smiled grimly.

'I shall be dead in six months, Charles. There – you can close your mouth now, you're gaping so you'll catch flies.'

'Bea –'

'*Charles.*'

He shook his head. 'Christ, Bea.' Her expression was so triumphant he almost laughed. Searching around for something to say, all he could manage was, 'You don't usually play your trump card so early.'

'I thought I'd get it out of the way.'

'Break the ice?' An over-powering sadness caused him to glance away from her. He set his cup down and fumbled in his pocket for his handkerchief – he could imagine crying, lately he was wont to – but this was only a precaution, his eyes felt as itchy and dry as his mouth. Reaching for his tea, he took a long drink. Sweet, strong tea – good for shock.

Quietly Bea said, 'Sorry, Charles. I don't get any better, do I? You don't have to say anything and I'd prefer not to have to answer the usual questions.' She laughed bleakly. 'I haven't prepared any answers, anyway. You're the only person I've told.'

'You must have told Adele?'

'No – and you mustn't, if you see her. No point in worrying her so soon.'

'She may have guessed – you look poorly, Bea.'

'Poorly!' She snorted. '*Poorly.*'

He began to eat the biscuit, an unthinking comfort. The sun withdrew, the room became as gloomy as he remembered it. Bea was in shadow now so that she almost looked like her old self. He reached for another biscuit and ate it in two bites – he could be an eleven-year-old boy in Bea's presence, a small retreat. Still, she had thrown him; all the things he was going to say didn't matter any more, he could hardly remember what those things were – perhaps an apology about the book, excuses. She had loved Margot so after all. He cleared his throat and took another sip of tea, washing away crumbs. 'Well,' he said at last. 'Well, well. I was ready for a battle, but it all seems rather pointless now.'

'You wanted to talk about your book – about Paul and Margot, all that.'

'No –'

'I'll just say that I have read it. I thought your portrayal of Margot was fair enough. She *was* very young, a silly child in many ways. Perhaps what happened was all her fault – if she hadn't tied Paul down as she did I suppose he wouldn't have got himself into so much trouble. He would have left Thorp in 1919, I think – gone somewhere more *accommodating*, no?'

'I don't think she tied him down. He told me he wanted to marry her, that he could see no other way out – keeping his dead brother's child was everything to him – and Paul's father wanted him to marry –'

'Understandably.'

'Yes. Easy to understand all their motivations.'

'And poor Margot, caught up in it all, pregnant and frightened.'

'Yes.'

'Paul should have stayed true to her – accepted the responsibility that was *everything* to him.'

He sighed. 'Yes. He should have.'

'You think so, Charles? Are you condemning Paul – the glorious Francis Law?'

There were biscuit crumbs compacted in his back teeth and he wanted to poke around with his tongue to get rid of them. He wanted to stand up and leave, to walk briskly to the station, to see with unadulterated relief the Kings Cross train approaching. But there was Bea, some of her old spirit returned – they could spar and he might even win. More than that, he wanted her to acknowledge the truth.

'What would have happened to Bobby if Paul hadn't married Margot, Bea?'

Her face was inscrutable. 'You tell me.'

'Oh, Bea! Would Margot really have preferred to give him up?'

'He might have had a decent home with adoptive parents who loved him.'

'Paul loved him! For goodness' sake, Bea – *Margot* loved him!'

'Did she?' She glanced away, no longer inscrutable, just bitterly angry, her face closed to him. At last she said, 'Adele once told me she wanted to kidnap Bobby. That year or so after Redpath moved her and Bobby in next door, she would watch Bobby wandering about in their garden and imagine taking him – or at least going to Margot and offering to take him off her hands. Bobby wasn't *loved*, Charles. And once Redpath had his own son, Bobby was packed off to school. Did your research reveal all that, Charles?'

'I know how terribly guilty Paul felt.'

'I bet he did.' Sharply she said, 'Margot felt guilty, too. It was all a horrible mess – perhaps if she hadn't married Redpath – that man preyed on her, saw a vulnerable woman he knew he could bully for the rest of time because she wouldn't have any defence: she was the woman who had married a pervert because she had a baby on the way. And now that pervert was in prison so what could she do? Only be grateful to Redpath for taking on her shamefulness.'

Unable to meet her eye he said, 'Don't keep calling him a pervert.'

'A queer then. Not even a very committed queer – how could he have married a young girl like Margot? How could he bring himself –'

'I don't know.'

'No. Me neither. I loathe people like that – people who will hop into bed with anyone – anyone. Nothing but selfishness and greed.'

Charles found that he wanted to laugh – her anger was so righteous and true. Men like Paul and Edmund were selfish and greedy – he had always thought so – and to hear Bea say it was marvellously gratifying.

Catching his eye, Bea said, 'Don't smirk – don't be all sophisticated and smirky.'

'I'm not smirking – I agree with you.'

'Good. So you should.'

They sat in silence for a while – old companions, after all. He thought about eating another biscuit – there were two left, she hadn't taken one – but decided not to look greedy. He was not a greedy man. He thought of Paul, who had entrusted him with the truth and had set him off on his course like a wind-up toy – to Edmund; to Patrick in Morocco; and now here, back to Thorp, if only to explain himself. Remembering his mission he said, 'I wrote to Margot. Although she wouldn't see me she wrote that she didn't care any more about the past and that I should write what I wished. You know how fatalistic Margot was. She thought Paul had told Bobby that he wasn't his son, only his nephew – she was surprised when I told her he hadn't. Neither could face telling him, I suppose . . .' He trailed off and Bea reached over to refill his teacup.

She said, 'Two weak people.' Glancing at him she raised her eyebrows. 'I know you agree, Charles. I know you loved Paul. I loved Margot – both of us mooning from afar, both of us nincompoops. But we can agree that they were weak. Well, most people are – weak and irresponsible.'

'Whilst we are strong and responsible?'

'Yes.'

'Strong, responsible nincompoops?'

'Have I offended you? Didn't you love Paul?'

He thought about this. At last he said, 'I had a terrific crush on him. I don't think I loved him, to be honest. I don't think I'm the kind of person who *loves*.' Remembering, he said, 'I loved Aunt May. I think I loved Uncle Arthur, in a way. They never made me feel any less their son than Eric was.'

Eric's name had the usual effect on Bea. She sat up straighter, her face became matron-stern, and yet she wouldn't meet his eye, wouldn't say anything as theatrical as *never mention that man's name in this house*. She simply closed down. But now that he had mentioned Eric's name he felt he had nothing further to lose. As lightly as he could he said, 'Poor Eric.'

'*Weak* Eric.'

'He was very ill, Bea –'

Her face became sterner still. It seemed that she was biting down hard on any sympathy she might have because her jaw clenched. At last she seemed to force herself to speak. 'Well, he isn't part of anyone's story – no one will write a book about him – long dead and gone and good riddance –'

'Oh, Bea –'

'Don't *Oh, Bea* me! Can't I have my say? No one would blame me for judging him harshly.'

Swiftly he said, 'Adele forgave Eric –'

'You presume Adele has forgiven him?'

He shook his head, thinking only that he had presumed her forgiveness because he knew Adele to be kind – forgiving; now he wondered why kindness and the inclination to forgive should be conflated. All he could do was placate Bea, he hadn't meant to stray so far into this dangerous territory. But he was with Bea, being with Bea always meant that Eric and Adele were around about them, just waiting to come up in conversation.

'Did you tell Adele I was coming?'

'No.'

'I would have liked to see her. I presume she's out – will she be back soon?'

'She's angry with you – she thinks you've dragged Margot's name through the mud.'

He had written that Paul Harris – who would change his name to Francis Law on his release from prison – had married his dead brother's fiancée on Christmas Eve 1919. A son had been born the following June. He supposed readers who had a mind to could draw their own conclusions. The scandal that was meant to sell was that Paul-who-became-Francis was homosexual. Not that anyone truly cared – an open secret after all. Francis Law's paintings were in all the great museums and galleries of the world, from New York to Tokyo, the only English painter to rival any of the continental artists. The paintings had become famous slowly, and then lately, or so it seemed, all at once, when Paul's war had become fashionable. Charles thought of the stage play – *Oh! What a Lovely War* – it seemed to him that he owed this play a debt, because no one had wanted to publish the biography until the production became such a hit, making everything about the first war interesting. There was even interest in the fact that this great artist had come from Thorp – Thorp of all places – how quaint, how amusingly unlikely, how preposterous. Yet Thorp was where all the true secrets were – Paul's life in Morocco was an open letter to the press in comparison.

Charles said, 'I could write a better book – about all of us, and Paul Harris–Francis Law would have only a walk-on part. I would try to be fair to us all –'

'Fair! Sounds like a dull read to me. You would put your own truth into it – your idea of fairness – that cousin of yours would be exonerated.'

'I would be fair to Eric, as I would be to you and Adele.' He laughed shortly. 'It wasn't Eric's *fault*, Bea! You remember what he was like before the war –'

'Let's blame everything on the war, then. Our good old war that gave us all an excuse for everything! You, me, Eric, Paul Harris – even Margot – even Adele. All of us so messed up by the war we couldn't tell right from wrong.'

He set his cup down gently on the tray and stood up. 'I should go, Bea, before Adele comes home. If you can bear to tell her I was here, tell her I said hello and that I was sorry I missed her.'

When he'd gone Bea carried the tray back into the kitchen, walking slowly, afraid that the tremble in her arms would send the whole lot crashing – she imagined all her mother's pretty china broken and jagged around her feet. But she held on tightly, determined not to be a fool – an invalid – and in the kitchen she washed the cups carefully, then slid the remaining biscuits into the old Quality Street tin, used as a caddy since its original contents were eaten one Christmas a couple of decades ago. There was the crinolined girl and her soldier beau. The Napoleonic wars this soldier seemed to represent were picturesque compared to her war – no one would put a picture of a 1914 subaltern on a box of sweets. Imagine Eric and Adele portrayed in such a way, arm in arm, smiling into each other's eyes as they strolled along Thorp High Street – perhaps in a hundred years, when all the horror had been forgotten and no one cared any more, just as she didn't care about Waterloo.

Eric had been her friend, taking her side when Charles was scathing and Adele was embarrassed. He would say to them *leave her alone, let her be a boy if she likes*. Eric should never have been a soldier. Charles was right: he could not be blamed. Yet still she hated him – couldn't stop herself, even now. Hatred of Eric was one of the things she shared with Adele.

She heard the front door open and Adele calling out a weary hello. She had hardly been any time at all, may even have passed Charles on her walk from the bus stop. If she had seen him then perhaps it was for the best – perhaps there was a conversation to be had about those two boys who used to live next door so long ago. It could be that Adele really had forgiven Eric and that their shared hatred was only a presumption. She looked down at the Quality Street tin and thought of Eric as he had been on the day he joined the army: a sweet, plain, jug-eared boy; she closed her eyes and a tear splashed onto the tin's embossed lid.

Chapter Eleven

Charles, 1923

Eric is dead. This morning I heard him cry out, and then what sounded like a sack of potatoes tumbling downstairs. I found him with his head at an odd angle against the hallstand, as though he was trying to peer beneath it for something lost. I knew he was dead at once – I've seen enough to know. I thought that I shouldn't move him, but let the doctor see that he had fallen – the actual *how* of it – I had a panicky idea that I might be somehow blamed, even that I might be suspected of his murder. I crouched beside him, shaking his shoulder just in case. 'Eric,' I said, and I could hear my own panic and despair in my voice as I repeated his name, shaking him that little bit harder. He was still warm, of course – one could imagine that he was still alive and that he would groan blearily and try shrugging me off, vexed that I had distracted him from his searching. He was barefoot and wearing his Christmas-present pyjamas, the material smelling of its stiff newness – he had never worn them before. He had shaved – made a good enough job of it, considering the thickness of his stubble, but there was a bead of blood on his cheek where he had cut himself. His hair was combed; there was a scent of Palmolive soap about him.

I crouched there beside him, my hand on his shoulder, and I felt a pain like none I had felt before: this was *Eric* – I had known him all my life; he had been happy and kind, buoyant – he had kept his orphaned cousin afloat. I forgot the horror of the last few years and saw only the boy I remembered from before the war. I admit I howled like a baby; staggering to my feet I thumped the wall with both fists.

Bea told me later that she thought I had made this racket to summon them. But when I heard her hammering on the front door and saw their shapes through the door's glass, I was only horrified. I stood stock still – as though I had really been caught in the act of murder – glancing around frantically as if for somewhere to hide. Bea stooped to call through the letter box and I called back that she should go – both of them should go. But the door was unlocked and Bea opened it; I almost ran towards her because Adele was there, trying to peer round her sister. I wanted to shield her from seeing her husband like that, from having the memory of such a sight. But already she was staring, her hand covering her mouth. Without a word, Bea took Adele's arm and led her outside again, closing the door behind them as deliberately and quietly as if leaving from any normal visit. A few minutes later Bea returned alone, having called Dr Harris who came almost at once.

Eventually I was left alone; in the silence after all the busyness of a sudden death, the house felt like a tomb: a many-roomed tomb, all of those rooms full of the things the dead leave behind. I have lived here for most of my life and despite May's efforts I never felt truly at home. Lying on my bed, staring at the ceiling, I thought I should leave – just get up and go with only a suitcase of clothes. I saw myself dropping the key through the letter box and walking off down the path, right at the gate towards Thorp Station to board the next train to London. I had the money my parents left me – I could survive while I looked for something to do in the city. London had always been my goal – only Eric had held me back. I closed my eyes tight, squeezing out the tears I'd been crying all day. I saw Eric again in his stiff pyjamas. Once again I tried to think through how I might have saved him.

Dr Harris had told me that he would swear that Eric's death was an accident – he had tripped on the stairs. 'You mustn't worry about anything else,' he said. His hand covered mine, a slight, brief squeeze of my fingers. 'He fell down the stairs, a tragic accident.'

I had been staring at the cup of tea growing cold in front of me and I jerked my head to look at him; I had an idea that he should know the truth. 'He killed himself.'

111

'We can't know that, Charles.'

'The pyjamas –'

'I'm not sure I understand.' Again he touched my hand, a tiny bit more briskly. 'There will be an inquest. I will say that I believe he tripped, an accident. So sad because he had been feeling better lately –'

'Did he tell you that? He said nothing to me –' I could hear my voice rising. 'Was he getting better?'

Dr Harris gazed at me. At last he said, 'Charles, I can offer you a sedative, or I could ask Miss Davis to come in and sit with you – she has already offered to.'

Tearfully I said, 'Won't you stay?'

'If you wish. For a little while.'

I blew my nose. Shoving the hanky in my pocket I tried to pull myself together. 'It's all right, doctor. You've been very kind – I won't take up any more of your time.'

He nodded, searching my face. At last he said, 'You couldn't have done more, Charles. No one could.'

'I'd given up on him.'

'You stayed, my boy. That isn't giving up.'

I had stayed, but it wasn't out of any kind of goodness on my part, only a certainty that I wouldn't find any peace, that wherever I was and whatever I was doing I would be thinking always about Eric: he would be starving himself to death, or something worse. Something worse – a malevolent, sly thing I couldn't think about, and so I directed my thoughts away – to leaving, dropping that key through the letter box, boarding that train – I would arrive in London and search out a garret. I would write to Paul Harris and invite him to live with me on his release from prison.

I couldn't decide whether it was obscene to think of Harris at a time like this, or a permissible comfort. I was alone in an empty house; if I chose to I could go next door and sit with Adele and Bea: the three of us could stew in silence together and all our unspoken thoughts about Eric, all our memories, would bang about between us so that his death would come to seem like a game – as children

112

we had always been great inventors of games. But I had only to think of Bea's grim expression, of Adele's bitter weeping, to put aside that idea. It occurred to me that I need never see either woman again; I pondered this; I could begin again completely afresh, as if I had no past but had been created a fully formed man in the Soho attic that was beginning to be so appealing.

All these thoughts – not least of them about Paul Harris – were knocking about my head so that when I heard the knocking on the front door I began to think the noise was just a physical manifest-ation of thinking. But the knocking went on and I kept still, until it came to me that it had to be Bea – come to interrogate me further – although the knocking wasn't what I would imagine from her: it was more patient, there was no rattling of the letter box as she called my name. Only the rat-a-tat-tat, then a listening pause, carefully judged before the rat-a-tatting continued. I sat up, sat on the edge of my bed, listening as I would to a piece of fine music I hadn't heard before that needed my complete attention. How easily I was dis-tracted from my grief – I needed to be distracted. I was still, listening when, all at once – because I realised whoever this caller was wouldn't keep knocking indefinitely – I sprang up and hurried downstairs.

How do I describe Havelock Redpath? I feel I don't want to describe him – he defies conventional description, albeit he *was* conventional: he was tall, well built, just handsome enough to be entirely unremarkable. He was older than most people I knew well, or had known well because many of them were dead. Yet, for all his ordinary appearance there was an air of unpleasantness about him as if he was always on the lookout for something he might hold against you. He had escaped the war for some reason – perhaps because of this age of his: a lucky age, not old enough to have lost a son, like Dr Harris, nor quite young enough to have lost himself. This luck of his was born with ill grace, I'm sure he thought he was being judged – he was, at least by me – for something he had no control of. And Havelock Redpath had so much control – as though he had written his own script. He must have found it infuriating to be looked down upon by someone like me, someone who was shorter, tubbier, with thinner hair and more irregular features, just because that tubby nonentity had *done his bit*.

This evening however, when I opened the door to him, he managed to hide all his contempt with an odd, unbecoming smile of condolence – I couldn't help thinking of Uriah Heep. Obviously he knew that Eric was dead and so I felt that I must accept his visit in the spirit it was meant. I led him down the hall to the kitchen and put the kettle on to boil, searching out clean cups, swilling out the stone-cold remains of the last pot of tea – the routine of the newly bereaved.

Havelock Redpath (I feel I must mostly use his full name to distance myself from him) sat down at the table and glanced around quite openly – I thought he might ask me how much I wanted for the old place. Yet he had bought the house next door to Bea, the dreadful ruin Adele loved so much. He had yet to move in – builders were still hammering away in its various rooms – I had even seen a man clambering about the roof. The whole of Oxhill Avenue was interested in the comings and goings, in the new owner himself, there were rumours and counter rumours; mostly we were pleased that the house was bought and wasn't falling into further disrepair: the Victorian Gothic of the avenue could easily become frighteningly derelict. Upkeep was needed, and Redpath was just the man, we all felt sure, having spied him strutting about the place.

I placed a cup of tea before him and he said, 'I hope I'm not intruding. I heard all the commotion, saw my two lady neighbours coming and going, et cetera, and thought I should drop in – be neighbourly, if there's anything I can do for you . . .' He sipped his tea, first blowing across its surface rather delicately. I could only think what a strange creature he was, that *et cetera*, for instance, his absolute lack of awkwardness in the face of bereavement; he might just as well be sitting in his own kitchen, alone. I pictured him surrounded by sacks of plaster and paint pots and not being in the least bothered by the mess because it was part of his plan and therefore under his control.

114

As I sat down he said, 'As I say, if there is anything I can do, you only have to ask.'

'There's nothing I can think of.'

'Of course, of course . . .' He smiled at me, although his eyes darted about; he had the air of a man who was working towards asking for a favour and I thought that he had better come out with it, whatever it might be, because I wanted to lie down, to sleep if I could. Perhaps I looked impatient because he laughed slightly and said, 'I saw you out the other day, in the park with a young lady – Mrs Harris, I think?'

I was astonished – what was this to do with anything? He had such a look on his face – I think he was trying for a kind of mild enquiry, yet his cheeks had coloured. He went on looking at me, though, bold as a blushing man can be, waiting for confirmation that yes, I was with Mrs Harris, Margot. I couldn't speak; he seemed absurd to me; I wanted him to leave.

At last he said, 'Mrs Harris – Margot, I think? And her young child. I believe she's the vicar's daughter. I attend her father's church, St Anne's, but I don't see her in the congregation – perhaps the child prevents her from attending?'

'I really couldn't say.'

'But you know her – you looked to be good friends, in the park.'

I could have asked him to leave, of course, and then the house would be empty and I would have no more distraction. I could go to bed and start on my memories, the tears would come again no doubt. But I found I was intrigued by him; his face had become redder still and he was watching me as if I held the key to the rest of his life. I thought I could pretend to be someone else – he didn't know a thing about me, after all – I could be Eric before his madness, jolly and sweet, or Dr Harris: calm and measured. Or Paul Harris, laughing at this man's presumption – *Why do you want to know about my wife?* I decided on being my best Captain Dearlove, inscrutable to hide the fact that he hadn't a clue what the blazes was going on. I said, 'I don't know Margot Harris well. I know her husband –'

'She's divorcing him.'

'I don't know about that.'

'*I* know.'

'Then you know more than I.'

'She doesn't talk to you, then? You're not – how shall I say – close?'

'I don't know what you're getting at.'

'I would like to be formally introduced.'

I gazed at him. His colour had returned to normal, he even seemed tight-lipped now that his hand was played. I thought of poor Margot; I felt that she didn't stand a chance if this man had her in his sights. Perhaps I should ask her to marry me, if that might save her, but then I thought of my escape and realised for certain that whatever happened I couldn't stay in Thorp – I would die here if I stayed.

He dropped his gaze from mine – at least I had made him a little uncomfortable. Brusquely he said, 'She has gone through a very difficult time – I would like to help her, if I can.'

'Don't you think it's too soon?'

'Too soon? She's not in mourning.'

I thought *Isn't she?* but said nothing.

Rather quickly he went on, 'Anyway, I saw you together in the park and thought – if there is nothing between you, of course – then I would invite you both to tea on Sunday. You and my neighbours – Miss Davis and Mrs Dearlove.'

'And the children?'

'The children?'

'Adele's boy, Tom, and Margot's child, Bobby.'

'Of course, if they wish to come.'

'I don't think they have such wishes at their age.'

He stood. 'I'll take my leave. Once again, you have my condolences. But just to say, I would like to be neighbourly – a good neighbour – and so I shall call on Miss Davis and invite her and her sister to tea on Sunday, at four p.m., if you would be so kind as to bring Mrs Harris along. I'm sure a little get-together will lift her spirits.'

I accompanied him to the front door and watched as he walked down the path towards his own home. I hadn't told him that I would attend his get-together, he seemed to take my presence for granted, to have forgotten all about Eric and the fact of my mourning. His strangeness intrigued me. Later, as I tried to sleep, I began to feel that he had been sent by my own guardian angel – a complicated creature and unfathomable – to prompt me into some action that would change my life for good or ill.

Chapter Twelve

Cathy said, 'Tell me something you have never told anyone.'

Tom seemed to consider this. He was up a ladder, wallpaper scraper in hand. He frowned. At last, beginning to scrape away at a particularly stubborn Humpty Dumpty, he said, 'Why should I do such a thing?' He turned to her. 'Would I fail some kind of test?'

'Depends what you told me.'

'All right. I was twelve before I stopped believing in Father Christmas.'

'That's not the kind of confession I had in mind.'

'No. I know.' He returned to his scraping. 'I have nothing to confess.'

She was gathering soggy wallpaper from the floor; for the last two hours they had been working together and almost all of the wallpaper was stripped. She had begun to think that they were easy together – they had talked about all kinds of things and she had begun to build a picture of an uncomplicated, straightforward man who loved his son and was kind to his mother and aunt; who worked diligently at a job he didn't much care for and told jokes about fellow teachers that were both funny and devastating – she wouldn't want to be on the wrong side of one of his character assassinations. But she had wanted to know more and so couldn't resist playing the secret game. She felt silly now – worse, she had succeeded in subduing the easy atmosphere he had done so much to create. She glanced at him as she thrust paper into a sack. He was scraping away with straight-faced concentration. Perhaps he didn't much care that she had tried to winkle something out of him – games were just that to some men, best left to children and a certain type of woman who was out to set traps. She wondered how he was categorising her, but he was inscrutable and she didn't know if she liked this inscrutability or not. Mark had been open – he would have played the game extravagantly. Mark was an actor. She had to keep reminding herself that Mark was different.

At last he said, 'I'll tell you one thing – I would very much like to down tools and go to the pub for lunch. Shall we?'

'I'd like that.'

'Good.' He came down the ladder and touched her arm lightly. 'We'll drive out to the Crown – I'll show you a little bit of the countryside.'

The countryside around Thorp was prettier than she had expected – quiet, tree-shaded lanes winding through small hamlets and villages with their pubs and Norman churches, here and there a manor house or Georgian vicarage tantalisingly glimpsed behind its walled garden. Fields of cows and horses gave way to moorland where sheep grazed the edges of the road and occasionally trotted out in front of the car so that Tom slowed and beeped gently on the horn. He glanced at her and smiled. 'How do sheep survive – I suppose they need their good shepherd. Well, don't we all.'

The sun shone and the breeze was soft through the car's windows as they climbed and climbed towards the summit of the hill. She thought of the good shepherd, a mild and gentle Christ with a lamb draped over his shoulders, and wondered if this calm, handsome man believed in anything. Now was not the time to ask him; now was only the time to be quiet because the daffodils in the hedgerows were so lovely and the green smells of spring were so intoxicating, the sky as blue as any she had ever seen. She realised her grief had receded: the sun's warmth was a balm, this journey into the hills a fine distraction. Perhaps he had meant it as such; perhaps he understood more than she.

He pulled up in front of a long, low, whitewashed building, a plain gold crown depicted on the sign above the door. Quick as a flash he was out of the car and opening the passenger door for her, bowing a little. She took his offered hand and noticed there was a scrap of wallpaper in his hair and picked it out.

'Will I do?' he asked.

'Yes. I think you will.'

Tom thought, I am not the man you think I am. But why did he think this – he had no idea what she thought – she was cool and self-contained; very beautiful, of course – rather out of his league. Did her sadness bring her down to his level – a flaw that would put off other men? *Lesser men*; he smiled to himself, turning his pint round and round on the beer mat. He was alone, she had gone in search of the lavatory – she had said that she should powder her nose; she would refresh her lipstick and brush her hair, no doubt, although she looked perfect to him – lipstick in fact would spoil her although he would never tell her as much. He knew some things about women – a little store of dos and don'ts. He would be careful, attentive: the stakes were high; he would try to be the quiet man she thought he was – suddenly he realised what she thought of him – an easy-going, no-trouble man.

Bobby Harris – her brother-in-law – liked this woman. He had said that she was good for Mark, that she brought him down to earth. Tom had wondered how she could do this – she was too intoxicating to be so dull. Bobby had also said that she was a good actress because her reaction to his disfigured face was quite perfect – not too much interest, nor embarrassment or fluster, not even a pretending that she hadn't noticed how badly damaged he was, just a well-judged acceptance. This was an achievement, Tom thought – Bobby Harris was quite a shock, at first. Sipping his beer, he remembered the first time he had seen him after the crash that had burnt away his face. He was sure he hadn't behaved as well as Cathy; he seemed to remember that he had tried very hard not to cry: no well-judged acceptance, then, but rather dismay and horror and grief because Bobby had been so handsome and he himself was shallow and frail and easily pushed over.

His ex-wife had screamed at him, *Where is your courage?*

She was French – she had a foreign turn of phrase, of course. But the question was valid – where had his courage gone? He had put it down somewhere when it became too much of a heavy burden and it had been a great relief; besides, there was no call for courage any more now that the war was over, duty done. But she had wanted something from him – ambition, drive, anger. She would slap him in the hope he would slap her in return, harder, so there could be no doubting his resolve. She was so tiny – a jumping, spitting sprite – he could have seized her flailing arms and thrown her down. His French was better than her English; he had some mastery of her. He could speak any language he cared to – French, German, Russian – he only had to listen to take it in, like a magic trick – there was no merit in it. But she didn't want to talk in any language – only to fight in order to make up. *How can you speak German?* she had said once. She might as well have asked him why he spoke at all.

Cathy came back. She picked up her gin and tonic and finished it and for a little while they sat in companionable silence. At last she said, 'Thank you for this – it was just what I needed.'

A drive out in the sunshine; a ploughman's lunch and a gin; some light-hearted banter – flirting, he supposed. Not much, really. Yet the pub was cosy with gleaming horse brasses and a coal fire, the locals solid and taciturn – good that they showed no interest in this lovely woman, as though women such as her drank in this pub all the time. There was a perfection to the day that he couldn't have invented – he would have left out some key element, or over-egged it so that the whole collapsed. He would not have imagined that she could smell so headily – rose petals steeped in hot, salty water – was that it? Hard to say – he would need to press his nose to her neck and breathe in deeply, try to figure it out.

She said, 'You're very pensive.'

He straightened his back. 'No, sorry – lost in thought, that's all.'

She smiled. 'Should we get back? Will your son wonder where you are when he comes home from school?'

Luc – he had forgotten he had a son; this hadn't happened before.

'I don't think he'll notice my absence.' He looked at her. 'I'd like you to meet him.'

She nodded. 'Soon.'

For a while he held her gaze; he thought about touching her face, a tender, actor-like touch, a prelude to brushing his lips lightly against hers. Who could he pretend to be? Mark, who *was* an actor; Bobby, who was brave. Other men he had known were ghosts watching over his shoulder – didn't he have a duty to the dead to live the best life he could? Hadn't he made quite a mess of it so far?

She said, 'Don't look so serious.'

'No, I shouldn't.'

Patting his knee she said, 'Let's go.'

As she stood he caught her hand. 'I'll take you out to dinner on Saturday.'

'I'd like that.'

'The Grand Hotel,' he hesitated, thinking how she made him want to be precise so there could be no doubt about what was to happen, there had to be an orderly schedule of events. 'Dinner and dancing – they have a band –'

She laughed. 'We'll dance, then?'

'Yes, if you'd like that.'

She was putting on her coat quite nonchalantly, as though she didn't need to pay so much attention. She looked across to the bar and the barman caught her eye and nodded, a curt appreciation. Tom could see her reflection in the mirror between the black and white whiskey dogs. And there he was too, a head taller, older but not so much that it could be remarked upon. He could be who she thought he was, if he tried.

He fished the car keys from his pocket and offered her his arm.

Chapter Thirteen

Adele had watched Tom help Cathy from his car, kiss her cheek, and wait until she was inside her house. He had stood for a few moments on the pavement – wistfully? – before climbing back into his silly little car and driving away. He hadn't looked up to see her standing at her bedroom window. If he had she knew he would have waved sheepishly and driven off all the same. He wasn't scheduled to visit her today; he wouldn't call in unannounced. Theirs was quite a formal relationship although she had no doubt he loved her. Sometimes she wondered if she loved him and she pondered how she would feel if he died. She wouldn't want him to suffer at all; she wouldn't want him to be very sad or frightened, but if he was merely absent – if she didn't have to think about him at all – she felt she wouldn't miss him. He looked too much like his father – that was the trouble.

There were photographs of his father in a shoebox on the top shelf of a wardrobe in one of the spare rooms. That wardrobe was full of things she would never wear or use ever again – old-fashioned things; broken things she should have thrown away, there were some forgotten reasons why she had kept them. She had kept the photos of Tom's father because she half-believed that one day Tom might ask to see them, although she couldn't imagine what might arouse his curiosity. Tom never asked about Eric, *had* never asked about him. He wasn't a curious man – she had never met a man who was. In the past she'd thought about taking the shoebox out into the garden and burning it, unopened, but even when she was young this had seemed too ritualistic and she didn't want to give Eric that much weight. The effort of going into that cold back bedroom, of climbing up on the flimsy chair to reach the back of the top shelf where the box lurked, of taking it downstairs (unopened) and outside to the brazier where Bea burnt the garden rubbish, matches in hand . . . too much effort requiring too much thought, allowing the escape of too many memories to torment her. Memories should be squashed into smallness, their clamouring ignored until they died and shrivelled to dust. She had trained herself in this squashing; she had become good at it, and she was proud that remembering didn't have the power to hurt her as much as she once thought it would. Rather she had the power, even if she looked soft and small compared to Bea.

Adele sat down on her bed and took off her going-into-town shoes and stockings. She changed from her good skirt and blouse into an old house dress and a pair of older, thicker stockings. Her mother had liked clothes and had taught her to take care of them and yet she had accepted Bea's eccentricities of dress without a word, as though Bea truly was a boy. Adele paused as she hung up her skirt on its padded hanger: she had inherited her mother's insouciance when it came to maternal feelings – she hadn't realised this before – did this mean she was off the hook or on it? She had also inherited her mother's round softness, that essential femininity that concealed her flintiness – the older she got the flintier she became. She was a beady-eyed old bird now and she had spied Charles Dearlove with her cool, flinty eye.

Charles: bold as brass, strolling along Oxhill Avenue like the dapper little man he was. Of course, she had known Bea was up to something, she just hadn't thought of Charles; she only thought of Charles in relation to that book he wrote, the book she had borrowed from the library – she had been the first to borrow it so that it was pristine; its brand newness would have been a treat had it been any other book. But it had been Charles's book, and she had hidden it from Bea and read it only in bed. She had to admit it was interesting – even something of a page-turner, even though she knew how it all would end: in Margot's humiliation. Except it didn't

124

end there, of course – Margot was an incidental a quarter way through.

Quarter way through and there was Margot – after the Great War and before The Imprisonment – a young, pregnant, desperate girl for Charles's hero to rescue. And he did rescue her. Margot had told her so herself.

Margot had said, 'I didn't much care for him at first – I thought he was fey, quite odd, angry much of the time.'

They had been sitting in the garden, a few days after *Machine Gunner* had appeared on Margot's kitchen wall. Adele hadn't prompted any of this remembering, but she wasn't about to put a stop to it; she enjoyed stories and the sun was warm on her face and the tea was hot and just as she liked it; there was a plate of newly baked shortbread between them. She remembered settling herself more comfortably on the garden bench, telling herself that this reminiscing was beneficial for Margot, that her memories were good and didn't deserve to be squashed.

Margot sipped her tea. She said, 'My mother thought Paul was extraordinarily handsome – well, lots of women did, I think, going by the looks they gave him.' She laughed a little. 'The first time I saw him he was in uniform, of course, smoking a cigarette as if his life depended on it. His brother Robbie introduced us and Paul asked me to dance. I didn't want to dance with him. I didn't think he was *extraordinarily* handsome. As I say, I thought he was odd, brittle with all that anger as if he might shatter into pieces.'

Adele closed her eyes against the sun, basking. 'What was he angry about?'

'Everything. But not angry like my father, or Havelock. He didn't lose his temper and jump about like them. There was just this kind of rage, burning away inside him – it drove him; he couldn't just be still with me and the baby.'

Margot became silent and Adele opened her eyes and looked at her. She was gazing at a pair of fat pigeons bumbling about the lawn. At last she said, 'Paul loved me, so he said. And he loved Bobby – oh, he loved him more than anyone or anything – but still he couldn't stay and I knew he couldn't, right from the start. And it wasn't anything to do with this homosexual nonsense,' she glanced at her then, her cheeks colouring a little. 'It was to do with what happened to him during the war, all the men whose names he called out during the night, out of his nightmares. He'd killed men – the machine gunner – well, they had given him a medal for that but he couldn't accept that he had killed. He couldn't be *still* for it.'

Adele had reached out and squeezed her hand, but Margot had pulled away, smiling apologetically. 'They all went through it – your husband, and Charles, all those boys . . .'

She hadn't wanted the conversation to turn to Eric and so she said what she hadn't intended to say, 'If you thought Paul was odd –'

'Why did I marry him?'

'Yes.'

'I had to keep my baby. I couldn't bear the idea of knowing my child was out in the world, not knowing what was happening to him . . . Paul suggested we get married and I could have fainted with relief. At once he stopped being odd, he became a kind, thoughtful man, and if I squinted he could almost be Robbie – they were brothers, after all.' After a moment she said, 'Do you think I was selfish?'

'No –'

Margot scoffed. 'I was. All I wanted was a nice, quiet life with my baby – the life Robbie had promised me, all peaceful and safe. But then Robbie was killed on that stupid motorcycle before he even knew about the baby – before *I* knew. And my life was shot to bits.' She laughed painfully. 'Never to recover. Paul only tried to help – he didn't know helping was beyond him. I think we all forget how young we were, babies ourselves, really. Naïve and stupid and selfish.'

Adele thought of Eric then. As the pigeons took off for no reason that she could see, she saw Eric, smart and happy in his uniform – a happiness she saw right through because he was afraid, too, and proud and surprised with himself – him, a soldier! All of it was extraordinary – a war, like something from the pages of a Russian novel, with all the men in preposterous uniforms and all the women

126

egging them on. *We don't want to lose you, but we think you ought to go* . . . Adele felt an old anger rise inside her, the anger she always tried to smother because it was so useless. She sipped her tea and reached for a biscuit; she would distract herself. She smiled at Margot and said, 'You did the right thing. I would have done the same.'

'Yes. Well.' Vehemently she said, 'I feel I should have known, if only I'd just opened my eyes to it – to him. Saw him properly for what he was. But we didn't know anything then. I sometimes think even my mother didn't know. I have to think that – that my mother didn't know. Although I suspect she did. She just wanted to see me married so all the shame could be avoided. Only for there to be a bigger shame.' She looked at Adele. 'What's the line? – *oh what a tangled web we weave when first we practise to deceive.*'

Adele wondered if she could confess her own deceptions; after all, she was old now, like Margot, and she could tell her about Eric and about Bea and perhaps Margot would only nod as if she had known all along. But still she was proud, and hadn't those memories turned to dust – there could be no resurrection. She would keep the conversation about Margot, and so she said, 'You've put *Machine Gunner* on your wall.'

Margot laughed shortly. 'Yes – well, a *poster*. I read that the original hangs in the Imperial War Museum, that Paul donated it to the nation in his will. It wasn't displayed for years – but his pictures became more and more valuable.' Bitterly she said, 'Paul became a lion led by a donkey, and that war became just a horrible waste of time, and aren't we clever to understand what a horrible waste of time it all was? Anyway,' she took a bite from a biscuit and set it down in her saucer. 'Anyway, I like the gunner's ferociousness. I wish Paul had willed the picture to me – I would have had the means of escape. And you know, if I'd written to him, asked him, I think he would have. But he left everything to Bobby and Bobby thought I didn't need anything and that I was well provided for. I was.' She sat up a little straighter, squaring her shoulders. 'Bobby doesn't love me – never has. I can only suspect that he realised I didn't love him. There. How's that for a confession?'

Standing in her bedroom, Adele thought how she should have made her own confession then, that she didn't love Tom and sometimes she wished he had never been born, but this didn't matter so much because Bea loved him more than life itself. But on that warm, sunny afternoon she said nothing, not even to protest that of course Bobby loved her – she was his mother – because she had seen the two of them together, and knew Margot's words to be true. She had only wanted ever to be a true friend to Margot and not have to offer false comfort as an acquaintance might, some avid neighbour, dismissing her words only to make Margot repeat them more adamantly. And if she had confessed in her turn it may have made less of what it had taken Margot so much to say – so what if you don't love your son, many women feel the same way, including me. No, she had to allow Margot her truth; they sat in silence for a little while and the pigeons returned, the tea was drunk and the biscuits eaten. She remembered that eventually they had exchanged a glance; it wouldn't have been surprising if they had both burst into simultaneous laughter. How funny the past can be – all our trials and tribulations once they are long over suddenly become quite the comedy.

Adele went to her dressing table and tidied her hair. If she decided to confront Bea over Charles Dearlove then she would need to look confident and not like an old lady who had been pulled through a hedge.

Chapter Fourteen

Charles, 1923

Havelock Redpath said, 'Margot, my dear, please do help yourself to cake.'

I watched as Margot shook her head, mute as her little boy who sat straight-backed and seemingly terrified beside her. I managed to catch the child's eye and winked at him as my uncle Arthur might have – like a music hall comic who has his audience in the palm of his hand. But I am a hopeless clown and the boy only looked even more stricken. After a moment Margot cleared her throat and her voice was faint as she said, 'Bobby, would you like some more cake?'

'Of course the child would like more cake,' Bea said, speaking over Redpath who was saying that yes, of course, the boy should help himself. The boy only moved closer to his mother.

Redpath said, 'Cat got your tongue?'

For a moment I thought he was referring to me – I had hardly spoken, occupying myself with the rather good fruit cake, and before that the ham sandwiches Redpath had provided. Bea and Adele had made rather desultory conversation with the man, Margot saying barely a word, only speaking softly to Bobby from time to time. I glanced at Redpath, about to bluster some apology for my silence, but I could see that he was staring at Bobby as though considering how he might reprimand him. Hastily I said, 'Well, the cake is exceptionally good – I could eat the whole plate full, but that would be greedy, eh, Bobby?'

Adele said, 'Did you make the cake yourself, Mr Redpath?'

Immediately she blushed, knowing what scorn would be heaped upon her. Bea said at once, 'Of course he didn't make it himself.'

To her credit Adele rallied. 'How do you know? Some men bake.'

'No, they don't.' Bea said this with great finality – nothing more could or would be said on this – men did not bake. *She*, Bea, did not bake, ergo no man baked. Her world would not be shaken on this. She turned to Redpath, 'I imagine you bought the cake from Hill's?'

'Yes, yes – from Hill's.'

'The bread, too,' Bea said. 'Their brown bread is very good.'

'Yes,' Redpath agreed solemnly, 'and their Eccles cakes are excellent.'

I looked down at my teacup; I had the feeling that I would laugh if I caught Adele's eye – we had always shared the same sense of the absurd. But I remembered that we were all supposed to be grieving in the wake of Eric's funeral and so I turned my thoughts to Eric and was sobered at once. We were all sober then, even little Tom who sat on his mother's lap sucking his thumb, his eyes flickering against sleep as if afraid of missing whatever interesting thing the adults might do next – the only one of us, I'm sure, who wouldn't have welcomed oblivion at that moment.

Redpath tried again with Margot. 'Margot, I very much enjoyed your father's sermon this morning,' here he smiled – an attempt at charm, I thought. 'But you weren't in church to hear it.'

Margot looked at him sharply, the first time I had seen her display even the slightest contempt for anyone. 'I don't go to church.'

'But your father –'

'What about him?'

Redpath was flustered; I wanted to cheer Margot on. He said, 'Doesn't he mind? Surely you want to show your support?'

I watched Margot keenly – we all did: at last the adults were interesting. Only Bobby looked wary, the only one who sensed the terrible danger. At last Margot said, 'I'll let my father know that you enjoyed his sermon. I'm sure he'll be pleased.'

I had to think of Eric again to stop myself from barking out a laugh. I knew that Margot wouldn't say a thing to her father; they never spoke: there was a war going on in the Whittaker household. Neither side was winning.

Adele broke in, the peacemaker. 'I've always so liked this house, Mr Redpath. We were all so pleased when it was finally sold to someone who obviously wants to take such good care of it.' She glanced around the room, at the striped wallpaper, at the large, ugly pot plant Redpath had set on a small mahogany table in the centre of the bay window. This plant – an aspidistra, I think – was the only decoration, if one could call it that. The striped walls were bare, as was the blue-veined marble mantelpiece, the only furniture the sit-up-and-beg horsehair couches we were perched on and another small table on which he had placed the tea things. There was a rather good Turkey rug in the centre of the room – he had told Bobby that he must not stand on it. Other than Adele, who held the now sleeping Tom in her lap, we all juggled crumbed plates and cups and saucers – Wedgwood, I was sure, although I hadn't had a chance to turn the plate over to check. The man had dull, decent taste.

Redpath managed to smile at Adele. 'The house needs a woman's touch, Mrs Dearlove. The edges need softening, if you will.' He glanced at Margot but she was studiously avoiding his eye. Quickly he added, 'I'm sure you ladies could give me some tips.'

Bea sniffed – a kind of subdued snort, no doubt Adele had told her to be on her best behaviour. She was wearing slacks and a blouse that managed to look like a man's shirt, topped with a grey cardigan. I'm sure her lace-up brogues had once belonged to the Old B. I noticed that Redpath could barely bring himself to look at her, although from time to time his curiosity would get the better of him and he would glance in Bea's direction as though he couldn't quite believe his eyes; he would look very young then, an innocent in the world, and it occurred to me that of us all he was the most pristine: hardly taken out of his wrapper. It seemed to me then that even Bobby had seen more of life than Redpath.

Bobby whispered to his mother and Margot nodded. To Redpath she said, 'My son needs to use the lavatory.'

Astonishingly, Redpath coloured – perhaps he never used the

word *lavatory* himself but rather a euphemism: I guessed he favoured *spend a penny*. I reached for my handkerchief to cover a smirk I really couldn't control just as Redpath stood up, quite flustered as he led Margot and Bobby from the room. As the door closed behind them Adele stood too, set the sleeping Tom on Bea's knee and began collecting the plates and cups, stacking them on the table.

Bea kissed Tom's head. Hugging him closer she said, 'What a dreadful old stiff the man is.'

'Yes,' I said, turning over my plate – Wedgwood, indeed – before handing it to Adele. 'What are we to make of him – other than stiffness?'

'He's a fool,' Bea said, predictably.

Adele turned to her. 'Have we decided to dislike him?'

Bea grunted. 'You make up your own minds.'

Adele glanced around the room again as though she wanted to rearrange the furniture. She went to the pot plant and fingered its glossy leaves. 'He's got his eye on Margot.'

'Of course – that's why we're all here.' I looked towards the door, wondering if I should go and find them, insisting we leave immediately.

Bea had the same idea because she said, 'We should go. I've had enough of the nasty little oik.'

I laughed. 'Oik? Well – he's covering up some past shadiness – he's too careful a minder of his Ps and Qs.'

Adele rounded on me. 'We should take him seriously. Margot is very vulnerable.'

'We hardly know her,' Bea said. 'Seems to me she can look after herself. Quite a sharp little thing under all that butter-wouldn't-melt.' She laughed. '*I don't go to church*! I thought the fool was going to choke on his tea. If he had any ideas he's probably abandoned them now. He wants some little mouse who doesn't answer back.'

Adele sat down again. 'We'll make our excuses and leave, as soon as they come back.'

I thought how drained she looked and remembered her at Eric's funeral, upright and dry-eyed. Adele, Bea, and I had sat on the front pew, Adele in the middle; Bea and I held her hands and I'm sure it wasn't just me who felt like a child again with the three of us holding hands as we used to, except Eric was missing and couldn't tease us for looking glum. I felt his loss so much as we sat there, linked like that − I had let go of his hand: the terrible sentimentality of this thought had sent the tears rolling down my cheeks and I'd swiped them away, impatient that such nonsense could hurt so much. Neither of the women cried. I could resent them, I supposed, if I allowed myself to wallow. But I only had to remember what Eric had become to bring myself up short, only had to think of the distance Adele put between herself and Tom, the way she gave up her maternal act and handed him to Bea as soon as we were alone.

Redpath came back, holding the door open for Margot and Bobby who were already in their coats. 'We're leaving,' Margot said, directing her words to me.

I stood up at once. 'I'll walk you home.'

Margot said, 'He wants to see me again.'

We had just left Bea, Adele, and Tom at their gate and were walking towards the vicarage, Bobby in his pushchair. The Sunday street was deserted but she spoke quietly, slowing her pace as if she had much to say before she reached her father's house.

Trying to keep my tone neutral I said, 'Do you want to see him?'

'He might be all right.'

'He might.'

'But you think not.'

'I don't know him, Margot.'

'I have to get away from them.'

Carefully I said, 'Out of the frying pan, perhaps . . .'

'Bobby needs a father.'

'He has a father, Margot.' I blundered on: 'If you waited for Paul, then if the three of you moved away −'

She stopped to stare at me. 'Paul doesn't want me, he doesn't want to be a husband, a father . . .' She laughed harshly and began to walk again, quicker now. 'You like him, I know. You think he only made a mistake and I should forgive him. But it wasn't a mistake! Marrying me was the mistake. *If I waited for him*! How can you suggest such a filthy thing?'

'Not filthy, surely . . .'

'I couldn't bear to have him touch me ever again. Ever, ever, ever!'

'All right,' I said, alarmed now. I touched her arm lightly but she jerked away.

'You're the same as him – don't think I don't know it. Don't think I'm so naïve.'

She shocked me; I didn't truly believe I went incognito, but I suppose I did feel that she was naïve enough not to see me, just as she hadn't seen Paul until forced to. I decided to say nothing on the principle of least said, soonest mended.

After a while she said, 'I'm sorry. But you must know I can't have him back, even if he wanted to come back, which he doesn't.' Suddenly she said, 'Do you think Adele wants to marry him?'

'Redpath?' I was astonished. 'No –'

'I'll marry him, then, I think.' She nodded, as though all was settled, and there was that same expression of fierceness I had seen on her face before. Bitterly she added, 'No one else will have me, anyway. Beggars can't be choosers.'

I couldn't argue with her – her expression forbade it; besides, all I had were platitudes and wild suggestions – she could ask Paul's father Dr Harris to take in her and Bobby, I was sure he would; or I would marry her and there would be no pretence between us – we would only be friends, a platonic partnership, I wouldn't cheat or disgrace her as Paul had, I wouldn't be that kind of beast. I stole a glance at her as she barged along, saw how angry she was, still, and I couldn't say anything: she was right and I couldn't be more completely wrong. Havelock Redpath was her only option.

All the same I couldn't quite give up and so I said, 'Someone else may come along.'

She shook her head, her mouth a thin, hard line. A moment or two later we reached the cemetery's main gate and its path leading to the vicarage. She stopped and turned to me. 'I'm sorry about Eric. I'm sorry for your loss.'

'Thank you.'

'I know you looked after him when you could have run away. You're a good person, Charles, a good, kind man and I'm sorry. But we both have the opportunity to start again, now. Will you go away?'

'Yes, I think so.'

'Good.' She looked towards the vicarage then back to me; she managed to smile. 'Good that you're getting away, I mean – no ties, no burden. Free as a bird.'

'Margot –'

'It's all right, Charles. Everything will be fine. Only,' she hesitated, 'only if you write to Paul don't be spiteful about Havelock. Don't mock him, or me.'

'I won't, Margot – of course not –'

She kissed my cheek. 'Goodbye, Charles.'

I stood at the gate and watched her until she reached the vicarage door. I was ready to raise my hand, a final salute, but she didn't look back. A few yards away I could see the bare mound of earth that was Eric's grave and it crossed my mind that I should stay in Thorp at least until his headstone was engraved and erected; I could put off my leaving indefinitely. But Margot was right: I was quite free to go, no one to stop me. I turned and walked home and in my head my suitcase was already packed and by the door.

Chapter Fifteen

Edmund said, 'So, how was Thorp? Just as you left it?'

He was leaning against the door frame in Charles's kitchen, watching as he made tea. Teacakes were toasting under the grill and behind him, in Charles's cramped yet immaculately tidy living room, the gas fire spluttered and gave off the smell of burning dust – a cosy smell, Edmund thought, like that of the teacakes, of the tea itself. He realised how intensely relaxed he felt in Charles's flat – he could fall asleep on the couch with his mouth open and there would be no shame, no fear of Roberts's smirking, only Charles to see him when he startled himself awake with a peace-ripping snore. Charles would be reading and would only look up from his book moment-arily: no comment, no snide remark, even though Charles never dozed – hardly slept, Edmund believed. No, Charles didn't judge him, didn't expect anything from him except that he take off his shoes when he arrived and put on the slippers he had bought him – expensive, sheepskin-lined leather slippers, very much more expensive than the tartan wool pair Charles wore himself. Edmund looked down at his feet – he never wore slippers at home, the novelty of slippers always amused him. At this moment though, with the comforting smells and the anticipation of toasted teacake, he felt moved by them. He glanced up at Charles who was gingerly sniffing at a bottle of milk and thought how fond he was of this man.

Charles said, 'A minor miracle – the milk seems still to be fresh.' He frowned at him. 'What's the face for?'

'What face?'

'Your moony face.'

'Nonsense.' Edmund pushed himself away from the door frame. 'Thorp. How was it?'

'Unchanging.' He began to butter the teacakes. 'But I think I'm forgiven, on the whole. No one wanted to lynch me for defaming Thorp's most famous son, at least.' He arranged the tea things on a tray, edging past him to carry it through into the sitting room. Glancing over his shoulder he said, 'Are you going to sit down?'

Edmund followed him and sat on one of the two red, boxy armchairs that faced each other across the beige-tiled fireplace. There was a maroon leather pouffe that Charles placed the tray on but otherwise there wasn't much in the way of furniture – the room was too small for the clutter of side tables – any kind of table, come to that. Charles ate from a tray on his lap, bathed in the yellow glow from an elaborately shaded standard lamp, listening to the wireless that squatted on a shelf and dominated the room with its knobby bulk. He wrote in the tiny spare bedroom, where more shelves were fixed on the walls all around his desk, cluttered with books (Edmund always thought of books as clutter). Edmund had glimpsed this room from the hallway only once, when Charles had forgotten to shut the door before his visit, closing it hurriedly when he noticed his interest. Even in that brief glimpse, Edmund had seen that this study was the least tidy of Charles's few, small rooms, but also that there was a framed photograph of Paul Harris, signed as *Francis Law, with the kindest regards* on the desk.

Settled in their chairs, they ate the teacakes in appreciative quiet. Edmund allowed his thoughts to wander, to the toasted teacakes served in a café close to the bookshop where he'd worked before going to university. *Bright's Café* – he smiled to himself, pleased with this flash of recall. He had taken Paul to Bright's and this had felt terribly daring at the time – more daring than he'd realised, young and very foolish as he was. He should have been more wary – such behaviour could have ruined him, as Paul's antics had ruined him, and although Paul had risen from ruination like a phoenix, Edmund knew he wasn't capable of such audacity.

Dabbing at his buttery mouth with his handkerchief, Edmund said, 'Paul's son visited me. He's after your blood, I think.'

Charles sipped his tea. He said, 'I know. He wrote to me via my publisher. He wanted to meet me – face to face. *Man to man.*' Nodding towards the teapot, he said, 'More tea?'

'No, thank you.' Not wanting to appear too eager he waited until Charles had finished his teacake before saying, 'Did you respond?'

'To Bob Harris? My publisher did – politely declining the invitation.'

'Aren't you curious?'

'No.' After a moment he said, 'Do you ever wish you had never met Paul Harris?'

Edmund laughed in surprise. 'No. Do you?'

'Yes, I think so. He complicated my life.' Charles seemed to consider this before saying quickly, 'I knew his wife quite well and I think that if he had only been true to her, been a decent, faithful man . . .' He drew breath. 'We should be decent, shouldn't we – and stick to the vows we make, no matter what? But I have always tried to find excuses for Paul, going against my own sense of what's right because he dazzled me.'

'Yet your book about him is warts an' all.'

'Is it? I wrote only what he wanted me to write, those things he thought excusable . . .' He shook his head. 'He makes me ashamed of myself.'

'I think you're being overly dramatic. What happened in Thorp to bring on such thoughts?'

'Nothing. I met a childhood friend who always cuts me down to size.'

'Sounds frightful.'

Charles looked at him shrewdly. 'Would you have married?'

'Never found the right girl.'

'Seriously, now.'

'Are we to be serious? What a bore.' Edmund sighed. He knew that Charles would give up on his interrogation if he continued to be glib but that flare of fondness he had felt earlier was still with him and so he said, 'I came close to marrying several times.' He thought of Caroline, of Jane, two debutantes he had squired briefly, in the 1920s. How tempting those lovely girls had been at first with their adoring eyes, their giddy flirtatiousness – they had flattered him beyond measure; and he had loved to dance, to quick-step Caroline or Jane around a dance floor, not having to speak to her, only to hold her in his arms and smile as he breathed in her perfume and knew that other men were watching. Yet when the music ended he wanted only to excuse himself, to go away and smoke in private and not suffer her attention, or her need for his attention.

He met Charles's gaze. 'I was too selfish to marry. *Am* too selfish. You know how most people bore me – women, men – sex is one thing; life-long relationships quite another.' He thought about Jane, who had wept when he finished their relationship. He had told her how selfish he was, and that she deserved a man who would love her unconditionally. She, clever girl, had asked him what his conditions would be, no doubt hoping that she could agree to them. He had never spoken of unconditional love again: how could there be such a thing?

Charles said, 'Men like us should never marry. Never.'

'I agree.' Edmund grinned. 'But I don't think Paul was like us – he could put his mind to *anything*.'

Bitterly Charles said, 'Then why didn't he? He promised to love, honour, and cherish that young girl.'

Edmund looked toward the gas fire, now burning steadily, the smell of burnt dust subsiding. He thought of defending Paul – he had an idea that there was a defence: the war; his youth; his good intentions. But in the end he couldn't help thinking that Charles was right. Paul should have done what he himself would have done – run away from his dead brother's pregnant fiancée. But that running away seemed cowardly and ungallant: so – there would be shame no matter what. Hesitantly he said, 'Who are we to judge?'

'Of course – God forbid any of us should be judgemental.' After a while he said, 'My friend in Thorp is dying. She seems quite sanguine about it, but she was always brave, much braver than I. I thought she

139

would outlast us all and organise our funerals with a no-nonsense efficiency. She would see us right – this was always a comfort to me. But the best of us go first . . . Forgive me,' he drew breath. 'I'm sad for my friend – and full of self-pity.' He laughed a little, glancing at Edmund. 'You came here to be entertained and here I am, casting the gloomiest of glooms.'

'I don't come here merely for entertainment.'

'No, I know.'

'If it's any comfort I will organise your funeral efficiently if you go first.'

'Thank you.' He became brisk. 'Now, should we have some brandy in our tea?'

After Edmund had gone Charles washed the dishes and swilled out the teapot. He shook out his pillows and straightened and turned down the bedcovers, opening the bedroom window a little so that later the room would be cool and smell only of the London evening. He noticed that Edmund had forgotten the little pile of loose change he had taken from his trouser pocket and left on the bedside table. Two shillings and fourpence. He would return it to him next time. Tonight he was sure there would be a next time, although he wasn't always so certain.

He went into his study and sat down at his desk – the first piece of furniture he had bought that didn't come from a junk shop, a solid piece, oak, with deep, lockable drawers. He lit the anglepoise lamp and picked up the framed photograph of Paul. Without looking at it he put it away in a drawer. Paul had always been out of reach; it was vanity that had him keep this man's image on display, as though they had been friends. Theirs had been a business relationship: Paul had wanted a truth to be known and he had told it.

Charles grunted. He took a pen from another drawer, a pad of paper, and began to write.

Eric, Adele, Bea, and I – often it felt that we were more than friends, that we were allies in a great war against the adults: my uncle Arthur

140

and Aunt May, and Bea and Adele's parents whom we thought of as the terrorist and his appeaser – that ineffectual woman who would take to her bed on the flimsiest of excuses. Eric, Adele, Bea, and I were left to our own devices on the whole because even the terrorist had to go to work. We called the terrorist the Old B and now, as an adult, I only think that it was a shame that no one loved him; after all, he was diligent in his bread-winning – his wife and daughters wanted for nothing and he didn't disown any of them, although he might have: his wife for her laziness, Adele for her silliness, Bea for her utter lack of conformity that must have been an exquisite assault on the Old B's senses. So, not a terrorist then but a put-upon man; a man who no doubt wished he had sons, some manly comradeship, and who could blame him? As it was the Old B suspected us all; no, he *knew* what we had done, yet he never said a thing.

What had we done? At the time our conspiracy seemed so gigantic we would never live it down – our lives would be blighted for ever more. But – if I can make the comparison – shame and guilt is like the corpse in the locked trunk, in the locked attic: at first the horror is so vital we can't understand why we aren't undone by it. But day by day, month by month, the horror recedes. The temptation to hang around outside the attic door working up the courage to confront the thing dissipates. Eventually there comes the realisation that even if the attic was unlocked and the trunk opened there would only be dust and dry bones and no horror, only sadness and pity. Poor old dead thing – dead as dead can be: burn the trunk on a bonfire; paint the attic sunshine yellow and throw open the window. Even confess. Yes, a confession would very much make light of the whole thing because weren't we all so young? Eric, Adele, Bea, and I, young enough to be excused and nowadays so much worse is done and no one bats an eye.

I joined the army in 1914 – jumping before I was pushed, as it were: I calculated that this jumping would be better, there might be some negotiation to be made with his Majesty's armed forces. I was right but only because I was deemed too flat-footed for the frontline, and, given a battery of tests, was found to be just the right sort for a job in the War Office. So, I was lucky – for a couple of years, at least. My life wasn't in danger yet I was given a smart uniform to wear – no white feathers for me, then, only smiles from the girls and salutes from the boys.

Eric wasn't so lucky.

Is it sentimental to write that Eric was a very much better person than I? I try not to make him into a saint but he was kind and patient and wouldn't speak ill of someone for sport. Most of all he loved Adele – the love he had for her shone from him so that even the Old B was half-blinded by it. And he was sure of his love and where it would take him – to marriage and children and a happy life of fulfilled uneventfulness, like a minor character in a George Eliot novel gifted a few artful, endearing quirks but loved by all his small world.

Eric married Adele in 1916. The war had already eaten away a part of him but still some of the old, happy Eric remained: on his wedding day we stood together at the altar, groom and best man, waiting for his bride, and he made a good show of it, not resenting me for my luck at all. He had a night or two with his new wife and then back to the front and the boom, boom, boom of the Somme. We have all seen the pictures and read the poems (although, God knows, I try to avoid exposure) and Eric was there, doing who knows what for who knows what purpose – there would be a line to cross or hold, a gun to capture, some order lost in disorder (I am writing from experience). I know he was there; I know he came back; at least *someone* came back, a man who matched Eric's description. The army said this is your cousin, your brother-in-law, your husband – yes, indeed, he's yours and no longer our responsibility.

For two years the army had tried to cure him and I think the doctors even believed his madness had abated – the straitjacket no longer required. I don't blame the doctors, nor even the army. I blame myself.

Charles put down his pen. He wondered if this was a good enough start, enough to be going on with. He wondered if it was truthful and so he read it back and decided he could be more truthful, but

142

that truth required imagination, a dazzling metaphor to distract from its mundanity. He couldn't just write that he was sorry – that he couldn't speak for the others but guessed they were sorry, too.

He folded the page and put it in the top drawer. There was a key to this drawer in a vase placed in front of a volume of Keats' poetry on the bookshelf. Keats equalled key – an aid to memory; he was growing old, he forgot things, although the past – some scenes at least – were becoming more vivid. He glanced up at the vase and decided he didn't need to lock the drawer, not yet. Turning off the lamp, he went into his sitting room where the scent of Edmund's expensive cologne still lingered, and poured himself a nightcap of brandy.

Chapter Sixteen

In the Grand Hotel Cathy watched as the fat man in the expensive dinner jacket fox-trotted a bottle blonde around the dance floor. Light on his feet, smiling – the very picture of confidence: how would she describe this man's expression to Tom when he returned from the bar with their drinks? Joyful, she thought – she wouldn't be catty; she wouldn't remark on his considerable size or the shapely woman's low-cut green velvet gown that gave her a smooth, firm look like a dressmaker's dummy: she would need to be well-corseted to keep this man at bay, perhaps, although he appeared to be chivalrous – his hand on her back didn't stray; he kept his eyes on his partner's rather than on her breasts. Perhaps he loved her to show such respect. Did she love him? She wasn't smiling but seemed only to be concentrating on her steps, less of a dancer than her partner. But then she grinned at him – he threw back his head and laughed. How happy they were. Cathy closed her eyes and had to stop herself from grinding her teeth, something she did to stop herself from crying – a habit she was trying to break. The happiness of others shouldn't be so painful; she shouldn't be so jealous.

Tom said brightly, 'Here we are. Gin and tonic.' He set down her drink and took his seat opposite her. A candle flickered between them; he placed a glass of brandy beside his coffee cup, moving the sugar bowl to one side. A bowl of sugar – very neat and orderly brown and white cubes, she imagined picking them out and building a sugar-cube wall between herself and this man who was lighting a cigarette with a studied air of indifference, shaking out the match, tossing it into the unsullied ashtray. He was giving up smoking because of his son – this was his first cigarette of the evening; he looked as if he needed it badly. The evening was descending into despondency and she wondered how she might salvage it. It occurred to her that he should be the one to think of something bright to say about the couple on the dance floor. She glanced towards them but they were gone; the band was playing a slower tune not suited to the fat man's joyous mood. He had taken his girl off somewhere.

After a while Tom said, '"Paper Moon".'

She glanced at him from stirring a brown cube into her coffee. '*Cardboard sea*.'

'It's a pretty tune.'

'Yes – although the words are sad.'

Tom looked towards the band. 'I've not heard it played at this tempo before.'

'No. Me neither.'

He laughed bleakly. 'God, but it reminds me of the war! Dances in Nissen huts, all the men drunk as fools, all the women . . .' He trailed off, flicking cigarette ash.

'All the women?'

He seemed to force himself to meet her eye. 'Girls, really – trying to understand why we were behaving like apes; scared of us and pretending not to be. Anyway – all in the past.' Trying to be bright again he said, 'Did you notice the man dancing with the woman in the green dress? I know him – Harry. I bet you thought she was his mistress, but she's his wife.' He laughed a little. 'Harry Jeavons. Never ever failed to pull the buxom blondes. No idea how he did it.' Drawing on his cigarette he exhaled and said, 'He was a translator, too. Both of us fellow interrogators.'

'Should you go and say hello?'

Tom glanced towards the dance floor. 'No. I liked him but we weren't friends.'

'He looked jolly.'

'Jolly. Yes. You just wouldn't want to be an SS officer on the other side of the table from him.' Again he met her eye. 'He truly did have ways of making them talk.'

The band began to play a Beatles tune in the same slow tempo. Tom snorted. 'From the sublime to the ridiculous.'

'We should try to be modern.'

'You are modern.' Quickly he said, 'You are young and modern and lovely and I'm sorry about how this evening has seemed to have ground to a halt.'

'My fault.'

'I know you are grieving.'

He was drunk, she realised, had been drinking when they should have been making conversation, flirting, even dancing. She watched as he ground out the cigarette. He said, 'You should say something, you know? Say that this was a bad idea, that you're not ready – it's too soon – that I should stop bothering you.'

'You're not bothering me.'

'I would like to bother you.'

She laughed; to her relief he grinned, lifted his glass and saluted her. 'All right. I shall say no more. Do you like the Beatles?'

'Quite.'

He nodded. 'Do you prefer Picasso or Constable – or – God forbid – Francis Law?'

'Picasso.'

Again he nodded. 'I see. Now, the waltz or the twist?'

'Depends.'

'On what?'

'My mood, I suppose. My partner.'

'I can dance. Not as well as old Harry, but still.'

'Would you like to dance?'

He stood up and held out his hand. 'Yes. I would very much like to dance.'

Harry Jeavons. Quite a shock to see him again, although Tom had known that, like him, he had ended up back in Thorp, back where they'd both been born. Harry in his major's uniform had cut quite the figure and although the man had out-ranked him Harry had always treated him as an equal, as though all the army ranking business was a nonsense they had to overcome. Major Jeavons spoke German like a Prussian officer and all those SS officers couldn't get over their surprise when Harry opened his mouth. Tom had liked to see their jaws drop. Weren't the English hopeless at languages? 'Your French is excellent,' Harry had once told him, 'but when you speak German you must try to be more confident – more like them, you know? Study the bastards.' Harry had barked out his scary laugh and slapped him on the back. 'And just remember – we won.'

We won, Tom thought. Or the Yanks, or the Russians, or perhaps even those German officers the Americans recruited to help build the bomb in the land of the free. Did he feel like a winner? Did Harry? He was in England, dancing with a beautiful woman, although she held herself rather stiffly away from him, although she was blank with sadness over missing another man. He wanted to hold her more tightly but knew he had drunk too much, enough to be maudlin but not enough to be uncouth. He had never in his life been uncouth. He smiled to himself. At least he was *good* – on the side of the winners. And oh, this woman was lovely; if he could stay on this dance floor with her in his arms for the rest of time all would be well. All will be well and all manner of things will be well . . . He was drunk; drunker than he had been in years and he was sorry and pleased at the same time because whatever came next, in the next few minutes, his drunkenness would take the edge off it.

The music segued and became slower, softer, as the bandleader said, 'Last dance, ladies and gentleman, last dance,' and began to sing 'Moonlight Becomes You'.

Tom stopped dancing to hold her at arm's length. 'I think you're lovely and if we go on, one day at a time –'

She nodded.

'I'm patient.'

Again she nodded; he could see there were tears in her eyes and he stopped himself from brushing them away, only took her in his arms again to lead her in the slow dance.

★

Later that night, in bed alone, it came to him that he had always known he would marry her, from the moment he had heard that Mark had been killed. That she had moved to Thorp to live next door to his mother only made the inevitable easier – and didn't this ease suit him? He was lazy, he knew, apt to give in, yet he knew also that he would have gone to her, found her wherever she was. She was his destiny. He drew breath, staring into the darkness of his bedroom; if he listened hard enough he would hear the sounds of his son sleeping: his bed creaking, his anxious murmuring; their bedroom doors were left deliberately ajar – he would never shut Luc out although the boy had long since stopped climbing into his bed in the small hours of the night. Tom exhaled sharply. *His destiny*, indeed! He would be sober in the morning, hung-over, certainly. He would think about her soberly, sensibly, if that were possible. No, not possible really. She would be the jewel he kept secret, a precious secret to take out to examine and marvel at. Tonight his life had changed; he smiled into the darkness; best to sleep now, before the doubts returned.

Chapter Seventeen

Making scones, Adele thought of the cook her mother had employed, briefly, before the first war, when people like her parents fancied themselves as the type to have servants. The cook, Mrs Hughes – the name returned to her suddenly, gratifyingly – had seemed to her extraordinarily old, slow, and fat and now here she was, old, slow, and fat in her turn, making the same scones that Cook (as her mother called her) made, the same generous, buttery, sugary recipe, heavy with sultanas, brushed with beaten egg. There had been great long stretches of her life when such generosity had been impossible – forbidden: the ships bringing sultanas were torpedoed, or commandeered to transport less frivolous goods. All eggs were powdered, or kept carefully to provide a meagre meal, and no butter or sugar, of course – hardly any, and that kept for her father and for Tom, if he was around, on leave.

Adele paused in her methodical work; she looked down at her hands, her fingertips still pinching at the flour, sugar, and butter. Where had her life gone? She had lived it all within this house and had never wished to leave it, never wanted to venture forth as Bea had. She had nursed her dying parents and always she had taken care of Bea, protected her with her acceptance and ability to face down and silence the gossips as best she could. They walked together, shoulder to shoulder, and she had always behaved as if there was nothing – nothing at all – unusual in her sister's appearance. Yet she had hated the pretence; she had wanted a sister and she had Bea.

'She's the bravest person I have ever met,' Charles had once said, and she could only agree. Except she had said, 'But where does bravery get her? One of us should run away – one of us should leave!'

'Where would you go?'

'Me? You think I should be the one?' She had looked at him, horrified, scared to death at the idea of leaving her home. What a coward she was – the foil to her sister's bravery. But neither she nor Bea could leave: the pantomime had to be played out to the end.

Adele threw the sultanas into the bowl, added a mix of milk and water (so not quite as generous as she might be) and turned out the dough onto the floured table. She picked up her mother's (Cook's?) rolling pin and dusted it with flour; she shaped and patted and cut the rounds with the metal cutter; she placed the scones (always the same number) on the baking tray and thought how Bea would be pleased; that fruit scones were her favourite – she didn't care for chocolate cake, for anything new-fangled or untested. No iced fancies for Bea, no Angel Cake or Millionaire's Shortbread; nothing feminine or flighty or fun. Ironic, really, when it was Bea who had proved her femininity beyond all doubt.

With the scones in the oven, Adele sat down in the chair by the range; usually at this point in the proceedings she would pick up her latest novel and read until she sensed the baking was complete. Lately, though, the stories bored her; she had begun to think she had read everything there ever was to read because all the stories were ultimately the same. Lately, too, she found she could allow her thoughts to wander, that she didn't need the distraction of made-up tales; she could sit and stare into space – something she had never in her life done before – and it was fine, enjoyable even. She had decided not to worry any more.

That day when she had gone to the library, when there was not a book to be found that interested her in the least, although still she had borrowed a couple – hope was not entirely lost. That day, when she couldn't be bothered to even step inside Robinson's to look for a new cardigan as she'd planned, that day, when the bus was exactly on time so that she had almost missed it, accepting as she did that it was almost always late – that day, the day she had spied Charles and had thought, quite acceptingly for a second or two – Oh, there's Charles, walking home because he never cared for buses and their capricious ways. That day, when the shock of Charles had dawned on her, she had confronted Bea before supper, saying only –

'I saw him.'

Bea had glanced up from the *Gazette*'s obituary column. 'Yes. There was a chance you might.'

'You knew he was coming – did you invite him?'

'You know, I can't remember. Perhaps he invited himself – yes, I think he did. And I was curious, wanted to hear what he had to say for himself.'

'And what did he have to say?'

'Nothing much. You know Charles, always careful with his words.'

'Why didn't you tell me he was coming?'

'I didn't want you upset.'

'*Upset!*' She was aware of the potatoes boiling too rapidly and that she should get up and turn down the gas. The gas began to splutter, the pan lid clattering as the water boiled over, but still she sat, watching her sister as she leafed through the pages of the evening paper with ostentatious deliberation.

At last Bea said, 'Is there something burning?'

Adele got to her feet. 'You and him – always scheming! So – what did he have to say? Is he to make a story of our lives? Give away all our secrets as well as Margot's?'

Bea looked up at her. 'No. The secrets will die with us – isn't that what we all promised each other years ago?' With sudden exasperation she added, 'Besides, it's my secret to keep or give away.'

Adele laughed harshly. '*Your* secret? Nothing to do with me, then?'

Bea tossed the newspaper to the floor. 'The potatoes are burning.'

'Good.'

'Oh, what do you mean *good*? Don't be so childish.' Bea got to her feet, brushing her aside to go to the stove. Turning off the gas she said, 'I went behind your back and I'm sorry. Charles said to say hello, and that he was sorry he missed you.' Turning to her she'd said, 'I don't want us to fall out – not over other people's secrets – and Margot's dead now so what does it all matter in the end?'

The scones were cooked, judging by the aroma from the oven. Just as Cook used to, Adele had earlier set out the wire cooling rack, her oven gloves beside it. She would get up from her chair, open the oven, confirm with her eyes what her nose had already told her, and take out the scones. She pictured herself doing this, running a little film of these actions through her mind, adding a soundtrack of herself singing, perhaps, or at least sighing with satisfaction, a clip of well-rehearsed domesticity: the housewife at home, orderly contentment. She wouldn't throw the tray of scones at the wall, nor grind their crumbs into the lino. She would only slip them onto the wire rack, turn off the oven (she was very conscientious), and boil the kettle for tea. Because who would clear up such mess? Who was there to witness it and feel concerned for her? Who would say, 'Here, let me sweep up the broken bits, you must sit down – I'll make sweet tea and in a few moments all will be well again.' No one. Her rage without an audience was more trouble than it was worth.

She took the scones from the oven and made herself a cup of tea. She thought of all the people she had taken care of: her parents – the Old B, who in the end had been so little trouble, making her realise he had only ever done what was best in his sights – worked to pay the bills, all the while holding his tongue, although he had known, of course he had known – but what was there to say? A few days before his death he had called her a good woman. Adele smiled to herself, remembering how she had changed his sheets and pyjamas that morning, that there was the smell of Persil washing powder and also of the Brylcreem she had used to smooth back his hair, just as he liked it. He had all at once clasped her hand, struggling to sit up against his too-forgiving prop of pillows; she had thought that he had lost most of his strength but his fingers tightened around hers, his eyes still sharp, his look intent as he said, 'A good woman and my best girl.'

At the time she had wanted more from him, but now those almost-final words were a fine memory, were, in fact, the most private memory she had. She would never repeat those words to Bea and not just because of the implied favouritism; her father had become someone else – someone who loved her, someone she loved in return: a wise man who recognised her own wisdom.

And she had cared for her mother and it seemed to her that the opposite had happened, that the one she thought she had loved best became instead someone she found contemptible. All her life her mother had never seen past her own pain and had no time for the pain of others and this truth outed itself on her deathbed; there were no last words, only demands and petulance, a slapping away of hands and cries of, 'Oh, oh, you're hurting me, you're hurting me,' so that Adele had wanted to push a pillow into her face.

There: she was wicked. Perhaps Eric, with the special insight of lunatics, had recognised her wickedness and that was why he did what he did. No, Adele thought, that couldn't be true because Eric never had the ability to see into her heart; Eric, even as a lunatic, was never very bright. Before the war she had thought that she could overlook his dimness because he was kind and handsome and so very taken with her that she had been immensely flattered. And anyway – couldn't she teach him not to be so foolishly inane? Wouldn't he grow up?

Adele sipped her tea, thinking of Eric on their wedding night: tender and kind and hopelessly shy, as gauche as could be. And she had held him and told him that it didn't matter, not at all, that they had all the time in the world, the rest of their lives and everything would be fine. From her words he drew strength because after a few minutes of lying quietly in her arms he all at once climbed on top of her and the deed was over and done in a moment. A moment after that and he was asleep and snoring and she had thought she would feel different, perhaps even look different, but she didn't; she knew this because she got up and went to the bathroom along the corridor from their hotel room and peered in the mirror. She was unchanged, there was only an unfamiliar smell and stickiness leaking out of her;

she took her gaze from the mirror and, with the resignation that was her hallmark, began washing herself thoroughly.

She had thought she might be pregnant then, that Eric would go off to his war and she would have a baby to care for. A lovely little lamb; a sweet cherub; an adorable little one to call her very own. But there was only her ordinary bleed and letters from Eric calling her his *dear, darling girl. I hope you are well.* Well, she wasn't; she was sick with disappointment and what was he going to do about that? *Come home*, she thought of writing, *roll on top of me again . . . Roll me over, in the clover . . . It won't take long.*

Bea had said, 'I never want anyone to know. No one, never ever, ever.'

Bea's face was swollen from crying, her voice shrill and almost hysterical, except that Bea was never hysterical, and Bea never cried or went on so like an ill-used girl. Adele could only sit beside her on her bed and hold her hand, although Bea kept pulling her own hand away to wipe her nose with a sodden hanky. 'No one will know, Bea,' she had tried to reassure her, and had even managed to laugh, 'not even me, not if you don't tell me.'

Bea had stopped crying then to look at her as though she had come to a horrifying realisation. 'I have to tell you – you of all people . . .' She began to cry more desperately.

Adele remembered that she had laughed again, a frightened, silly noise. 'Yes, me. You know you can tell me anything. Please stop crying, Bea. Please try to be calm. Try to be calm and tell me what on earth has happened.'

Calm! There would be no more calm, not for months – years. Not until Eric was lying in his grave, having done for himself – she had no doubt that he had found at last the adult man inside himself and finally done the decent thing. And everyone said *Poor Eric*, as they so often had since he had returned home. Everyone but her and Bea, everyone but Charles and her father; the four who knew the most said the least, said nothing at all, in fact.

Adele remembered how Bea had all at once grasped her hand in both of hers. 'It wasn't my fault,' she said. 'I was only trying to make

154

him do the right thing – the right thing by you. I wanted him to do his duty by you . . .'

'Are you talking about Eric?'

Bea bowed her head. Adele felt her fingers tighten around hers. 'I had to speak to him – finally have it out with him – tell him . . . I only wanted to speak . . .' She shuddered and began to cry again. 'I'm sorry, I'm so sorry.'

And Adele had felt some sense of it then, some intuition, and it seemed to her that she had always known what Bea and Eric were going to do – their actions were entirely inevitable. She had drawn her hand away from Bea's, she had sat up straighter and her voice was level, stern even. 'Did he hurt you?'

Bea tugged at the handkerchief, smoothing it over her knee only to crumple it into a ball again, her eyes intent on this fidgeting. She nodded.

'He took advantage of you?'

Again Bea nodded. A tear dropped onto her hand.

Roll me over, roll me over, do it again. Adele said, 'It's just an unpleasantness, that's all. A thing all women must endure. It's done and over with. You must put it behind you.'

Bea had jerked her head up. 'I can't.'

Of course she couldn't. None of them could. But Adele had found herself saying, 'We'll pretend. We'll pretend we can.'

'We?'

'You and me.'

'I'm pregnant.'

Adele stared at her, taking in her sister's white, puffy face, her red eyes. She looked down at her sister's body, hidden beneath a too-large jumper. She snorted. 'No. He hurt you, but that's all. It doesn't mean a baby comes from it.' She almost laughed. 'It happened once, only once – didn't it, Bea? You didn't go back for more! Surely only once –'

'Once!' Bea's voice rose in panic or anger, or the horror of remembering, Adele couldn't tell. 'Of course only once –'

'So you can't be pregnant. You're not to be silly and imagine such things.'

155

'I'm pregnant.' Her voice was steady now. She sat up straighter. 'I am. Three months.' A look of horror crossed her face, she began to cry again. 'What am I going to do? What shall I do? Should I go away? Where? There's nowhere.'

They had sat for a while without speaking. Adele listened to Bea's quiet crying, a more subdued noise now, a more ordinary kind of grief now that her secret was out. She thought of Bea storming next door, to 'have it out' with Eric, as she put it, of her sister finding her husband alone, in that room he sat in day after endless day, of standing in front of him, demanding his attention. She would say *When are you going to be a husband to my sister, Eric? When are you going to pull yourself together and be a man?* Perhaps she had touched him, punched his shoulder, shaken him – something. Adele wondered what had provoked him so, Bea's words or actions.

Adele said, 'Why? Why did you go there?'

'For you!' She sounded indignant, swiping her tears away with the back of her hand. 'For you – I did it for you! He should take responsibility!'

Adele laughed. 'What made you think I wanted him to *take responsibility*? What makes you think I care what he does?'

'He's your husband.' She sounded outraged.

'We went through a ceremony in a church. He was never a husband to me.'

'He was – he is – I did it for you –'

'You should have asked me first. And anyway, what did you think would happen, that he'd suddenly come to his senses just because you told him to?'

'No, I don't know – I was angry . . .'

'Angry – always angry. And where does anger get us? Into trouble, into misery and trouble.'

'I'm sorry.'

'Well, it's done now. Nothing to stop it. We'll pretend. Pretend the baby's mine. We'll just lie to everyone and everyone will have to accept it.'

'No, no, I can't.'

'You have to. We'll have a baby to bring up. Our baby – yours and mine, together.'

'No. No, no, no.' Bea began to cry more loudly.

Adele got up and stood before her. How strong she was then, how clear-sighted and indomitable. She would have her way; her idea would work beautifully – who would dare to doubt her?

And a few weeks later Charles had said, 'I know what's going on –'

'What? What could possibly be *going on*?'

He'd laughed despairingly. 'Adele . . . I *know*. Eric told me what he did. I will help you.' Looking down at the pretending, cushioned bulk of her body – she had thought it so convincing – he had shaken his head. 'It's a good plan. The *only* plan.'

'The Old B has guessed, I think.'

Charles exhaled heavily. 'Perhaps everyone has. For once the world might be kind and turn a blind eye.' Reaching out he took her hand and squeezed it. 'I'm sorry, old girl. And Eric would be sorry too, if he was the old Eric.'

In her kitchen, so many years later, Adele remembered that this was the only time she had cried over it all; she had thought of the old Eric and had cried, and Charles, crying too, had drawn her into his arms and told her he would help her, old friends after all, 'Dear old friends . . .' Drawing away from her he had wiped her eyes and then his own. He had tried to laugh. 'We are the stars of our very own melodrama.'

'I'll have a baby.'

He nodded. 'Something good will come of this.'

Adele had thought so, at the time. She had thought she would love another woman's child – that woman was her sister, after all; the child would be her blood, after all. She hadn't realised then that feelings couldn't be so neatly controlled.

She thought of Tom: a good man with no imagination. Surprising that he hadn't guessed, but for the best, she supposed. And Bea loved him as she should, and didn't hold his father against him, as she herself did.

She heard Bea coming down the stairs and got up. She would make a fresh pot of tea and butter a scone for her sister. Memories must be kept at bay, locked in a box, whatever metaphor served best. There was the present to see to, and the future to worry about. She smiled at Bea as she sat down at the table. 'Scones are just out of the oven,' she said, for all the world as if scones were the most important things in the world.

Chapter Eighteen

Bobby had turned up at her door, out of the blue, saying, 'I had to come and see you, Cathy.' They had embraced and he had held her tightly, standing back after a few moments to hold her at arm's length, an inspection. 'How are you coping?'

Now they sat on a bench in her overgrown garden (was it really hers?) and he smoked his way through a pack of Players as she told him about her new life in Thorp, how there was a surprisingly good department store – Robinsons – and that the park at the end of the road was like a picture postcard one would send to an elderly aunt: gaudy with begonias and marigolds and with a bandstand focal point. She should buy a dog, she told him, a Pekinese she could pick up and carry under her arm if their walk proved too long for its short legs. She went on very long walks – to the park, to the High Street with its shops and marketplace, to the cemetery. She glanced at him, then, telling him she had seen his ancestors' graves.

He nodded. 'The weeping angel. She has a pretty face.' Flicking cigarette ash into the long grass he said, 'Thorp isn't a bad place. For a quiet, pleasant life I would recommend it.'

'Yes, it's nicer than I expected.'

'But it's not London.' He glanced at her. 'There are no theatre companies, no TV studios.'

'I think my ambition was bigger than my talent.'

'But you are very young to give up on that ambition.'

She nodded. 'I feel old.'

'That feeling will pass. Soon you'll realise how young you are.'

The bench was wrought iron and more comfortable than it appeared. Opposite them was what was once a flower bed – a few rose bushes had grown leggy and bristled with grey thorns. Her mother grew roses – her mother who lived in Kent, who dreaded her husband's retirement – *What would they do all day?* Who had said to her, 'Darling, you must do what you think best, but Daddy and I can't imagine why you want to live so far away.' So far away in the north, a place her parents had never deigned to visit. They would come, eventually, she supposed. And her father would say, 'You should sell that picture – far too valuable to be left lying about.'

Her parents were impressed that she had married Mark – their friends and neighbours knew him off the telly – and his link to Francis Law was another feather in their cap. On her wedding day her father had barged up to Bobby and shook his hand with great enthusiasm. Her father, who had been just too young for one war and just too old for the next, had told Bobby how much he admired him. 'Can't be easy,' he had said, 'no, not easy at all.'

Not easy, of course not, to look like Bobby, although he was easy with the attention that came his way – gracious, she thought. Mark had adored him, as he had adored Bobby's father, Francis Law. Mark had spent a summer in Tangiers with Bobby and Law, the last summer before Law's death. 'It was heaven,' Mark would say. 'Such a place!' Words seemed to fail him, as they often did – he was used to speaking the words of others, after all. But the look on Mark's face when he remembered that summer was enough – his eyes shone with excitement. She had told him that he must take her there, one day, and he had grinned, of course! Of course. Tangiers was just one of the plans they had.

Bobby stood up and began to walk along the garden path towards the house. He stopped and looked up then turned to her. 'That was my bedroom, that attic window, up there. My stepfather wanted me out of the way.' He laughed. 'But I liked it up there. I could see right across all the gardens, spy on everyone. And if I saw Tom in his garden I'd sneak out and call for him – his mother was always very kind – always cakes and biscuits just baked.'

160

Cathy thought of Adele, she hadn't seen her since she'd delivered the eggs. She had seen the sister – that odd, manly woman – from her bedroom window, the window below Bobby's attic. Adele's sister was walking around her garden, a stooping, slow kind of walk, and then she had sat down on a rickety-looking bench and stared into space, over the garden she must have tended all her life, but not seeing it, it seemed to Cathy, only a pageant of the long-dead parading across the lawn. Cathy imagined she could see them too and the thought occurred to her again that she should leave this place to live somewhere pristine, brand new, without any history at all. But then she had thought of Tom and whether she could leave him.

Standing next to Bobby she said, 'You and Tom were good friends, then?'

'Yes. For a while, when we were children. Then he came to see me, when I was in hospital at the end of the war. He was a very diligent visitor, a cheery bringer of beer.' Bobby glanced at her. 'He's a good man. Do you like him?'

'I think so.' Quickly she said, 'I feel disloyal, when I'm with him – not that I've been with him much, but all the same. Disloyal.'

'Then perhaps it's too early.'

'Should I go back to London?'

'Only you can decide.'

'But this house is ridiculous, isn't it? Just me, rattling around, not knowing anyone . . . I could just as well be one of the old ladies next door, waiting to die.'

He laughed. 'You'll have a very long wait.' He took her hand. 'You are so young, you have time to decide what to do.'

They went back inside the house and ate a makeshift lunch of bread and cheese and tomatoes bought from Thorp market and Bobby talked a little about his wife, Jane, and of their children, two boys and two girls, how the eldest boy was a little wild, a rebel, the younger boy just started at Oxford, the girls barely into their teens, both obsessed with the Beatles. He described a crowded, lively life, a life full of life, smiling as he talked, taking out a photo from his wallet of the two boys and two girls, his wife in the centre, their

161

arms linked. Putting the photo away after she had admired it, he became serious. 'I came to Thorp to see you, but also to see your neighbours, to talk to them. I don't think they will want to talk to me, but nevertheless.'

'Tom's mother seems very sweet, I haven't met the other one –'

'Bea. She's scary – always was: very brusque. She was in love with my mother, Margot.' He glanced at her, flicking cigarette ash into the ashtray. 'What is it with Thorp? Packed to the rafters with crazy, queer people. Something in the water maybe? My father –' he shook his head, '*Paul*. Paul once said that Thorp was always there in the back of his mind as somewhere he should have returned to, if he'd been brave enough. Brave enough to stay with my mother and be faithful.' He laughed shortly. 'He fantasised about such a life, I think. Being Paul Harris, a husband and father, a schoolteacher – not painting, except perhaps as a hobby, giving evening classes . . .' Looking up from rolling his cigarette around the edge of the ashtray he said, 'And not being the famous Francis Law, living his famously queer life. Anyway, Paul liked to think about what might have been, spinning stories instead of admitting the truth.'

She had read the biography, of course. She wondered what she might say, whether she should pretend that she hadn't read it, that she knew nothing except what almost everyone knew – a young war hero who had left England for Morocco to paint his astonishing pictures; who became an appeaser – but what did that mean, except he wanted peace, for his son not to be killed in another war; who died before his time and left his legacy and was eventually rehabilitated by a world shot to pieces by the war he'd spoken against.

Cathy lit her own cigarette and waited for Bobby to speak and at last he said, 'So, Bea – Tom's aunt – was in love with my mother, so obvious if you ever saw them together, although not obvious to my mother, who was oblivious to most things. But it was Adele – Tom's mother – that my mother was closest to. She confided in Adele. Adele knows the truth, I think.' All at once he said, 'Now I'm here, though, I wonder if it matters at all. If Paul was only my uncle then that absolves him of so much, but he let me go on believing he was my father right to the last, I held his hand when he was on his death-bed and he said that he was proud that I was his son . . .' He drew breath. 'I'm sorry, I shouldn't be telling you all this, but being here again, in this house . . . I hated this house, hated Redpath, hated her, sometimes . . . Sorry.' He smiled at her, 'I loved Mark. Mark made living here bearable.'

'Do you want Paul to be your father?'

'If he was then I hate him for leaving us. But if he wasn't, well, he still left, but his leaving is more understandable. But I've lived my life being his son – that's how everyone knows me, the keeper of my father's flame.' He stubbed out his cigarette. 'And it all makes me wonder what on earth I've done with my life.'

'You have your wife and children –'

'Yes, of course.'

She grinned at him, wanting to lighten the mood. 'And you were a war hero. One of the few who saved us all.'

'Oh yes, of course I did *that*! All that goes without saying, of course. That old warmonger Churchill thought we were the bee's knees. He – and everyone else – owes me, apparently.' He stood up. 'So, I should go next door.' He glanced towards the wall that divided her kitchen from that of the old ladies'. 'Wish me luck, eh?'

'Good luck.' She stood too and kissed his cheek. 'You must come and see me anytime.'

He gazed at her. 'Promise me that if it all gets too sad you will return to London – you can live with us, until you get settled, we have room now the boys have left.'

'I promise.'

She showed him out and watched as he turned towards the Dearlove house. He seemed hesitant and she almost ran after him, saying he didn't need to confront his past – no one did, everyone should only look to the future, looking back could turn you into a pillar of salt. Then he raised his hand and saluted her as she stood in the doorway, and she realised that no advice could be given or taken; everyone was on their own.

163

Chapter Nineteen

Charles, 1923

I have had word from Eric's solicitor and of course Eric had made a will during the war, leaving this house to Adele. That he had made a will, and the fact that I had never even thought of him doing such a thing, left me leaving as foolish and naïve as it is possible to be. The house isn't – and never was – mine, such an obvious state of affairs, but often we don't think of the obvious things, only the obtuse and unlikely. The solicitor had seemed a little embarrassed – he was turfing me out of my home, after all, although he murmured that of course, he was sure Mrs Dearlove would give me time to put my affairs in order. I thought of Adele then, who would need the money the sale of the house would bring, and I told the man I would leave within a few days, and that I had plans, well-established, well-thought-through plans. He nodded, looking up from the documents with their ribbons and tassels, their embossing and sealing wax and curly, barely readable script. 'Splendid,' he said, as though he didn't believe me but admired my brave bluster. He stood up from behind his desk and ushered me to his office door. 'If there's anything I can do, Mr Dearlove, and my condolences, of course, at this unhappy time.'

The solicitor had told me, too, that Eric had left me £50: *as a token of our friendship*, Eric had written in his will. I suppose he had expected at the time to still be my friend on his death. And he was, I told myself as I walked down Thorp High Street, underneath all his insanity he was my friend, as I was his.

As it was Wednesday the market spread itself about and the

164

crowds slowed me and I allowed myself to be slow, to look at the apples and tangerines piled on the stalls and to consider what might be a suitable gift for Dr Harris. I was on my way to visit him, having telephoned to ask if he would be home one afternoon, as I should like to say goodbye before I left Thorp for good. He'd told me that Wednesday afternoons were best, the one weekday afternoon each week he kept free of patients. Perhaps he was surprised when I telephoned him, he sounded puzzled, I think, as if he was trying to remind himself of who I was. At the flower stall I chose a bunch of yellow and white chrysanthemums and their peppery scent reminded me of gravesides so that, halfway along Oxhill Avenue, I almost threw them over a garden wall.

Dr Harris answered his door in shirtsleeves rolled to his elbows and although he smiled and was as gracious as ever, he seemed distracted as he showed me in. Walking ahead of me along the dark hallway he said over his shoulder, 'I was in the garden. Weeding. I think I'm weeding, anyway. Maybe I've just destroyed incipient flowers.'

He led me into the kitchen where a kettle was already beginning to whistle on an ancient-looking stove. A tea tray had been set out on the table, a cake already sliced on a plate. On the mantelpiece was a framed photograph of Robbie and Paul, posed back to back, unsmiling, stern beneath their army caps: it would be difficult to tell them apart. I placed the flowers on the table and Dr Harris smiled at me. 'Flowers,' he said. 'Lovely.' He stood them in the sink amongst pans and plates and cups. 'I have a vase, somewhere, later . . . Anyway, sit down. Tea? And cake − a patient makes this cake for me, very kind of her, but I can barely keep up with the eating of it . . .'

I sat, trying not to look around too obviously, to the bookcase with its books behind dusty glass, to the pile of newspapers beside the opposite chair − his chair, obviously, well-worn, its cushion crumpled, a reading lamp angled over it. Besides the picture of his sons a porcelain pug dog goggled its mate at the other end of the shelf. I couldn't imagine Dr Harris buying such ornaments, then I remembered that of course, once he had a wife. There was no other womanly touch; the room had a neglected, slightly unclean feel; I guessed that he lived in this room and that he didn't much care about its lifelessness, his chair an island of dim light and shabby comfort surrounded by the gloom of unloved, unused stuff. The pug dogs' expressions were as stern as his sons' and I wondered what those boys had been thinking of – they should have smiled for their father and not posed so artfully for the camera's stark flash. I looked towards the flowers in the sink, a splash of colour, and was pleased I bought them: they could be a small inspiration.

He sat down opposite me, nodding towards the tray of tea and cake he set on a side table. 'Do help yourself. Victoria sponge. Goes stale damnably quick. Still. I take some to Paul, he always had a very sweet tooth . . .'

'How is he?'

'Oh, you know.' He laughed painfully. 'He says to me that it's not as bad as France. No one is trying to shoot him and the bed is more comfortable. So, I tell myself that at least he will get out of this alive. I don't have to worry so much.'

'No. No, I can see that –'

'He's very thin, has a worrying cough . . . But it's not for ever . . . Not for ever.'

I took a cup of tea, but the cake, unnaturally yellow and bright with raspberry jam, seemed untouchable, like one of those fake desserts set out for show on a restaurant trolley. I couldn't imagine myself eating a slice and he didn't press me, only looked at me frankly as though I had visited him for a consultation and he was waiting to hear my symptoms. Unnerved by this I said quickly, 'I wrote to Paul but he replied to say he didn't want visitors.'

'No.' He sighed. 'I insist on going, of course, and he knows he can't stop me. But no, generally he doesn't want anyone. There's an army friend who seems very faithful, he visits. Patrick Morgan?' He looked at me as if I might give something away at the mention of this name.

'I don't know him.'

'No? Well, anyway. He's very loyal to Paul.' A closed, pinched expression settled on his handsome face and he turned towards the fire; taking up the poker he shifted the coals a little and orange flames flared, a spark landing to smoulder on the rug; he didn't seem to notice, just placed the poker down gently and sat back in his chair. He had collected himself, there would be no more mention of Paul's loyal friends, and he turned his professional gaze on me once again. 'So,' he said, 'what are your plans?'

'Well,' I blustered, trying to make light of myself. 'I'm leaving – the house is Adele's now and is to be sold, so I'm homeless – but I prefer to say fancy-free.'

He nodded. 'Where will you go?'

'To London – I've had a couple of pieces accepted in a periodical that has offices near the Strand . . .' I trailed off, thinking how tenuous this sounded. In truth I had decided that I would live on bread and water in the cheapest of rooms, to spin out the money I had until I could establish myself as a writer. But no one could admit to wanting to be a writer without sounding preposterously pretentious. I grinned at him foolishly. 'I'll muddle along, as ever.'

'Good. That's good.' After a moment he said, 'I saw Margot the other day, in the park, walking with a man. Your new neighbour, I think? You've met him?'

'Yes.'

'Is he decent?'

It was my turn to take an interest in the fire. I thought of Havelock Redpath and tried to think of something positive that might be said about him. At last I said, 'I barely know him.'

Dr Harris snorted. 'He looked like a prig. And Margot only looked embarrassed, pretending not to see me. I don't blame her, she's very young. Too young to have a baby, I think, too young and sheltered, and I wish my sons had never laid eyes on her. There. I'm very bitter. And you are right to leave Thorp. Away from all the humbug and secrets.'

He knew all the secrets. I pictured him on the night Tom was born, how he had hurried up the stairs to Bea's room, his black bag, his coat all splattered with the rain that was pouring down outside, his air of concern – I am sure I had worried him to death with my garbling, the panic I'd caught from Adele. I had fetched him, as Adele had begged me to, saying that things were going wrong, that Bea might die if help wasn't fetched – and who else could we trust? Adele, almost hysterical, grabbing my hand and pulling me towards the open front door she'd just barged through. 'Go now. Now. Dr Harris will come. Tell him it's life or death!' I was in my slippers, my braces hanging down, my collar undone because it was evening, almost time for bed. Adele only allowed me to shrug on my coat but not to change into my outdoor shoes. I ran in my slippers, slithering and sliding on the rain-soaked, leaf-blown pavement all the way to the end of the road and Dr Harris's house.

Sitting beside his fire, my tea growing cold, I managed to say what I had come to say. 'I wanted to thank you. For what you did for Bea and Adele. And for Eric, too, really.'

'I didn't do very much.' He smiled a little. 'She's an exceptionally brave woman and I can't fault either of them for their audacity. I can't pretend I wasn't a little shocked, but I only wish she'd taken me into her trust earlier.'

'Bea insisted.'

'I'm sure.'

The telephone began to ring and at once he stood up. 'Would you excuse me? Sometimes there's an emergency.'

I stood up. 'Of course, I must go, anyway.'

He held out his hand. 'Good luck.'

As I followed him into the hallway where the telephone was still ringing, I said quickly, 'May I send you my address when I'm settled – in case Paul needs a bolthole.'

He glanced at me as he picked up the phone, nodding, covering the mouthpiece with his hand. 'You may, of course. Goodbye, Charles.'

I imagined Paul knocking on the door of my Soho room; he would have a prison pallor; he would be thin, trying not to cough too alarmingly into his handkerchief. He would say how it would only be for a few days, a week at most, until he found his feet again. And I would hold the door open wide, saying that of course, of course, he must come in, out of the cold. I would try not to smile too much, not to fuss, to be calm and not too awed. This broken, ragged god on my doorstep would not be wearied by my worship; there would only be a refuge.

Walking home – no longer home, now – I thought of Paul's father, how he had not really dismissed me, only went on with his life, speaking to the caller with practised reassurance as I let myself out. If he had forgotten me in that moment perhaps later he would think of my visit and imagine my postcard on his doormat, how, having noted my new address, he would tuck the card behind a pug dog and it would be there for Paul's return. I thought about the loyal man he had mentioned, Patrick Morgan, who had been at Paul's trial, as I had. We had exchanged glances, Patrick Morgan and I, a curt nod or two; he knew me just as I knew him. And of course Paul would never turn up on my doorstep, not as long as Morgan existed in this world.

I paused outside Adele and Bea's house. I knew I should call and say goodbye to them, too, but I couldn't face Adele's questions or Bea's indifference. I would write to them – another postcard with a second-class stamp and a dashed-off signature. My life was about to start again.

Chapter Twenty

Adele said, 'I really don't know anything about it. Your mother was a very private person.' She wanted to say that he was too bold, and that he shouldn't ask such impertinent questions. He should drink his tea and be quiet and be on his way as soon as politeness allowed. Off you go now, she might say, as she had when he was a child and had stayed too long, impinging on Tom's teatime. She glanced towards the door, hoping that Bea might appear to rescue her; but Bea didn't know that Bobby Harris was here; earlier that afternoon she had taken herself off to her room without a word of explanation.

Bobby Harris said, 'Would your sister know anything?'

For what seemed like the first time in her life she didn't even make a pretence of politeness. 'My sister doesn't know anything either and I won't have her disturbed.'

He matched her coldness. 'I'm sure I wouldn't disturb her.'

'Well, you're disturbing me.'

To her surprise he laughed. 'No one has ever said that before.'

'I didn't mean –'

'That's all right. I knew what you meant. And I didn't mean to remind you of things you might want to forget, but all the same – I had to ask.'

'I don't want to forget your mother. I only have fond memories of her. But we didn't discuss such very private matters.'

He nodded. 'No, of course.'

He sipped his tea. She hadn't wanted to serve him tea but it seemed she couldn't help herself – tea must be offered; but she hadn't put out biscuits, hadn't even asked if he took sugar, but had only set a cup of tea on the side table beside his chair. He had asked if he might smoke, but she had told him that Bea wouldn't allow smoking in the house and at once she had felt foolish and so added that she didn't care for the smell of it, either, and all this had seemed petty and even spiteful, because there he was, so right and proper in his expensive and elegant clothes, smelling of some marvellous cologne; he was the prince transformed into the beast – she quite understood what a Beauty would see in him: he had walked through hell – wasn't that powerfully compelling?

Putting down his cup gently in its saucer he said, 'I've tried to speak to Charles Dearlove but he's avoiding me. I suppose I hoped that you would tell me that everything in his biography of Francis is true because my mother had told you about that time when she met my father – or that it's all lies, again because she had told you what happened. But of course, as you say she was a very private person.' He placed the cup and saucer on the side table – she couldn't help noticing his hands and thought again of the beast – and stood up. 'I should go. Thank you for the tea.'

She showed him into the hall and handed him his coat and hat. He put his hat on, but only folded his coat over his arm and held out his hand. She took it hesitantly. Was she repelled or afraid? – either way both responses shamed her. His grip was firm and cool, brief, businesslike, he wasn't about to be overfamiliar even though she had known him as a small child and had wanted to take him as her own, knowing that his mother behaved towards him almost as if he was a stranger's child.

All at once she said, 'I'm sorry I couldn't be more helpful.'

'I understand.'

'Margot tried her best, I'm sure she did, it's just that your stepfather . . .'

He touched her arm. 'Mrs Dearlove, I understand, truly. Please don't worry. I didn't mean to upset you.'

She was crying and this was ridiculous. She fumbled in her skirt pocket for her handkerchief and wiped her eyes impatiently. 'I miss your mother.'

Again he touched her arm. 'You were a good friend to her.'

'Oh, I don't know about that.' She looked at him defiantly. 'We could have done more.'

'No. I don't think so. Our lives are our own, after all.'

Later she tried to think about what he had meant by this and whether she had told him the truth about doing more for Margot. But all she could think about was Havelock Redpath and how he was like a guard at Margot's door, deciding who was allowed to visit, at what time and for how long. She had been afraid of this man, afraid of his coldness and nasty tongue, afraid most of all of the repercussions for Margot if she behaved too much like a busybody, knocking on the Redpath door for any reason or none, peering along the dark passage as Redpath held the door open a crack. 'My wife is indisposed,' he had told her once, when she had summoned the courage to call because she hadn't seen Margot for days. She hadn't questioned him, only nodded meekly and scurried home. She had never wanted to be a trouble to Margot; perhaps she should have been a trouble to *him*. If she had been a man she would have punched Redpath in the face. But that wasn't what men did, none of the men she had ever known, at least. The men she'd known had side-stepped and made excuses and only wars made them brave.

Bea had worried so about Tom when he enlisted. For her own part she was certain that Tom would return because she couldn't imagine Bea without him. From the moment of his birth it had seemed to her that Bea would vanish into thin air if anything happened to Tom. Bea's son, after all; it was Bea's face that was transformed by love the moment this scrawny, bloodied creature was pushed from her body. And Dr Harris said, 'You have a son, a fine boy,' and Bea had held out her arms at once although she was exhausted, her eyes blazing with that love that was all at once and all powerful and utterly shocking. She hadn't expected *love*. Perhaps Bea had, although Bea hadn't wanted him. *She* had wanted him, but that want – that terrible need – had disappeared the moment he was born.

Adele went upstairs with the idea of knocking on Bea's bedroom door to ask if she needed anything – whether she would like a sand-wich or a cup of tea. Or anything – anything at all: a hand to hold, a listening ear because she was certain that Bea needed someone to hear her out. Bea was ill, Adele had guessed this weeks ago, and she wondered if there should be some conversation between them, some restructuring of the truth – who was hurt more and who was hurt less and who should be forgiven and who should say that none of it mattered, now, now the day's over.

The hymn they had sung as children came back to her as she hesi-tated at the bottom of the stairs, her hand on the banister, all ready to heave herself up. *Now the day is over, night is drawing nigh*, sung every afternoon at the end of the school day so the hymn heralded not darkness but a release from the terrible boredom of the class-room, the capricious anger and spite of her old-maid teachers, and so she had loved every sentimental word, the shadows stealing across the evening sky meant nothing to her then. She looked up and the stairs were too much effort to climb, the landing dark and as forbid-ding as Bea's closed-tight bedroom door. Bea would be asleep, she told herself, and she needed her sleep, sleep lent one strength and forbearance; in an hour or so Bea would come downstairs refreshed and would ask about supper, hungry because she had missed lunch. Perhaps she would tell her about Bobby Harris's visit, because she wasn't one to keep secrets as Bea did. It occurred to her then that perhaps Bea knew the truth of Bobby's paternity and she imagined Margot making her confession to Bea because Bea had been a nurse and was unshockable; but this imagining presumed that Charles's book was true. Adele believed it was. Charles was not a spiteful man, nor a liar; most of all he kept secrets as if they were his own.

Adele went back into the kitchen; there were chores to complete, supper to consider. She would buck up and be positive and build up a good front for Bea.

*

For her own part, Bea sat on the edge of her bed, willing herself to stand, to straighten her sleep-rumpled clothes and make her way downstairs. Adele would suspect something if she stayed in bed all day; she would come knocking, perhaps with a tray of tea and sandwiches. Bea strained to hear her sister's footsteps, beginning to wonder why she hadn't ventured to her door. Perhaps she had looked in on her when she was sleeping; Bea glanced at the door to see that it was still firmly closed: Adele would have left it ajar so as to make as little noise as possible. Weren't they pussyfooting around each other lately? But then they had always avoided confrontation.

Reluctantly she stood up. There were her slippers where she had left them, side by side, ready to step into, she had been careful earlier, wanting to make the putting-on of slippers easy; every action she took now was slow and careful and deliberate, always with this future ease in mind. But the slippers seemed a very long way away and the room had begun turning and all at once the dead were everywhere, all talking at once, the Old B smiling and smiling with relief as he held out his hand.

Chapter Twenty-one

Patrick Morgan read Bobby Harris's letter – such thick paper: expensive, blue as the skies Bobby had once flown. Bobby was always so lost. Lost as a child, as an adult – that dashing young air force officer: even his uniform couldn't conceal Bobby's lostness. Is that a word, Patrick thought, lostness? He was growing old and words sometimes presented themselves to him in a manner that seemed right but was actually quite wrong. Perhaps he was creating his own language. He remembered there was a language that was created for men like him: Polari. He knew a few words, learnt from the men who frequented those dreadful Soho clubs Paul would sometimes take him to. Oh, the two of them had attracted such interest. Paul was so beautiful, after all, and as for himself, well, not to be immodest, but he had been a very striking man. Those Polari speakers had taken him for a king's guard. But he had never lied to them, they had only presumed. He had never minded presumption – the presumptions of others could be used as a cover, a disguise, no one ever guessed who he really was.

He read Bobby's letter again, struck again by how childish Bobby was – he wanted truth; he wanted there to be no more lies, no more secrets – there should be confessions. Patrick thought of his summer visits to Ireland to visit his mother's family, the Irish priests of his childhood who would tell him to go and sin no more. There was one particular church in Belfast where his mother would kneel for so long, her back so straight, her hair covered by a vain piece of black lace, her head bowed, her rosary fidgeted through her fingers, each bead a prayer, perhaps the same prayer – Lord save me – at least that was his own silent chant. In that church the confession screen almost revealed the father confessor's face, if one were to squint and hold one's head just so, if there was a certain light slanting through the stained-glass windows. No, perhaps he had imagined this revelation of the priest's stern face. Weren't priests always stern? No; sometimes they were kind; they reassured his mother, or at least he sensed they did, from the expression on her face when she left the confessional box.

Bobby. Paul's son, who wanted to know whether he truly was Paul's son, as Paul had always claimed. Everyone couldn't help wondering if this claim was true or not. For his own part Patrick believed – had always believed – that Paul and Bobby were father and son; he had never, as some did, put fatherhood past Paul. Paul would have seduced Margot, Bobby's mother, in the blink of an eye – the wink of an eye. Margot would have been so taken with him – wasn't everyone? Paul was never exclusive but a sexual adventurer. Never satisfied, never content; promiscuous: Paul could see promise in almost anyone. And once he had been so jealous of Paul's proclivities, and once Paul had told him that that was who they were – homosexual men – promiscuous dogs. Paul had told him this with an exasperated air, as though he couldn't believe that he didn't know this and couldn't excuse it. We're queer, Paul had said, with all that impatient exasperation. No, Patrick had thought, I'm queer, you are something else, but what? He seemed to be outside nature, beyond even his own understanding. An angel; a god. A devil. Patrick smiled to himself; Paul, dead for so many years now and still causing trouble. He looked down at the letter; he would have to think carefully about his reply, remember carefully; or he could simply write: You are Paul's son; he always insisted on that to me and I never doubted him.

Patrick got up and went to the window. There was the plane tree, there the London sparrows flying in and out of the bare branches. A young mother pushed her baby's pram towards the park; a black cab pulled up across the road and his opposite neighbour climbed out, harassed as ever, fumbling for his wallet. Catching Patrick watching him this man raised his hand in a brief salute; this was a friendly neighbourhood; names were known, pleasantries exchanged; there was even a cocktail party or two at Christmas or New Year. His neighbours were curious about him, the tall, upright old man who lived alone in the fine Georgian town house Paul had bought in 1938, before such houses were fashionable. The place had been bastardised into poky bedsits; it had reeked of damp and hopelessness and Paul had stood at the kitchen window, spun round to him and said –

'Well? What do you think?'

'That you're crazy. There's going to be another war. We can't come back here. We can't live here –'

'We won't. I will – when I need to, when I'm in England.'

'And if there's a war?'

'If. Patrick – we have to be hopeful.' He grinned at him. 'Believe in Mr Chamberlain.'

Patrick snorted. He looked around, at the cracks in the ceiling, the bare, paint-splattered floorboards; a picture of the little princesses had been cut from a newspaper and pinned above the filthy-looking cooking range. An old maid had lived here, Patrick thought, in this one room, alone; he could weep for her. Instead he went to the picture and tore it down, crumpling it into a ball. He said, 'We have a home, in Tangiers.'

'Patrick, I need to be here, in London. If I'm to make a real name for myself –' He crossed the room and took his hand. 'This is about the painting, that's all. There'll be no other men here, I promise.'

'Don't make promises you can't keep.'

'All right.' Paul let go of his hand and glanced around the room just as he had, only with more enthusiasm – thoughts of old maids obviously never occurred to him. 'I've found a builder. I've asked him to restore it to how it was – well-proportioned, elegant. Look,' he turned to the grimy window, 'There's a garden – a bit over-grown now, but it could be lovely – I'll show you –'

'I've seen enough.'

Paul laughed as he often did in the face of his mulishness. 'Oh, come on, Pat. Let me give you the tour. This could be our home. In England. Home.'

'England's never been a true home to me.'

'Are you playing the Irish card now?' He lit a cigarette. Tossing the match down he said, 'I'll divide my time. Summer here, winter in Tangiers.' After a moment he said, 'And then there's Bobby. If I'm here – well, he could visit me.'

'He barely knows you exist!'

Paul gazed at him. 'He knows I'm his father.'

'You think so?'

'Why don't you just fuck off, Patrick, eh? Back to Tangiers and all the fucking heat and the fucking flies and your fucking dusky-skinned boys.'

'You think I'm unfaithful to you?'

'Unfaithful! For Christ's sake, you sound like a bloody woman! We're not married, Patrick. I didn't make any vow – this is not till death do us part.'

'So, this is the end of it?'

'No.' Paul sighed. 'No. I just need to be here. I'm good at what I do, Pat. I have to be good at this or else there's nothing.'

'Nothing? You and me – we're nothing?'

'Oh, for Christ's sake. You know what I mean.' He breathed out smoke, impatient now: his anger was always quick to live and quicker to die. 'Let me show you the rest of the house. I've put your name on the deed – it's ours, whether you want in or not. If I die it's all yours, it's in my will.'

Watching the flitting sparrows Patrick remembered how Paul would think of everything, plan everything, even going as far as making a will, although he was only forty – still young and vital. That afternoon he had trailed after him, from room to partitioned room, and all he could think was how dirty the house was and dark and that there would be rats in the cellar and mice beneath the floor-boards and pigeons in the attic. An English house, in other words: cold, damp, sunless, with too many stairs leading from a narrow passageway; and then, on the first floor, Paul opened a door onto a lovely room, with twin windows looking out over the plane trees, with a blue-veined white marble fireplace and a high ceiling, and this room was full of light and there was a tantalising scent he couldn't place, one he now knew came from the oak floorboards. Paul had turned to him, grinning, and held his arms out wide to his sides, like an actor declaring the happy ending to the play. 'Isn't it grand? A room for fine dandies.'

Patrick stood in that same room now. If he turned from the window he believed he might see Paul standing there, as he had that day, when Paul approached him cautiously, his footsteps light on those broad boards that didn't creak. Reaching out Paul had touched his arm and said, 'Patty. England is my home.'

Patrick had said, 'All right. If that's what you want.' How could he deny him anything? Paul was the only person he had ever loved, if love meant giving up one's own life for the beloved.

The room was still grand, although a little shabby around the edges, he supposed. One of Paul's self-portraits hung above the fireplace: that one with the serious, intent expression, all the colours muted. On the wall above the sofa was a painting of their courtyard in Tangiers and this picture was all colour and life and gaiety. There were little birds, if you looked closely, and once seen they could not be unseen but seemed always as if they were about to fly from the picture to settle in the palm of your hand. Patrick crossed the room to this picture, straightened it; sometimes the house shook from the traffic on the road below, removals vans made the place shudder like a frail old woman. Lots of vans, these days, lots of young couples moving in, renovating, smashing the fireplaces into rubble and tearing out cupboards – even walls. Paul had restored the house to its original state, but such restoration seemed to be unfashionable now.

Now he was close to his three score years and ten – *the days of our years*: the psalm came back to him as psalms were wont to do, lately. He had lived longer than his father, his mother, his grandparents for all he knew, because he hadn't known them, had barely known his parents, although he knew his father was cruel, his mother ineffective against her husband's fists and boots and spittle-flecked tirades.

They had died whilst he was off fighting a war his father had so heartily scorned. His mother had prayed for him, she told him so in her infrequent letters. Perhaps he should have prayed for her, but God was too much of a joker in those days – those stern priests really didn't know Him at all.

He turned from the picture of their home in Tangiers, went to his desk, and sat down. He took out a pen and writing paper from a drawer and wrote the date: the time was now and the past mattered not one jot. All the same, he would write to Bobby Harris; he supposed it was the least he could do.

The least he could do but still, words failed him. He thought of his twin brother, a poet who had long since rivalled Kipling in his international fame. This twin of his would write a fine letter, somehow he would know just what Bobby wanted to read: a parable about a young man who wanted only to do what was right, as long as right actions didn't inconvenience him too much. Could there be such a sting in his words? Patrick tapped the pen against his teeth; really he had no idea what Bobby wanted from him. He wrote, *Dear Bobby, I hope you are well. I know you have read that book by that man with the unlikely name – Dearlove – would such a name make one feel better about life? Anyway, you have read his book as I have and it was odd to read about oneself in such an entertaining way. I was amused and flattered, I felt important for a while. A rainy afternoon and an otherwise dull evening was passed strolling along a memory lane where the landmarks were only vaguely recognisable yet the people vivid enough for me to lift my hat to. Your mother and grandparents were more than ghosts – Paul's father George in particular – I think Dearlove must have loved him as we all did.*

But you want to know if Dearlove's story is true.

Patrick put the pen down. He turned to the window and the little birds – their immediate busyness was compelling, far more so than the past and all its complications; who said what to whom; who was the villain, the victim, the martyr – surely all of them all at once. Outside the sun was shining, bright as could be. Tempting simply to walk out; he could write to Bobby tomorrow, or the next day.

Standing up, he decided he would visit his twin, Mick, who lived, after all, only a few streets away. Perhaps the two of them could write the letter together, concoct a version of the truth that would sit well with Bobby.

Mick wheeled himself to the door of his drawing room as his house-keeper, Mrs Wood, ushered Patrick in. As he almost always did, Mick thought how his brother hardly aged at all, was always so straight-backed, hadn't lost any of this height, no stooping, no rounding of his shoulders – still the stern, taciturn sergeant major; irritating that he should be so handsome at their age, so virile. Was he jealous? Jealous of his two legs. Mick placed his palms on what remained of his own legs, amputated just above the knee by an army surgeon in 1917, a man who had told him to be grateful he wasn't dead. Well, he was grateful: he thanked God every day for the life he had been given since the war; this thanking was important to him. He wanted God to know that he knew he had been spared, that His mercy was miraculous. He could be dead, lying beneath a white cross, one of thousands and thousands and thousands of such crosses, his intact body slowly decaying into a foreign field. Not intact, then, but alive – that was the miracle, and so what if his brother had legs? Patrick lived an intact life Mick wouldn't ever wish for.

Mick said, 'Well, to what do I owe the pleasure?' He wheeled his chair back and indicated the visitor armchair beside the fire. He glanced at his housekeeper. 'Could we have some tea, Mrs Wood?'

Patrick sat down. He said, 'It's cold out – quite blustery.'

Mick looked towards the window and saw that the blustery wind had splattered raindrops across the glass. He had been writing at his desk and had noticed that the light had changed but was too caught up to switch on the lamp. Lately words came to him well and quickly and hardly needed revising – hardly. He inhaled sharply, thinking this vanity would be the ruin of him. But these poems were better, if he put them to one side and tried to forget about them he knew that they would impress him when finally he went back to them, like the work of a better, younger poet. Again he drew breath, he might be wrong, he might be wasting his time. But the words were so quick and lively –

'Mick?'

He had forgotten his brother. He looked at him. 'Pat. You're here. Put some more coal on the fire, would you? I don't like asking Mrs Wood. She remembers scullery maids and parlour maids, or at least those maids-of-all-work who wore different caps and aprons for all the different jobs . . . although I'm sure she doesn't mind . . .' He was aware of saying too much, as though he hadn't spoken for days – he hadn't, not really; there was only Mrs Wood after all and precious few visitors. He watched as Patrick put more coal on the fire, poking the embers so that the flames flared. He hadn't noticed the fading of the light and he hadn't noticed how cold he had become; he realised he was hungry and hoped Mrs Wood would serve teacakes with the tea, wondering if he should send Pat to the kitchen to ask if she would. But Pat was settling himself back into the armchair and it seemed wrong to have him get up again like a servant. Mick remembered that time just after the war when the two of them had lived together, when Pat had done everything for him, everything – this was a time before Mick realised he could do most things for himself, a time when he still felt institutionalised, just out of that hospital full of legless men. Pat had rescued him. How ungrateful he had been.

Mick studied his brother, said at last, 'So – what's the face for?'

'What face?'

'The worried face.'

'No, not worried.' Patrick smiled. 'How's Hugh?'

Mick thought of his son who telephoned from time to time and from time to time visited him with his children. 'Hugh's fine. Nina and the children, they're fine, too, as far as I know – no news is good news when it comes to Hugh and his family.'

'That's good. Give him my best wishes, when you see him.'

'I will.' Mick glanced towards his desk, his notebook and pen just where he had left them when he heard the front doorbell ring and had wheeled himself to the window to see Pat standing on the door-step. He had been trying to unravel a thought he'd had about sunlight on grass, how the light shifted through the trees; he had needed to be distracted, the thought was going nowhere, the words, for once, not as swift as they could be. Best not to think about it. He turned back to Patrick. 'Are you keeping well?'

'Yes, thank you. You?'

'Mustn't grumble.'

Patrick said, 'I had a letter from Bobby Harris.'

Mrs Wood came in then, bumping through the door hip-first, the tea tray loaded with teapot, cups, and saucers and also, gratifyingly, the teacakes, toasted in that expert way she had, a little pot of jam set next to the butter. He had an idea he should ask Mrs Wood – Mr Wood's widow – to marry him; he often had this idea and knew how sentimental it was. He said, 'Oh, thank you, my dear. Wonderful.'

She smiled at him, set the tray down and left without a word. He *should* marry her; he had always been drawn to discreet, capable women.

Patrick waited until Mrs Wood had shut the door behind her before saying, 'Do you remember Bobby Harris?'

Mick looked up at him from buttering a teacake. 'Of course I do. I'm not senile yet. He wrote you a letter, you say? What did he write?'

'It was all questions about Paul.'

Mick laughed, knowing he sounded harsh and dismissive but unable to help himself. *Paul Harris.* That bugger; that sodomite that would have landed his brother in prison for all that he said he cared about him – only good luck had kept Pat from that particular deg-radation. And Harris had been dead for years, yet still Pat carried his torch, still his brother's face showed such devotion to the man. At least there had been no one else in Pat's life, no woman, no other *man.* It was as if Paul Harris had used up all Pat's heart: there was nothing left for anyone else. He began to eat the teacake, deciding to allow Patrick time to say what he had to say, because despite Pat's love for the Harris creature – or whatever such infatuation should be called – he hardly ever mentioned him; Mick couldn't help but be intrigued by this turn of events: a letter, indeed – like a twist in a novel, dredging up rotting secrets.

Patrick poured the tea. After a while he said, 'Have you read that biography by Dearlove?'

'No. I never read stories I already know too well.'

'But you know him?'

'Dearlove? Slightly. We move in the same circles – literary events, book launches, that kind of thing.'

'He's from Thorp.'

Mick snorted. 'Yes – he approached me at a party once, I think he had the idea that our coming from the same town meant that we shared some kind of bond, or something. Anyway I told him I never went back to Thorp, tried to forget all about the place. He's a queer little fellow, everyone knows him, or rather he knows everyone – an enigma?'

'Bobby thinks the book is a pack of lies.'

'Do you?'

'No. Paul trusted him. *I* trusted him.' He sighed. 'He stayed with us in Tangiers when Paul was dying. Paul would talk to him, for hours and hours, exhausting himself but I couldn't stop him from talking. And then, when Paul died, Dearlove went away and after a while I forgot all about him, forgot all about those notes he took, reams and reams of notes. And then, suddenly, after so many years, he publishes Paul's life –'

Mick interrupted. 'He waited until the time was right – haven't you noticed how suddenly we are in fashion, we great heroes?'

'That silly play – musical, whatever it is, you mean?'

'Yes, and Paul's paintings. His anti-war pieties are in vogue.' Mick lit a cigarette, tossing the packet to his brother. As Patrick took a cigarette, Mick said, 'Why do you think Paul married that girl Margot? He was hardly fit to look after himself back then – let alone a wife. You really think he got her pregnant – the state he was in – the kind of man he was?'

Pat shook his head, looking away from him. '*The kind of man he was!* You can't stop, can you?'

184

'Oh Patrick – stop what? Speaking the truth? *Was* he a woman-iser, chasing skirt? Fresh from the mad house and girls were throwing themselves at him? He no more fathered that child than I did. He married her to save her face – Christ, Pat. If you hadn't guessed that . . .' Mick frowned, a truth occurring to him. 'My God, you thought badly of him! Who did you want him to be? The great sin-ner you had to save?'

Pat managed to look at him but he couldn't keep the sullenness out of his voice. 'He swore to me Bobby was his.'

'Yes, his – but did he swear that he'd sired him?'

'Words – you play about with words – he should have told me the truth.'

'Perhaps he expected you to figure out the truth for yourself.'

'Well, I didn't. I believed him because I knew him. I knew what he was capable of.'

Outside a car horn sounded, tyres screeched, a man shouted obscenities and if he had been alone Mick would have wheeled his chair to the window and looked outside for a glimpse of the commotion – any excuse to distract himself from writing, no matter how well the words were arranging themselves. But Pat sat before him, such anger on his face because he had riled him, although he hadn't intended to, and to go to the window, to take an interest in the world, would make him appear frivolous. Could a legless man be frivolous? He was certain that the world thought not. Yet he was, and always had been, and his poetry, his plays, everything he had ever written were like iridescent soap bubbles, pretty, even mesmer-ising for a little while, but ultimately frivolous. He sighed. 'Patrick. Does any of this matter now?'

'It matters to Bobby.'

'Let him believe what he wants to believe. Only Paul and Margot knew the truth of it. And Paul told you one thing, and Dearlove another thing, and none of us can know anything for certain.'

Patrick stood up, quick and agitated as he ever was, and went to the window as though his own curiosity couldn't be contained for a second longer. 'A car's gone into the back of a taxi.'

'Much damage?'

'Not really. A lot of gesticulating going on. PC Plod's approaching.' He glanced at him before returning his gaze to the street. 'When I see a policeman my stomach lurches – even now. Do you remember the military police during the war? I used to wonder whose side they were on. Vicious bastards.'

'They kept order, I suppose.'

'Because without order we would have all run home to Mammy.' He turned from the window and went to the bookshelves, standing in front of them as though books had ever held his interest. At last he said, 'I should go back to Thorp, visit Mammy's grave. I think of it left untended and lately it seems wrong. I don't care about him – Dadda – but her . . . Well. She deserves something, I think.'

Mick watched as his brother took a book from the shelves, flicking through it only to put it back, to squint at another, taking it down, turning it over, putting it back, unable to make any connection. 'Books,' he said suddenly, and laughed. 'Never got the hang of them.'

Mick manoeuvred his chair towards him, only to stop a few feet away. He felt shy of this man he saw only so often, they could lose touch so easily; there had been times in their lives when they only exchanged letters, and sporadically at that; times when he had despised the life his twin brother had chosen, times when he was too caught up in his own life to care. Yet always a letter would be sent or received, a visit made, and they would talk like neighbours meeting on the street, catching up on inconsequential gossip. He couldn't remember Patrick ever mentioning their parents before, at least not since they had both left Thorp. *Mammy*: the Irishman stirred in him, sentimental and maudlin: *Mammy* – he could shed a tear using that word for the woman who had brought them into the world. He had hardly thought of her for years.

'Anyway,' Patrick became brisk. 'I should go home – you were busy,' he nodded towards Mick's desk. 'Busy writing. I shouldn't have disturbed you.'

'Will you go to Thorp?'

'Stroll down memory lane? Put chrysanthemums in the urn? Maybe. Probably not.'

'We could both go. Lay the past to rest.'

'There's a plaque dedicated to Paul in the Parish Church. Thorp is proud of him now.'

'Then let's go – salute the plaque. That would have amused him, no?'

Patrick laughed a little. 'Should we go?'

'Why not?'

He nodded. 'All right, all right then,' he smiled, 'I'll see myself out.'

But Mick followed him to the front door and waited as Patrick walked down the path, closed the gate behind him, and turned to walk along the road towards his own home. He waited until he was out of sight and still he sat in the doorway, thinking of Thorp, of going back there after so many years. There was the house where he was born, where he had lived after the war with his wife Hetty and their newborn son, where he had written the play that had made his name, his fortune, and all that feverish writing had cost him his marriage and the settled family life he had only half wanted in the first place. That play, *Theory of Angels*, had been revived lately, playing to full houses in the West End, and he wished that it had been left, quietly forgotten, because it seemed juvenile to him now, too much a part of his manic, thrown-away youth, his thrown-away wife and child. He glanced back along the dark hallway, he had been blinded by the sunny afternoon and nothing could be seen of his lovely home, in this well-heeled part of London, except closed doors and a staircase he couldn't climb leading to rooms he never used. He would go to Thorp, the past could have its say, and then he would return home and ask Mrs Wood to marry him. He smiled because the idea was vain and silly, like him, and because his life was comfortable and easy and he knew he would never take any drastic step to change such a happy state. He wheeled himself back to his study, to the tray of tea, to the warm fire and his writing desk; there was still work to be done.

*

Adele said, 'She didn't suffer. The doctor said it was so sudden – she wouldn't have known anything about it –'

Tom shook his head, 'No? Well, that's good . . .'

He looked as shocked as she had ever seen anyone look, all the colour gone from his face, and he glanced around as though he had never sat in her kitchen before, as though all the sense had been knocked out of him. Upstairs Bea's body lay on her bed – she and Dr Walker had managed to lift her up from the bedroom floor where Adele had found her after hearing that alarming thud. She had known her sister was dead, all the same she had knelt beside her and taken her hand, saying 'Oh – what have you done? Can you get up, if I help you?' Bea had only stared at her, such a surprised expression on her face. 'Oh, Bea,' she had said, 'Oh, *Bea*.'

For a little while she had knelt beside her, holding her hand; she couldn't think of anything else to do. Then she noticed that the legs of her pyjamas had ridden up and she let go of her hand to straighten them; then she had the idea that her poor body shouldn't become too cold so she reached for the eiderdown from her bed and covered her with it; then she closed her eyes so that she wouldn't look so surprised any more and it appeared as though Bea had decided she would sleep on the floor – isn't that just the kind of thing that Bea would decide to do for some stubborn reason of her own? Adele touched her cheek – was she already becoming cold? 'Bea,' she said, 'I have to go and call the doctor.' Yet still she didn't move, it had seemed too cruel to leave her alone, and so she stayed until she felt if she didn't scramble to her feet she would never move again.

Now the doctor had gone and she had called Tom's school and he had come so quickly, such a flustered look about him – he had been given some garbled message. She had sat him down and told him that Bea was dead and he had said no, that couldn't be. And now he looked around the kitchen as though he might see her, hidden in a dark corner.

Again she said, 'I'm sure she didn't suffer, it was so quick –'

'A stroke, the doctor said?'

'Yes.'

'It's hard to believe.'

'Yes. It is.'

She was standing over him – hovering, having set a cup of tea in front of him. All at once he said, 'Should I go up and see her?'

He looked panicked and she touched his arm. 'Only if you want to.'

'I don't know – I don't think I do.' He laughed painfully. 'She was always so full of life . . . Indestructible, you know?'

'Yes, I know.'

'Mum, sit down, this is such a shock for you.'

She sat because her legs did feel odd and there was a pain in her side as if she had strained herself helping the doctor lift Bea's body. 'Can you take her feet?' he had said, and taken almost all her weight. A kind man, gentle, taking care as if Bea could feel all the indignity of the situation. He had called the undertaker. Bea would be taken away soon.

Tom sipped his tea. She watched him; without Bea asking her questions and taking an interest she hardly knew what to say to him, but their silence was bearable and better than all the things they might say to each other at such a time. Perhaps he would blame her for Bea's death, for not noticing that she was ill, not nagging her to visit the doctor, to eat more, to rest more – she should have guarded her sister more closely. But the truth was she was tired of the nagging and cajoling and she had decided to allow Bea to go her own way without her interference – interference that had always come to nothing anyway. Watching Tom she wondered if he realised how little she could have done. She glanced up, towards the room above them where Bea was lying neatly on her bed; she thought that she should be sitting with her – wasn't that what was done by normal, proper people. Proper people would cry for their only sister, the woman they had lived with all their lives. She had never lived alone, and now she would be all alone; she should be afraid of this and not feel any relief at all, as a proper person wouldn't.

Tom said, 'Mum, do you want to stay with us tonight?'

'No,' she almost laughed in astonishment. 'No, of course not. I'll be fine.'

'Or we could stay with you –'

'No, best to keep things normal for Luc. Let's not have him too upset.'

'Staying the night here wouldn't upset him.'

'No, probably not. All the same.'

'I'd be happier if you weren't on your own, tonight at least.'

'Why? What do you think I'm going to do?'

He didn't reply, only glanced up as she had done, as if he hadn't already decided that he wouldn't go upstairs. He must have seen dead bodies, and not peaceful, still old bodies either but far worse than that. Yet the body upstairs, peaceful and still, belonged to his mother: she had always believed that he knew, in his heart, that Bea was his mother and that he kept their secret because he was a good, kind boy. She wondered if he would say something, now that his mother was dead and if he did whether she would apologise, because really, theirs had been no way to bring up a child – all that confusion leaking out like the milk from Bea's poor breasts. Adele closed her eyes – she would not think of that time; Bea was dead, none of it mattered any more.

'Mum?'

'I'm fine.' She looked at him, appalled to see that he was swiping tears from his eyes. 'Please don't cry. She would want you to be strong.'

He laughed brokenly. 'Yes, I know. No nonsense.'

He began to cry properly and she got up and went to him, placing her arm lightly around his shoulders. 'She loved you very much.'

He nodded.

'Very much – more than all the world. You were her lovely boy, her one true love.'

Again he nodded, fumbling in his pocket for a handkerchief and wiping his nose. She squeezed him to her, the first time she had more than merely touched him in years; she kissed the top of his head. 'We'll be strong, you and I, and remember that she loved us and that she had a good life.'

'She was brave.'

190

'Yes,' she laughed a little. 'Very brave.'

He drew breath. 'I have to get home – for Luc –'

'Yes, of course.'

'But we'll come back, sit with you for a while.'

'Yes, I'd like that.'

He looked up at her and she thought that he was about to speak so she smiled, as brightly as she could and said, 'Best you get off, now, I don't want Luc to worry –'

'He'll be fine –'

'All the same.' She patted his arm and drew away from him. 'I'll call you, after the undertaker has gone – Luc doesn't need to see that – then you can both come here.'

He stood up. 'Will you be all right?'

'For an hour or two? Of course I will.'

After he'd gone she went upstairs, pausing at Bea's bedroom door – she had almost knocked, just as she always did, privacy was important to them both. But the doctor had left the door ajar and she pushed it open gently, and stood for a moment, seeing that the sun was streaming in through the windows, a bright patch of light lying across Bea's face.

She went to the window and opened it, then took Bea's hairbrush from her chest of drawers and went to her, hesitating a moment before brushing her short fringe back from her face, as Bea liked. She said, 'I love you, more than anyone else in my life.'

There, she had said it, and the room was so still, only a slight billowing of the curtains, shadows of branches shifting across the wall. She was alone now, yet there was a presence – the sun's warmth and light, the swaying shadows, the green scents from the garden – all were part of it and if she turned around she would see Bea, standing in front of the mirror above the chest of drawers, and her reflection would smile at her – such a smile she had – and then she would be gone. But the warmth would remain for a little while, the sunlight, the scent – lilac blossom? – Bea would know – and she would remember these moments and not bury them in a box.

All that remained was to choose an outfit for Bea – the under-taker would ask for this, an outfit she would most like to be buried in. Her best tweed suit; her checked shirt, and dark green knitted tie. Adele went to Bea's wardrobe and began to gather these clothes together.

Charles sat opposite Edmund who was staring out of the train's window, seemingly totally absorbed in the repeat of fields as they sped north to Thorp. In first class, a finished pot of tea between them, he thought again of thanking him for accompanying him on this journey – he felt as though he really couldn't thank him enough and that Edmund's travelling two hundred and fifty miles on a train for him was far beyond what he would've expected of him and their relationship. And he couldn't imagine Edmund in Thorp: he was too startlingly grand. He had forgotten how grand he was outside in the world; for years he had only ever seen him indoors, most often in his own poky flat where Edmund would visit in his soft, old clothes, incognito. Now, on the train, Charles found it difficult to take his eyes off him, more difficult still to keep himself from blurting out his thanks again.

Edmund caught his eye and smiled. 'How are you bearing up?'

'I'm fine.'

'I know funerals are ghastly but the anticipation is the worst.'

'Yes, quite.'

'And I'll be there, you know – or not, if you want to be discreet. Of course I could be *discretely* there, too. Whatever you want.'

'I want you there, of course.' Charles tried to keep the desperation from his voice, all the time imagining going to Bea's funeral alone, while Edmund stayed in the hotel, or strolled around Thorp, or did whatever Edmund thought most appropriate. He said quickly, 'Unless you'd rather not –'

'Gosh, it's a long way to travel to stay away from the main event.' After a moment he said, 'Sorry, that was crass.'

'No, no. I'm very glad you're here.'

Edmund nodded. He lit a cigarette and returned to watching the countryside go by. He seemed to be completely absorbed in this watching when he said, 'Tell me about Bea.'

'Bea?'

Edmund turned to him. 'Yes, unless you'd rather not.'

'No, no, you should know something –' He thought of telling him of the first time he had set eyes on Bea, in her garden; how he and Eric had climbed their own garden wall to catch a glimpse of the new people who had moved in next door, only to see this girl – obviously a girl to him if not to Eric – dressed in boys' clothes, kicking at the ground, her hands thrust deep into her trouser pockets, head bowed. Was she angry or sad, or both – hard to tell with Bea.

Edmund said, 'Charles?'

'I'm thinking about the first time I saw her. So good-looking – you know when girls dress up as boys and become something else entirely? She wore her hair like some girls do nowadays – elfin, except I think she had cut it herself. I had never seen anyone like her. She bought her boys' clothes herself, from jumble sales – saved up her pocket money. We teased her, of course, to hide our awe.'

'We?'

'Eric and I.'

'Eric your cousin?'

'Yes.'

Edmund tapped cigarette ash into the British Rail ashtray. 'Quite something, to be in awe of someone.'

Charles remembered the feel of that old brick wall against his legs, its cool damp, and the cushion-like clumps of the brightest green moss. And there was Bea, who looked up and glared at him as though he had done something well beyond the pale. Awe was quite the right word he realised when it came to Bea, and though he knew that Edmund was waiting to be told more he found he couldn't think of more words. He would stray into territory that was better left – a kind of no-man's land, fraught with hazard. He smiled at Edmund and because he looked so expectant he came up with the words that would keep Bea and his memories safe.

'She was a very good person – worked hard and supported her

193

widowed sister and her sister's son, Tom. And we were very good friends. I liked her very much.'

Edmund returned to gazing out of the window. They would be in Thorp in a few minutes; there would be the short walk to the Grand Hotel, the fuss of signing the register, of taking the lift to the two rooms he had booked, the concern that Edmund would find the hotel lacking in some way, although, of course, he would be much too polite to complain. Perhaps Edmund wouldn't care at all, making Charles think that he really didn't know him very well. Yet he was here, demonstrating a friendship that made his doubts seem mean. He should allow himself to believe that he was worthy of friendship and stop being the orphaned child who had climbed that garden wall.

Edmund glanced at him. 'All right?'

'Yes.' He managed to smile. 'Yes. I think I'll be fine.'

Cathy stood back from the mirror and smoothed down her black dress, the same dress she had worn to Mark's funeral – a dress bought in a hurry, snatched off the rail; she hadn't tried it on for size, wouldn't have been able to describe it even later that evening when she had thrust it into her wardrobe. It seemed that she had lost weight since then, the dress was loose and hung about her like sackcloth. All the same, it was the only thing she owned suitable for a funeral. On the wardrobe shelf there was a black handbag, also bought for Mark's funeral and not used since. She took it down and opened it; there was a neatly folded handkerchief, a forgotten lipstick, and an order of service.

She took this out and stared at it; how had she kept such a relic, such a reminder? But she couldn't throw it away; nor did she ever want to see it again. She stood for a moment, at a loss to know what to do. It should be kept, but hidden, she decided, and although she realised how illogical this was, she pushed it to the back of the wardrobe shelf. Some future version of her would find it. That future Cathy would be strong and her heart wouldn't beat as rapidly as her heart was beating now. That future Cathy would be someone else.

She sat on the edge of her bed and took the handkerchief from the bag. It smelt of the perfume she used then and hadn't used since, but faintly; she thought she might be able to bear it and so she put it back inside the bag still folded. She hadn't used it that day; somehow she had remained dry-eyed because she had been given a pill by some actor friend of Mark's that had worked in the way she supposed it was meant to; the day had passed as though it was someone else's day: she was merely an observer of all the comings and goings. Certainly she hadn't taken out the handkerchief or the lipstick; after that little pill the very idea of applying lipstick seemed extraordinary. Who was she to look in a mirror, to pout, to fluff up her hair, to practise some brave, bearing-up expression? She was no one, a ghost, someone who shouldn't have been there at all.

Cathy snapped the bag closed on the handkerchief and lipstick. She would refresh her lipstick today, for Tom: a brave, presentable face for him.

Last night he had come to her and they had sat in the kitchen and talked as they hadn't before as though his aunt's death had revealed the world's truth, that everywhere there were lonely people who should try not to be lonely but reach out to others; she believed that was the gist of it – although she already knew that he loved her, from the moment that she had opened the door to find him on her doorstep. There was a look of relief on his face – the one person in the world he wanted to see was there, opening the door, wordlessly standing back to allow him inside. That look of relief had shifted her heart: here was a good, fine man who loved her and her own relief was as sweet as it was surprising.

His aunt's funeral was at 2 p.m. and she would be there at the back of the church. Afterwards at the wake she would meet his son. For the first time since Mark's death she had the feeling of life going on; there was a future to be had.

Luc said, 'Are you all right, Dad?'

Tom looked up at his son from polishing his shoes. 'Yes. Are you?'

'Yes.' Hesitantly he said, 'Do you think there will be lots of people there today?'

'Not so many, perhaps. Are you worried?'

'No!' He looked slightly outraged and Tom smiled.

'No, of course – nothing to worry about.' He returned to polishing his shoes; he knew that Luc would speak if he allowed him enough time. The boy was wearing his school uniform, he had polished his own shoes and combed his hair. Always neat, he was especially so today. Tom was moved by this care Luc took: a soft, vulnerable feeling kept rising inside him every time he looked at his son, a kind of terrible sentimentality he struggled to contain. He kept his eyes on his best, black shoes, concentrating on the yellow duster – such a bright contrast, the smell of the Cherry Blossom shoe polish grounding him in the mundane. Part of him wanted Luc to be satisfied with their short conversation so that he might leave him alone to clear away the polish tins and dusters, the newspaper he had spread out on the kitchen table. A larger part wanted him to voice the concern he must be feeling.

There had been no funerals to attend in his own life until he was much older than Luc. His grandmother had died when he was ten and all he remembered was being sent to a neighbour who had taken him into town on the bus and bought him an ice cream at Rea's Café. His grandfather's funeral had taken place when he himself was cowering on the beach at Dunkirk. He had not loved his grandmother; she had seemed so old, so distant; her illnesses made her less than human in his eyes. As for the Old B, he supposed he had been afraid of him, as one might be afraid of a ragged, tame bear, a bear that slipped him mint imperials with a wink of his watery eye.

But Luc had loved Bea and she had never taken to her bed or complained about the noise a child makes. He remembered how Bea would take Luc's hand and lead him into the garden. 'Let's see where that robin's made his nest, shall we?' Carrying him on her shoulders, Luc's small hands clutching at her hair, Bea would stride out across the lawn and Luc would shout out for her to go faster. Tom closed his eyes, didn't she carry him like that – up on her shoulders so that he could see all the world? And the robin's nest was a wonder to him, as if Bea had created it herself just for him.

'Dad?'

'I'm fine, Luc. Don't worry.'

'We'll be OK.'

Luc was standing at his side, very close. Tom put down the duster and pulled his son to him, his arm tight around his shoulders. 'We'll be fine,' he said. He managed to smile at him. 'Together, you and I.'

Luc nodded and Tom kissed the top of his head. 'Best foot forward, eh?'

'Best foot forward.'

It was what she used to say, always that valiant momentum. The words would carry him through the day, perhaps even the rest of his life. Fleetingly he thought of Cathy – he couldn't help his unruly thoughts returning to her – but she was for the days ahead and for now he kissed his son's head again and let him go; he began to clear away the polish. 'I think we may need our coats today, still a chill in the air, after all. Would you go and fetch them?'

Alone, Tom sat down and put on his shoes. He straightened his tie and smoothed back his hair and went into the hall where Luc was buttoning his coat. They would drive to his mother's house and from there the funeral car would take them the short distance to St Anne's. The sun was shining and this was good, fitting, because Bea had always loved the sun: she said it made the world more forgiving.

He drew breath and ushered Luc out into the spring sunshine.

Time to say goodbye.

Acknowledgements

With many thanks to my editor, Greg R, whose kindness and patience helped bring this novel to fruition.

Look out for the heartbreaking novels in Marion Husband's
The Boy I Love **series**

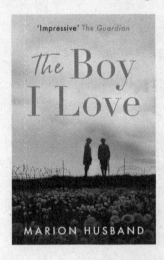

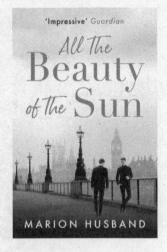

Available now from

ACCENT

Discover Marion Husband's moving novel,
NOW THE DAY IS OVER

In my more lucid moments I know I'm dead . . .

So begins Edwina's story, a young woman whose
spirit is trapped by guilt.

Edwina recounts the story of Gaye and David Henderson,
the adulterous couple whose house she haunts.

But Edwina also has her own story to tell, gradually revealing
the terrors that keep her from finding peace.

Set between the present day and the First World War,
Now the Day is Over **is a moving novel of adultery,**
love and redemption.

ACCENT